Measle
and the
Dragodon

Ian Ogilvy

Illustrated by Chris Mould

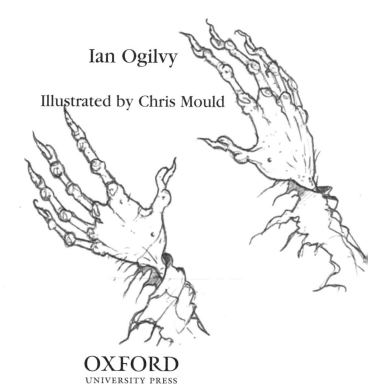

OXFORD
UNIVERSITY PRESS

FOR BARNABY AND MATILDA – again

OXFORD
UNIVERSITY PRESS

Great Clarendon Street, Oxford OX2 6DP

Oxford University Press is a department of the University of Oxford.
It furthers the University's objective of excellence in research, scholarship,
and education by publishing worldwide in

Oxford New York

Auckland Bangkok Buenos Aires Cape Town
Chennai Dar es Salaam Delhi Hong Kong Istanbul Karachi
Kolkata Kuala Lumpur Madrid Melbourne Mexico City Mumbai
Nairobi São Paulo Shanghai Taipei Tokyo Toronto

Oxford is a registered trade mark of Oxford University Press
in the UK and in certain other countries

British Library Cataloguing in Publication Data available

ISBN 0 19 271953 X

1 3 5 7 9 10 8 6 4 2

Manufactured in China by Imago

CONTENTS

The Searchers

The dingy, dreary street was still there, with its two rows of dingy, dreary houses. The houses were still abandoned and derelict, their doors and windows boarded over with rough planks of wood. Weeds grew tall in the sooty back gardens and the fences that separated the properties sagged and rotted in the damp air.

Nobody had wanted to live there—not since Basil Tramplebone had moved into the biggest and nastiest looking house at the far end of the street, right down by the railway tracks.

And still they didn't want to live there, even months after Basil's death, when he and his pet bat Cuddlebug had fallen from their high attic window and splattered on the pavement below. Before Basil had ever arrived in the street, it hadn't been a particularly pleasant place to live—poor and mean and too near the railway tracks, for a start. But when Basil had moved into the big, black horror of a house at the far end of the street, the few inhabitants who were already living there found themselves wanting to move away—far away, and quickly, please. And soon, every house in the street had been abandoned and boarded up and, in all the years that Basil Tramplebone had haunted the street, nobody had ever wanted to buy a house there again. And even now, months after Basil was no longer a bother to anybody, there was still something about the street that made prospective house buyers turn away and go and look for somewhere to live in another part of town— preferably a part of town that was as far away from the dingy, dreary street as possible.

And now, today, on this warm, late summer's evening, it seemed at first glance that the street was as empty of human life as ever. But if you looked a little closer, particularly there, down at the far end of the street, where a great rotting pile of black rubble lay by the side of the road, you might have noticed some movement.

On the pavement, in the shadow of the

great rubble-heap that had once been Basil Tramplebone's horrible house, two dark figures sat on a pair of folding camp stools. They held open umbrellas over their heads and they huddled together under the rain that dribbled down on them.

The rain that dribbled down on them—*but on nothing else in the street.*

Elsewhere in the dingy, dreary street, the early evening sun cast a golden glow over everything, turning the gloomy road (at first glance, at least) into a nicer place than it really was. But over the two huddled figures there floated a strange object—a small black cloud in the shape of the figure 8. This odd-looking little double cloud dribbled a constant stream of water down over the two black umbrellas and the huddled figures beneath them.

Wrathmonks! Members of the third—and most feared—branch of Sorcery. First among the sorcerers were the wizards, who were kind and friendly and usually very secretive, living private lives and not bothering anybody very much; then the warlocks: proud, ambitious—and a little greedy, perhaps; and last came the wrathmonks, the most terrible of all the magical beings, for they were mad.

Besides the small movements made by the two wrathmonks as they sat quietly talking to one another, there was other movement too. Another pair of figures were scrambling about on the huge pile of dirty rubble. Their heads were down and their backs were bent and their hands were picking over the bricks, as if they were looking for something. Every now and again they would cast anxious eyes in the direction of the two figures under their umbrellas on the camp stools and then, just as quickly, they would avert their eyes and continue their search.

The pair of searchers were men, both in rough working clothes and heavy boots, with cloth caps on their heads. They looked frightened and exhausted—and a little puzzled, too.

They had been searching for a very long time and now, for a moment, each man took a few seconds to rest. They both stopped quite near to each other and both straightened their aching backs and tried to rub a little of the dirt from their sore hands.

'Did I tell you to ssstop, Robert?'

The first man jerked at the sound of the hissing voice. He looked fearfully down at the figures on the pavement. One of them—a short, round, fat little blob of a person—had folded his umbrella and had stood up from his camp stool and was now glaring up at him from under hooded eyelids. The eyes were like two little black holes in a smooth expanse of white, white skin. There wasn't a single strand of hair on the shiny round head. The ears were small and round and lay close to the skull. The nose looked like a little ball of white wax. A pair of pale, pudgy little lips occupied the lower half of the face and, below them, the chin sloped away backwards so that it looked as if the figure had no chin at all. Below the non-existent chin was a non-existent neck and, below that, a well-pressed black suit, a white shirt, a black tie, a pair of black leather gloves, and, on the small feet, a pair of shiny black lace-up shoes.

'Well, Robert? I asssked you a quessstion, Robert.'

The man on the rubble pile shook his head fearfully. 'No, Mr Gristle, sir—I wasn't stopping, Mr Gristle, sir. I was just taking a breather, Mr Gristle, sir. Won't happen again, Mr Gristle, sir.'

Griswold Gristle twisted his mouth into the semblance of a smile.

'No, Robert, it won't happen again. And would you like me to tell you *why* it won't happen again, Robert?'

Robert swallowed hard and whispered, 'Oh, yes please, Mr Gristle, sir.'

'Well, Robert—it won't happen again because, if it does, you won't be taking a *breather*, as you call it, ever again. You won't be taking a *breather*, Robert—because you won't be *alive*, Robert, you'll be dead—and dead people don't do all that much *breathing*, you sssee. Hee hee.' Griswold's fat little body jiggled up and down a couple of times and a wheezing sound slipped from his mouth. 'Hee hee.

Do you follow me, Robert?'

Robert nodded, lowering his eyes to the ground. 'Yes, sir, Mr Gristle, sir. Very, very sorry, Mr Gristle, sir. Beg your pardon, Mr Gristle, sir. Won't happen again, Mr Gristle, sir.'

Griswold wrinkled his tiny round nose in disgust. 'Sssee that it doesn't. Well, get on with your sssearch, then,' he muttered and sat back down on his stool.

Robert didn't dare throw a look at his fellow searcher on the rubble-heap. He simply stared hard at the jumble of bricks, crumbling plaster, and rotting timbers beneath his feet and went back to his seemingly endless quest.

'Sssuch lazy creatures, these common working humans,' hissed Griswold to his companion. 'We let them sssleep at night, don't we? And they've only been sssearching for five days. That's nothing, Cedric—why, when I'm at my bank, I regularly work non-ssstop for ten or eleven hours without even a break for doughnuts and lemonade—and I never, ever take a holiday.'

Judge Cedric Hardscrabble nodded approvingly. 'The average human,' he said, 'is an idle brute.'

Judge Cedric Hardscrabble's appearance was the absolute opposite of Griswold Gristle's. Where Griswold was short and round and fat and as bald as a billiard ball, Judge Cedric was long and thin and twiggy, with a mass of pure white hair on his bony skull. It stood out from under his black bowler hat in a frizz, so that it looked as if he'd just touched a live electric wire and was still trying to recover from the shock. His face was the colour of old candles. His ears were long and curiously pointed. His nose—which always had a drip of disgusting-looking greenish liquid hanging from the end of it—jutted from his face like the beak of an eagle and the tip bent down, as if trying to join itself with the pointed chin beneath. He wore a long, shabby black overcoat that completely covered the rest of his clothes, apart from the glimpse of a grubby white collar around his bony throat at one end and a pair of scuffed black shoes at the other.

Judge Cedric swivelled on his camp stool, moved his umbrella out of the way, and peered up at the two searching men. 'And what about you, Harry?' he called. 'Are you working hard up there, Harry?'

'Working very hard *indeed*, your worship, sir,' called Harry.

'Have you found what we are looking for yet, Harry?'

'Er... well, I can't rightly say, your honour, sir. Since—begging your pardon, your lordship, sir— we don't exactly know what it is we're looking for—'

'Sssilence, you insssolent creature!' snarled Judge Cedric. 'It is not for you to know what it is we ssseek! It is enough that you sssimply obey your inssstructions!'

Harry swallowed hard. The last thing he needed was an angry Judge Cedric Hardscrabble. The last thing *anybody* needed was an angry Judge Cedric Hardscrabble.

'Yes, sir. Sorry, sir.'

'You don't want me to *breathe* on you again, do you, Harry?'

'Oh—no, sir—please, sir—don't do that, sir—'

Judge Cedric had once breathed on Harry and Harry had never forgotten the experience. In fact, he remembered it with horror. He'd done something wrong—he'd made Judge Cedric a cup of tea and he'd put in three lumps of sugar instead of four—and then Judge Cedric had become very angry and had started *breathing* on him, and the judge's breath had smelt horrible, of dead fish and old mattresses and the insides of ancient sneakers—but that hadn't been the worst part. The worst part had been that, within a few seconds, Harry's face and his hands—and then, moments later, his whole body—had suddenly become covered in disgusting and very painful, bright red, pussy boils which had taken a whole month to clear up.

Harry didn't want that to happen again.

'We'll find it, your highness, sir! Don't worry, your greatness, sir! Robert and me—we'll search all night, all week, all month—but we'll find it, your supremeness, sir!'

'Sssee that you do, Harry. Sssee that you do.'

Harry moved away, shifting bricks as fast as he could.

The two wrathmonks sat in silence for a few moments. Then Judge Cedric sniffed and leaned a little closer to Griswold Gristle.

'Griswold, old friend—I've jussst had a thought.'

'Really?' said Griswold, in a surprised voice. In his experience, Judge Cedric hardly ever had any thoughts at all.

'Yesss. I was wondering, Griswold—when we find this thing that we ssseek—what are we going to *do* with it?'

Griswold Gristle sighed. He had explained all this several times to Judge Cedric but, ever since his old friend had been transformed from warlock into wrathmonk, Judge Cedric had become very forgetful. He had also become very stupid, as well. Lately, Griswold Gristle had begun to wonder whether being friends with Judge Cedric Hardscrabble wasn't—well—rather *pointless*.

Griswold decided he certainly wasn't going to go through the whole thing again—at least, not until they actually found what they were looking for. So, instead, he just whispered into Judge Cedric's pointed, whiskery old ear, '*Do* with it, Cedric? Why—we shall do wonderful things. Wonderful, *wonderful* things.'

Judge Cedric was about to ask *what* wonderful things when, from somewhere above them, there came a muffled scream, quickly followed by running, stumbling footsteps—then another muffled scream—then silence.

The two wrathmonks looked at each other. Then Griswold Gristle said, 'It would appear that they have found something, Cedric.'

Judge Cedric smiled, revealing a mouth full of brown and crooked teeth. The three upper teeth on either side of his mouth came to sharp points. 'Let usss hope they have found what we were looking for, Griswold.'

'Then let usss wait a moment, to be quite sure,' said Griswold.

The two wrathmonks sat in silence, listening for any sound of movement on the rubble-heap behind them. There was none.

'Robert?' called Griswold.

'Harry?' called Judge Cedric.

Silence, apart from the sound of the rain drumming against their umbrellas. Griswold got to his feet and rummaged in a leather bag by the side of his stool. He took out a small hand mirror and a pair of long barbecue tongs. 'We mussst be very careful, Cedric,' he said.

Judge Cedric nodded and stood up, wrapping his long coat tight around himself. 'Careful, yesss,' he said.

'You hold the tongs,' said Griswold. 'I shall manipulate the mirror.'

'Do you have the container ready?'

'Of courssse,' said Griswold, holding up a small

cloth bag. 'I have thought of everything, Cedric. Now, let usss retrieve the preciousss thing forthwith.'

Leaving their umbrellas by their camp stools, the two wrathmonks climbed up the rubble-heap until they both reached the top. In front of them, about ten metres away, was a strange sight. Two grey stone statues, representing a pair of working men in flat caps and heavy boots, were standing in a small pit in the brick rubble. The statues bore remarkable resemblances to Robert and Harry. Both were bent double at the waist, as if intent on some object on the ground in front of them. Both had their arms standing stiffly away from their bodies and all four hands were splayed, their fingers wide, as if trying to ward off some horror they could see in front of them.

Griswold Gristle and Judge Cedric Hardscrabble approached cautiously. When they got to within a couple of metres of the two statues, Griswold held the hand mirror out in front of him, angling it towards the ground. He took his eyes off the broken surface of rubble and stared instead into the mirror, inching his fat little body forward step by careful step.

'Can you sssee it yet, Griswold?' whispered Judge Cedric, creeping slowly behind him.

'Not yet, Cedric. Be patient.'

Griswold was now on the edge of the small pit, crouching between the two statues. His short, fat right arm—with the mirror clutched in his right hand—was sweeping backwards and forwards over the surface of the rubble. Slowly to the left... then slowly to the right... then Griswold took a cautious step forward and swept his arm again... slowly left... slowly right—

His arm stopped. Very carefully, he moved his arm back a few centimetres.

'There!' he hissed. 'Do you sssee it, Cedric?'

Judge Cedric stepped forward, his eyes glued to the ground in front of him. Griswold seized his arm. 'No, no, you fool! Look in the mirror! Look in the mirror!'

The two wrathmonks stared intently into the little mirror, still held at arm's length in Griswold's right hand. There, in the reflection, a small, grey, wrinkled object lay among the dirty bricks.

'Careful now, Cedric,' whispered Griswold. 'Bring the tongs forward...a little to the left...forward a few centimetres...now a touch to the right...down a bit...down a bit...there! Now, gently sssqueeze the tongs together—that's it— you have it! Now lift ssslowly...ssslowly...I have the bag ready...bring it ssslowly towards me... that's right...careful now...that's excellent, Cedric...keep looking in the mirror...a little closer...good, good, you're now directly over the open bag...lower it ssslowly, ssslowly, excellent... now, carefully open the tongs and—there! It's in the bag, Cedric! We have it! It's in the bag!'

A few beads of sweat stood out on both wrathmonks' white foreheads. The drops of sweat were a pale green in colour and, instead of trickling down their faces (like ordinary sweat), these drops stayed where they were, as if stuck there with glue.

'A dangerousss business, Griswold,' said Judge Cedric, his voice a little shaky.

'But worth it, wouldn't you agree, Cedric?' Griswold tightened the drawstring around the neck of the cloth bag and stuffed it carefully into his jacket pocket. 'What was once Basil Tramplebone's is now ours! With thisss object, we have a mighty weapon at our disposal—one that can ssstop an army in its tracks! Imagine, Cedric— an entire army, all turned to ssstone before our very eyes!'

Judge Cedric looked a little doubtful. 'And…
what army would that be, Griswold?'

'Well…not necessarily *any* army, Cedric!' said
Griswold, sharply. 'The point is, with thisss rare and
preciousss object, we will be able—if we ssso
choose—*literally* to petrify a large number of
humans, whenever we want to!'

'*Petrify*, Griswold? Surely it does more than
merely petrify?'

'The word has two meanings, Cedric,' said
Griswold, with the air of somebody who is proud
of their education and likes showing it off. '*Petrify*
means to frighten—but it also means *to turn to
ssstone*. A preciousss object indeed! And, best of
all, Cedric—it uses up none of our own magical
powers!'

'We shall use it against my enemies!' hissed Judge
Cedric, excitedly. 'My wicked, evil opponents!
Twelve of them in particular—all mossst unpleasant
persssons—they sssit in a sssort of box in my
courtroom and disssagree with everything I sssay!'

'You mean…the *jury*?' said Griswold, in the sort
of voice people use when they find it hard to
believe what they've just heard.

'Indeed, yesss!' cried Judge Cedric. 'The jury! We
shall petrify the jury!'

'We could indeed,' said Griswold, carefully. 'But
first things first, Cedric. First, as I told you before,
we musssst take our revenge against those who
hurt usss the mossst!'

Judge Cedric grinned wolfishly. 'The jury, yesss!'

Griswold Gristle sighed. Sometimes he wondered how his friend had ever managed to remain a judge at all.

'The jury, yesss,' said Griswold, patiently. 'But later, Cedric—*later*. First we mussst deal with the enemies of *all* of usss. Of all wrathmonks, wherever they might be. I am ssspeaking, of course, of those who persecute us! Who hunt us down! I am ssspeaking of the family of Ssstubbs!'

Judge Cedric's thin white face crumpled in hatred. 'The Ssstubbs family! Yesss! We mussst deal with the Ssstubbs family!'

'And, in particular, Cedric, we mussst deal with the boy! That wretched child, Measle Ssstubbs, who murdered our beloved Basil Tramplebone! We mussst avenge poor Basil's death!'

'Yesss! Yesss!' cried Judge Cedric, dancing an unsteady little jig on the uneven ground. Then he stopped and leaned towards Griswold, his bushy eyebrows raised. 'But how, Griswold? How shall we get our revenge?'

For a moment, Griswold Gristle seemed at a loss for words. He frowned, his fat face crumpling like a soggy cake.

'I am not yet sure, Cedric,' he said. 'I mussst think of a plan and you shall help me. You and sssome others who will join us. But ressst assured, Cedric—we shall find a way. Oh yesss. We shall find a way! Now, let usss leave this place—we have what we came for.'

'And what about those two?' said Judge Cedric, inclining his head towards the pair of stone statues.

'Leave them, Cedric,' said Griswold, beginning to scramble back down the rubble-heap. 'They have ssserved their purpose. They are no use to usss now.'

Judge Cedric sniffed and nodded. Then he took a couple of steps towards the statue that had once been his servant Harry. 'Ssstupid, idle creature!' he sneered. He lifted one foot and kicked the statue hard—and the statue teetered for a moment, then lost its balance and fell slowly sideways. It thudded against the statue that had once been Robert, pushing against it—then the two stone figures fell together, down onto the jumbled bricks beneath them.

'Come along, Cedric!' called Griswold Gristle. He was down at the pavement level now, picking up his umbrella and folding his camp stool. 'Come along! We have a plan to make!'

'A plan, yesss!' muttered Judge Cedric. His toes hurt a bit from kicking the stone statue and he hobbled down the side of the rubble-heap, retrieved his own umbrella and his own camp stool and then limped slowly after Griswold Gristle.

And the little black rain cloud, shaped like the figure 8, drifted along overhead.

Happy Birthmas Day

Measle Stubbs was having the time of his life.

It had all started the moment he'd come home.

Home to Merlin Manor.

It had taken Measle exactly three days, six hours, and seven and a half minutes to get used to living at Merlin Manor. It's much easier to get used to things and places and people if they're nice—and everything about Merlin Manor was extremely nice indeed.

To Measle, who had spent most of his life living in a really horrible house, with his really horrible wrathmonk guardian Basil Tramplebone, Merlin Manor seemed to be nothing short of perfect. It was a big old house, way out in the countryside, made of warm red bricks. At the entrance to the

Stubbs estate was a pair of massive iron gates, then a long driveway made of crunchy gravel. A sweeping lawn in the front of the house. Tall trees at the back. Big stone urns, full of red and white and blue flowers, stood on either side of the front door—and, inside the big old house, everything was just as good, with enormous, bright rooms full of soft, squashy furniture you could flop into, gleaming bathrooms with fluffy white towels and endless supplies of hot water—and a light and airy kitchen, out of which came the best food that Measle could ever imagine eating.

In fact, Merlin Manor was just about the most fabulous, comfortable, and friendly house imaginable.

And it was Nanny Flannel who was mostly responsible for making it so.

Nanny Flannel was small and old and round, with grey hair, pink cheeks, and a pair of bright blue eyes that twinkled behind her wire-framed spectacles. She had helped to look after Measle's father when he was a baby and, when Sam had grown up, she had simply stayed on at Merlin Manor, cooking and cleaning and organizing everything ever since. She had helped look after Measle, too, when he was a baby—so, to have him and his parents—in fact, the whole

Stubbs family—back again at Merlin Manor, after all this time, was just about the best thing that had ever happened to her.

So, what with Nanny Flannel fussing over him—and his father Sam Stubbs and his mother Lee Stubbs loving him so hard that sometimes Measle thought they all might burst from the strain of it—Measle couldn't have been happier.

'I say, Measle—isn't it about time you had a birthday?' said Sam, lowering the newspaper he was reading and peering at Measle over the top of it.

'Er...' said Measle, who hadn't the faintest idea when his birthday was.

They were all sitting at the big pine table in the kitchen, having breakfast. Nanny Flannel was cooking sausages and bacon and eggs at the stove and Lee was buttering a big pile of toast.

'Nonsense, Sam,' said Nanny Flannel. 'You know perfectly well when his birthday is. February the twelfth and that's months away.'

Ah, thought Measle, *February the twelfth, eh? That's nice to know.*

'True, Nanny,' said Sam, thoughtfully. 'But he's missed an awful lot of them, hasn't he? Let me see now—why, he's missed at least six birthdays, hasn't he?'

'At least six,' said Lee Stubbs, smiling happily at

Measle. 'And Tinker's probably missed a few as well.'

At the sound of his name, Tinker—who was lying on the kitchen floor, with his head resting on Measle's feet—wagged his stumpy tail. Like Measle, the little dog was having the time of his life, too. Oh, he'd been perfectly happy with his dear old lady—but life out here in the countryside, with the smelly kid to play with, was much better. (Prudence Peyser, the old wrathmonkologist, had given Tinker to Measle—in gratitude for saving her life. Tinker was the best present Measle had ever been given.)

'I tell you what,' said Lee, 'why don't we have them all right away?'

'Have all what?' said Sam.

'All their birthdays, of course,' said Lee, putting a big plate of buttered toast down in front of Measle. 'Over the next six days, Measle and Tinker could have six birthdays, couldn't they?'

'Terrific idea,' said Sam, firmly. 'Six days, six birthdays. And, come to think of it, six Christmas Days as well. They've missed them too. We'll put them together and call them—um, let me see— yes, we'll call them their *Birthmas Days*. Oh, we *are* going to have fun.' He turned to Nanny Flannel. 'How about it, Nanny? All right with you?'

'Perfectly all right, Sam,' she said. Nanny Flannel's eyes were twinkling behind her spectacles. 'I'm all for a bit of fun. Six Birthmas

Days! That means six Birthmas *cakes*! And a call to the butcher, too. Well—I *will* be busy, won't I?'

Over the next six days, Measle and Tinker got a whole lot of birthmas presents. Tinker's presents were all bones—big beef bones, each one nearly as big as Tinker himself. (And, if Tinker was the best present that Measle had ever been given, then those big beef bones were the best presents that *Tinker* had ever been given.) Tinker would chew each bone, with passionate concentration, for most of the day, until there wasn't a scrap of meat left on it—and then, in the evening, he would dig a hole under an ancient oak tree in the garden and carefully bury the bare bone among the tangled roots.

Measle's presents were the sorts of presents that a boy of his age might expect to get—a bicycle, a skateboard, a football, some new clothes—but he also got one very unusual gift indeed.

'Here you are, son,' said Sam, handing Measle a small, oddly-shaped package, all done up in bright birthday wrapping paper, with a big blue bow on the top. 'This used to be mine, a long time ago. I had a lot of fun with it when I was your age.'

It was a strange little object, called a VoBo. It was shaped like a tiny trumpet and, like a trumpet, it seemed to be made of polished brass. But, unlike a trumpet—which has three valves you can press—the VoBo had only one very small button, set into the side of one of its brass tubes. It also had a little hinged sighting device—a circle of brass with a pair of crossed brass wires, one vertical, the other horizontal, set inside the ring. The sight was fixed with a brass hinge on the top of the trumpet's bell, and you could flip it up and down.

'Look,' said Sam, 'I'll show you how to work it. You hold the VoBo up to your mouth, press the button, and then speak into it.' Sam lifted the little trumpet to his mouth, pointed it towards the ceiling, pressed the button and said, 'Happy Birthmas Day, Measle.'

To Measle, it seemed that nothing particularly special had happened and he wondered what, exactly, the little trumpet was for. He was about to ask that very question, but Sam held up his hand to stop him. 'Wait a second, Measle,' he said, 'there's more.' Then Sam turned the trumpet and pointed it at Lee. 'You have to get it aimed exactly at a person,' he said, grinning like a schoolboy. 'That's what these sights are for. Right—look, I'm now aiming it at Mum—and now I press the button again and say the same thing—'

And once again, Sam said—in a near whisper, 'Happy Birthmas Day, Measle,' into the VoBo's tiny mouthpiece.

And, at exactly the same moment, Measle heard Lee say, quite clearly, 'Happy Birthmas Day, Measle.'

The only thing was—she hadn't opened her mouth.

Sam grinned at Measle's look of astonishment. 'The VoBo imitates voices. All you've got to do is point it at the person you want it to imitate, press the button, and speak into the mouthpiece. The VoBo even makes the voice seem to come from their direction, too—and it's got quite a range on it as well. I used it on my maths teacher, once. I had her tell our whole class that we had the rest of the period off—so we all ran outside and played football in the playground.'

'Don't give him evil ideas, Sam,' said Lee, trying hard not to laugh. 'I'm sure he'll think of some all on his own.'

The one present Measle *didn't* get was a model train set.

They all went on long car trips round the countryside to show Measle the interesting places nearby. The Stubbs car was...well...it was *different*. It was big and comfortable and fast—but it didn't have the manufacturer's name on it anywhere and it didn't look like any other car on the road. It was long and low and sleek and painted a dark, metallic green. The engine rumbled and roared like an angry lion and when Sam started it up, he didn't turn an ordinary, dull ignition key—he pressed a large red button in the middle of the dashboard. The big wheels had spokes like a bicycle and the sides of the tyres were painted bright red. The windows were tinted grey, so you could see out of them but it was hard for somebody on the outside to see in—but what Measle liked best about the car was the bonnet ornament: on the front of the bonnet, over the radiator grille, was mounted the skull of what (to Measle) looked like a giant lizard.

'It's a very small dragon,' said Sam. 'Actually a baby one.'

'Oh, wow. Did you kill it?' said Measle. The idea that his father might have killed a dragon—even a baby one—was extremely cool.

'Oh no,' said Sam. 'No, that's been dead thousands of years. There aren't any dragons around any more. Pity, really. They must have been amazing creatures. No, we were given that by the Wizards' Guild.'

'Wow,' said Measle. 'That's so cool. They gave you a dragon's skull.'

Lee laughed. 'Actually—they gave us the *car*,' she said. 'The skull was already on it.'

'The whole car. Wow.'

'Yup,' said Sam. 'And what's really "wow" about it—you never need to fill the petrol tank. In fact, it hasn't even got one. The engine is—well, let's just say it's a bit different from the usual sort of engine. Apart from not needing any fuel, it's completely silent. The red button does two things—it starts it up and also makes the engine noise, so nobody gets suspicious, you see.'

'Wow.'

'And here's another "wow" about it. It's got a sort of autopilot. It remembers where it's been—so, if I can't be bothered to drive myself, I just press the switch marked A/P, say the name of the place and it'll take me there. Of course, I have to sit in the driver's seat and *pretend* to drive, otherwise there could be all sorts of problems.'

'Your dad refuses to use the autopilot, Measle,' said Lee. 'When it's turned on, the car behaves itself beautifully. It goes at *normal* speeds and obeys all the traffic rules.'

'And where's the fun in that?' laughed Sam. 'No, I like driving it myself. But it could be useful, I suppose—if you were really tired, or something, and didn't *want* to drive.'

'Wow. But *why* did the Wizards' Guild give this car to you?'

Sam and Lee glanced at each other. Then Sam turned back to Measle and grinned. 'For services rendered.'

Sam didn't explain what the services had been—and Measle had the sense not to ask. He'd been learning a lot about his mother and father—

mostly from little snippets of information that they both let drop now and then. Measle now knew that Sam and Lee Stubbs were bounty hunters, employed by the Wizards' Guild to ferret out wrathmonks. What they *did* with the wrathmonks when they found them, Measle didn't know. Once he'd asked his father—and Sam had smiled and winked and had then changed the subject. One thing Measle *did* know—Sam and Lee Stubbs were the only ones around doing what they did—and the Wizards' Guild rewarded them very well indeed for their work.

On the last day of Measle and Tinker's six consecutive Birthmas Days, Nanny Flannel gave Tinker the biggest, juiciest bone he'd ever seen—and Sam, Lee, and Measle set off early in the morning and drove in the big Stubbs car to the Isle of Smiles.

'We've saved this until last,' said Sam, weaving the big green car round a slow-moving lorry. 'Because it's the best. You're going to love the Isle of Smiles. It's by the sea—well, actually, it's sort of *in* the sea—and it's the biggest and the best amusement theme park in the country. It's got every ride you can imagine. There's carousels and water rides and haunted mansions and a Ferris wheel and spinning saucepans and bumper cars and a go-kart track and a whole lot of different sorts of roller coasters—'

'Those are the ones your dad likes best,' said Lee.

'Well, of course,' said Sam. 'Everybody likes the roller coasters the best.'

'Not me,' said Lee. 'They're too fast for me. Or, at least, they are when your dad's on them. I prefer the water rides myself.'

'I bet I like them all,' said Measle, a little nervously. He'd never been on a thrill ride in his life and he wasn't sure how he was going to handle the experience. He also wondered what Lee had meant when she said they were too fast—*when your dad's on them*. He looked at his father. Sam was grinning and, for a moment, Measle thought he looked as excited as a small boy.

Lee said, 'This is your dad's favourite place in the whole world, Measle.'

'And it'll be Measle's too,' said Sam. 'I guarantee it.'

The isle of Smiles

They had been driving fast for some time along a motorway when Measle saw the sign—a billboard that read: ISLE OF SMILES—NEXT EXIT.

Sam swung the car into the slow lane and, a few minutes later, they left the motorway and took a winding road that led through thick pine woods. The trees grew dense on either side of them and they cast a gloomy shadow over the road—but then Measle saw a chink of light ahead, which grew wider and wider as they came out of the pine forest. The great, gleaming green car roared out of the shadows, out into the blazing sun—and there, a little to the right and far below, between a dip in the distant hills, lay the sea.

They drove down a long winding road, descending steadily towards the sea. There were a lot of cars on the road now and Sam had to slow down and take his place in the queue. Suddenly he lifted one hand from the steering wheel and pointed ahead. 'See? There it is.'

Measle saw a bay, with a little town and a harbour full of fishing boats. Starting by the harbour—and extending right out to the middle of the bay—was a broad causeway made of piled-up rocks. There was a wide, multi-laned road along the top of the causeway and lines of cars inched their way along it towards their goal—a big, almost circular, rocky island set right in the very centre of the wide bay.

'That's it,' said Sam. 'The Isle of Smiles.'

'More like the Isle of *Screams*,' said Lee. 'You should hear them on the roller coasters. Like a lot of banshees.'

'You scream louder than anybody,' said Sam, laughing.

'Only when you *tamper*, Sam,' said Lee, prodding him in the ribs.

For a moment, Measle wondered what his mother meant by *tamper*—but then he caught sight of the distant Ferris wheel and the loops and curves of a roller coaster and he began to feel a growing excitement. Today was going to be *fun*.

And it was. The island was full of visitors and the park was crowded—but somehow Sam managed to lead them to rides where (at that precise moment) the queues were very short—so they never waited more than a few minutes, which seemed to Measle just a little bit—well, *magical*. Which (with Sam Stubbs being his father), of course it was.

They went on every ride at least twice and on one or two of the more thrilling ones three times. They rode all the water rides—the Crashing Rapids, the Log Flume, the Giant Splash—and got very wet. They rode the tall Ferris wheel. They ate popcorn and hamburgers. They went on the Ghoulish Grange ride and laughed at the wailing ghosts and the clanking skeletons. They rode the Spinning Saucepans, which made Measle feel a bit sick. They took a turn on the old-fashioned carousel, riding the garishly-painted carved wooden horses. They tore around the go-kart track and Measle won all three races. They shot airguns at paper targets and Lee won a big, squashy, pink-furred hippopotamus.

And then they went on the roller coasters.

There was the Thunderer, a traditional wooden ride, that shook their stomachs and rattled their bones; then the Screaming Eagle, with tight loops and vicious curves that made them dizzy; the Golden Nugget ride, which plunged them into the darkness of a mineshaft and then out again into the bright sunlight; the Dinosaur Diver, which featured a life-size, animated model of a Tyrannosaurus Rex that roared and lunged and snapped its massive jaws as the riders rattled by; and finally, the Big Daddy of them all, the Juggernaut.

The Juggernaut was a steel roller coaster, painted bright red. It rose to dizzying heights, dived to unspeakable depths, whistled round gut-churning curves, and somersaulted and cork-screwed its riders so often that, by the end of the ride, they didn't know up from down or right from left. At the end of it, Measle felt like a piece of beef that had been through a mincer. His eyes didn't seem to be working properly, his spine was acting like a length of wet string, and his legs appeared to be made of jelly.

'Want to go again?' said Sam, cheerfully.

'Oh sure,' said Measle.

'Not me,' said Lee, flopping down onto a bench. 'I know when I've had enough. And besides—I don't trust you, Sam Stubbs. My pink hippo and I shall wait here for you two lunatics.'

Sam and Measle managed to get themselves into the front seat of the leading car. As it clanked its way up the long incline, Sam said, 'It was a bit slow last time, don't you think, Measle?'

'We-e-ell,' said Measle, quite unable to imagine that anything could possibly go faster than the

Juggernaut—except perhaps light itself. 'We-e-ell, maybe it was a bit slow.'

'I thought it was *very* slow,' said Sam, a small, wicked grin turning up the corners of his mouth. 'We ought to do something about that, don't you think?' Then, before Measle could reply—and very quietly so that Measle almost didn't hear it—he muttered, '*Velocitum increasabile fractotum con seguridus.*'

The clanking sound of the chain lifting-mechanism underneath the cars had been going a steady *clank-clatter-clank-clatter*. Now, all of a sudden, it went *clankclatterclankclatterclankclatter*—and Measle felt a slight pressure on his back as the car began to speed up. 'Er...Dad...we're going faster,' he said, a little nervously.

'So we are,' said Sam. 'Isn't that fun?'

'Er...yeah. Great fun. What did you say back there?'

'Oh, it's a little go-faster spell, that's all.'

Measle swallowed hard. 'Go faster?'

'Yup,' said Sam, airily. 'And, if you think this is fast, wait till we get over the top.'

'Er...' said Measle.

Sam grinned down at him. 'It's all right, Measle,' he said, quietly. 'We'll survive. I added a safety clause.'

'Oh good,' said Measle. 'I'm glad you added a safety clause.'

They clanked their way rapidly towards the top of the long rise. Measle glanced behind him, taking quick looks at the other passengers. They all seemed to be unaware of the increased speed of the car and were smiling and chattering among themselves.

Measle felt Sam nudge him in the ribs. 'Don't look back, Measle—look *forward*. This is the fun part.'

They had reached the top. For a moment, it seemed to Measle that everything was going to be the same. Their front car topped the rise and began to descend slowly on the other side, just as it had before—held back by the remaining cars in the rear, which were still on their way up the steep slope behind. But then the last car in the line reached the top and gravity took over—gravity, with a little bit of help from Sam's go-faster spell.

The car lunged forward. The wheels screamed. The wind tore at their hair. Their eyes watered with the blast of air that hit them. They howled down the first, impossibly steep, precipice at terrifying speed, then ripped back up the short slope opposite, then screamed over the top (Measle felt his bottom leave the seat by several centimetres and he gripped hard onto the safety bar that held him down) and next to him Sam was yelling and laughing and waving his hands over his head—then came the first loop and Measle felt his body slam back into his seat as the centrifugal forces took over—then a rattling curve to the right—another to the left—then a sudden dive into the bowels of the ride and then up again into the blazing sunlight—and all this at such a dizzying speed that Measle wondered how the wheels could possibly keep their hold on the track—and Sam seemed to read his thoughts, because he suddenly bellowed into Measle's ear, 'Don't worry, Measle! There's that safety clause!'—and while that did manage to make Measle feel that perhaps they weren't actually going to die (at least, not immediately) it didn't stop his stomach leaping about inside his body as if it was trying to escape through his ribcage—and it only began to settle back down into its proper position when they started to slow down as the ride ended back at the station.

'Now, that's what I call a *ride*,' said Sam, as the safety bar was raised and they climbed out of their seats. They both looked at the other passengers who were also emerging from the cars behind them. Most of them looked pale and a little startled—and one or two had faces the colour of lettuce leaves.

When they rejoined Lee, she got up from the park bench where she'd been sitting and touched Sam lightly on his hand. Then she looked into Sam's face and said, so quietly that Measle almost missed it, 'Sam Stubbs, you're a wicked little wizard.'

Sam laughed and bent down and gave her a quick kiss on her lips. 'I know I am,' he said, smiling happily down at her. 'But it was a lot of fun.'

Lee shook her head and tried hard to look disapproving. 'If I wasn't here to recharge you—'

'But you are,' said Sam. 'You *always* are.'

'Yes—but what if I'm *not*?' said Lee. Then, before Sam could reply, she turned and peered closely at Measle.

'I bet you feel sick,' she said.

'No, not really,' said Measle, although he did a bit. The thing was—he felt more *puzzled* than sick. *What had that little, half-whispered conversation between his mum and dad been all about?*

They did every ride all over again—and when they boarded the Crashing Rapids water ride for the third time that day, Sam—just for a joke—thickened the water to the consistency of treacle, which meant that their raft floated v-e-r-y s-l-o-w-l-y down the stream and they didn't get wet at all.

'Very funny, dear,' said Lee.

They had a wonderful time.

But, had they known what was following them, they might have felt rather differently about the day.

The *thing* (whatever it was) had started to shadow them ever since Sam and Measle had emerged from the Juggernaut's exit. From then on, it followed close behind them, riding with them wherever they went. And none of the three Stubbses noticed.

It certainly wasn't human, this creature, because no human could do what this creature could do. The reason that Sam, Lee, and Measle failed to notice the creature was because it changed its appearance every few minutes. One moment it was an ordinary-looking middle-aged man in a blue tracksuit and a baseball cap—then, in the blink of an eye, the creature became a ten-year-old girl with a freckled face and pigtails—then a fat woman in a cotton dress, carrying an ice cream cone—then an eighteen-year-old boy with long hair and a spotty face—and on and on, through a whole range of human disguises, each one being as ordinary and unspectacular as the last, so that the Stubbs family (and everybody else in the park) hardly noticed them at all. The thing sat close behind them on every ride they took—and it stared at the backs of their heads with a strange, unsettling intensity in its deep, black eyes. The eyes were disturbing things. There was no colour to them—only the deep, black emptiness of outer space. The thing's eyes were the only features that it retained each time it changed its appearance and it was careful to hide them behind a succession of different sunglasses. And since it was a sunny day, at least half the visitors to the Isle of Smiles were wearing sunglasses, too—so it was hardly surprising that the Stubbs family never noticed that they were being watched so intently.

And, for the rest of that wonderful day, wherever

they went and whatever they did—the *something* was never far behind them.

Then, that evening, when all three Stubbs family members were dog-tired and ready to go home, the *something* made its move.

There was quite a crowd round the exit turnstile and everybody was squashed tightly together as they slowly filtered through the clicking revolving gate. Sam was in the front, with Measle close behind him. Lee brought up the rear.

Behind Lee—and separated from her by a young mother clutching a sleeping toddler—was a thin woman with a pinched, sallow face. A pair of sunglasses, with rhinestones glittering on the frame, covered her eyes. As the Stubbs family inched forward, with the rest of the crowd pressed around them, the thin woman slowly extended her hand, past the mother with the toddler—and on towards Lee's slim back.

'You'd think,' muttered Sam over his shoulder, 'that they'd have a few more exits working. This really is a bit of a squish—'

Then suddenly, behind him, Measle heard his mother gasp—as if somebody had trodden hard on her toes. Then he heard her voice, urgent in his ear.

'Push through, Measle! We've got to get out of here!'

Sam looked back. 'What's the matter?'

'I don't know,' whispered Lee, over Measle's head. 'Something touched me—and now I'm ... I'm ... well, here—feel.'

Lee extended her hand and Sam took it—and a look of shock passed across his face.

'You're ... you're *freezing*!' he hissed.

'I *know*, Sam. We've got to go—now!'

Sam nodded. Measle saw that his face had lost some of its natural tan and he was now looking a little pale.

'Come on,' muttered Sam. He turned his body sideways and put his shoulder between two people who were in front of him and then pushed firmly through them.

'Excuse me,' he said, loudly. 'Sorry—can you let us through? My wife's not feeling well—that's it, son, help your mother—thank you—thanks—'

The crowd parted obediently in front of him and the Stubbs family were quickly through the turnstile and out into the car park. Sam hurried them to the car and they all quickly got in—and closed and then locked the doors.

'What happened?' said Measle. 'What's the matter?' His mother looked fine to him. She wasn't smiling like she usually did and there was a look of anxiety in her green eyes—but otherwise she seemed all right.

'Something touched me,' she said, her voice a little shaky. 'I think it was trying to take my mana.'

'Your what?' said Measle.

'My mana,' said Lee.

'It's what fuels magic, Measle,' said Sam. He was holding Lee's hand and looking at her like a concerned doctor might look at his ill patient. 'That's what separates us wizards from the rest of humanity—the mana. Wizards have it stored inside them and they use it up when they invoke magic. A big spell can use it all up instantly. It comes back slowly—after a major invocation, most wizards are ready to go again after about twenty-four hours. Think of it as a sort of self-recharging battery, if you like.'

'You mean Mum's a wizard too?' said Measle, looking at Lee with new respect.

Lee shook her head. 'No, I'm not, Measle. I can't do any magic at all—and I don't want to either.'

'She's better than a wizard,' said Sam, proudly. 'She's much rarer than that. She's a manafount.'

'A what?' said Measle.

'A manafount. There are only three others in the world—one in China, one in Australia, and a third in Bolivia. They're all very old—your mum's the only young one.'

'But—what *is* a mana-what-you-said?'

'A manafount. Literally, a fountain of mana. Your mum has a constant supply of mana, which never runs out. Manafounts can't invoke magic themselves—but they can pass their mana on to somebody who can. But not just to anybody. They have to be married, you see. A husband manafount can pass to his wizard wife, or a wife manafount can pass to her husband wizard. That's us, of course. That's what she did when we came off the

Juggernaut ride. She touched my hand—and recharged me.'

'I knew he'd done a spell, Measle,' said Lee. 'I could feel he'd used up all his mana, so I just put it back.'

Sam gazed admiringly at Lee. 'Let me tell you, Measle,' he said, proudly, 'every wizard and warlock in the world wanted to marry your mum. Luckily, she chose me, which was very nice of her, since I'm a pretty minor wizard. Of course, I was by far and away the best-looking one.'

Lee leaned over and kissed Sam on the cheek.

'No, Sam darling,' she said, with a smile, 'you *weren't* the best-looking one. Justin Bucket was.'

'*Justin Bucket?*' yelped Sam, trying to look hurt. 'Justin Bucket was a total nerd! A geek! A dweeb! A dork!'

'Yes, Sam darling,' said Lee, stifling her laughter, 'Justin Bucket was all those things. But he looked like a film star. He was easily the handsomest wizard in the Guild. He was also the most *boring*. Not like you. You weren't boring at all. Of all the wizards in the Guild, you were by far the most interesting. And you were certainly the *funniest.*' Lee turned to Measle and said, 'Your dad made me laugh, Measle—and I liked laughing. I still do, actually.'

'You do, don't you?' said Sam, happily. Then he turned back to Measle. 'Anyway, a wizard who is lucky enough to have a manafount on his side can continue to perform spells without stopping—but there has to be an unbroken contact between them all the time he or she is doing the magic. That's why we work together, your mum and I. As I said, I'm not a particularly powerful wizard, Measle—but hand-in-hand with your mum, I can keep up a constant stream of small spells, while my enemy can only perform one big one at a time.'

Sam broke off. He looked hard at Lee's small hand, buried in his big one.

'You're getting a bit warmer,' he said.

Lee nodded. 'Slowly, though.'

'Thank goodness for that. What do you think happened?'

'Somebody—or some*thing*—touched me. I felt a finger tap me very gently on my back—and then—'

'How did it feel?'

'Very cold, very empty—like I had nothing inside me but icy air. Everything—except my mana—just sort of left me. All my emotions, all my feelings—we've been here all day and I was getting a little tired and a little hungry too—and then, when I was touched, even my hunger and my tiredness disappeared! It didn't hurt—but it was a shock. How could that happen, Sam?'

'I don't know,' said Sam, 'but there's obviously something here—and I don't think we should stay to find out what it is.' He stabbed his forefinger at the red button on the car's dashboard and the engine rumbled to life. He turned and glanced at Measle. 'First rule of wizardry, Measle—if you don't understand what's going on, don't try to be brave—run for the hills!'

Sam stamped hard on the accelerator pedal. The engine roared. The big car's rear wheels spun for a moment on the smooth tarmac of the car park. Then the rubber gripped the surface and the car leapt forward.

'Hold on to your hats!' yelled Sam, gripping the big steering wheel so hard that his knuckles turned white. 'We're going to be breaking a few speeding rules!'

'So what else is new?' said Lee—and Measle was relieved to see that a small version of her familiar smile had returned.

Sam laughed. 'Of all the rides we've been on today,' he shouted, over the roar of the engine and the squealing of the tyres, 'this one could be the most exciting!'

Sam spent the next few days locked in his study, head bent over his dusty old books. He also spent a lot of time on the telephone, talking to senior members of the Wizards' Guild. When at last he emerged, he looked tired and worried.

'Family conference,' he announced. 'Everybody into the kitchen.'

Lee and Measle sat down at the big pine table. Nanny Flannel sat halfway down on one side and Tinker lay down at Measle's feet, his ears pricked forward, so that it looked as if he was listening. Sam sat at the head, looking very serious.

'Did you find out anything?' said Lee.

'Not much, no. But, according to the Guild, the Isle of Smiles is something of a mana well.'

'A mana well?' said Nanny Flannel. 'And what, pray, is a mana well?'

'It's a rare, natural source of the stuff, Nanny,' said Sam. 'According to the Guild, the whole island is quite rich in mana. I must say, I wasn't aware of it myself—but the Guild has apparently known about it for years. They didn't know there was a magical entity actually living there, though. They think that, whatever it is, this entity feeds on the mana—which means it probably can't leave the area, not without losing most of its powers. Whatever *they* may be. Meanwhile, until they've done a lot more research in the archives, nobody from the Guild is to go near the place—which means no more trips to the Isle of Smiles. Sorry about that, Measle. Not that it makes much difference—they close the place next week, for the whole winter—so we couldn't have gone again for several months anyway. Perhaps they'll have cleared up the mystery by the time they open again in the spring.'

Later that same evening, they were watching the news on the television. At the end of the news came the weather forecast. It had been a hot day and the whole screen was covered in little pictures of the sun.

'A glorious day all over the country,' said the weatherman. 'Record breaking temperatures here—and here—a real Indian summer. Not a drop of rain anywhere—apart from one rather unfortunate little spot, right here on Borgrove Moor, where it's actually pouring with rain right now. It only started a few minutes ago—but it's really bucketing down. A rather odd meteorological phenomenon actually—a very small, localized low-pressure system, that seems to have come out of nowhere and doesn't appear to be going anywhere either. Very interesting and quite rare. Anyway, it's a foretaste of what's to come, I'm afraid—this lovely weather won't last and by tomorrow afternoon the wintry weather will be with us all over the country, with lots of wind and rain everywhere, just like what poor old Borgrove Moor is suffering at this very moment—'

Sam pressed the mute button on the television

remote and the sound died. He turned to Lee and said, 'What do you think?'

'Well ... wrathmonks, obviously,' said Lee. 'Must be rather a lot of them, too—for them to show up on the meteorological radar like that.'

Measle felt a sudden chill. On his own, Basil Tramplebone had been bad enough—but a whole bunch of wrathmonks, all together in one place?

'What are they doing?' he said, nervously.

Sam shook his head. 'No idea, son. Nothing good, that's for sure. I'd better notify the Guild.'

Sam got up and went to his study to telephone his superiors. Lee and Measle and Nanny Flannel were watching a game show when he came back.

'We're to sit tight,' he said. 'At least for the time being. They're keeping an eye on the place.'

Griswold
Gristle

Judge
Cedric
Hardscrabble

Buford
Cudgel

Scab
Draggle

Mrs
Zagreb

Mr
Zagreb

Frognell
Flabbit

THE CAVE

The air inside the cave was damp and cold. It was the kind of cold that slowly seeps into your body, chilling your toes and fingers first and then creeping gradually through your whole frame, numbing you until you can't even shiver any more. It was dark in the cave too, the only light coming from a few guttering candles stuck in crevices in the rock walls.

Griswold Gristle sat, uncomfortably, on a narrow piece of rock that stuck out from the cave wall. The projecting rock was just high enough from the floor of the cave to give Griswold a small height advantage over Judge Cedric Hardscrabble, who stood next to him—and this gave Griswold the look of a small, pale, fat king, sitting on his throne, with his trusty Court Chamberlain at his side.

In front of Griswold and Judge Cedric stood five figures, of various shapes and sizes and ages. All were dressed in black, all had white faces and staring, fishy eyes—and all of them looked cold and uncomfortable and not a little irritable.

'But what I don't underssstand, Griswold,' said one of them, in a scratchy, self-important voice (he was a tubby man with a thin hank of long, greasy hair combed over his scalp in a futile effort to hide his baldness), 'what I don't underssstand, is who put you in charge? I don't remember usss holding any elections. Ssso, who put you in charge?'

There was a murmur of agreement among the others. Griswold sighed. What was it about wrathmonks that made them so quarrelsome? Why could they never agree about anything? *If only*, he thought, *we could all get along with each other— why, wrathmonks could probably rule the world! Instead, all he was getting from them were arguments!*

'The reason I am ssspeaking for all of usss, my dear Mr Flabbit, is because it was I who called usss all together here on Borgrove Moor. It was I who found the thing—'

'I found it too,' said Judge Cedric, shooting a hurt look at Griswold.

'Indeed you did, Cedric,' said Griswold, in a soothing voice. 'Cedric and I found it together. Found it in the ruins of the very house recently inhabited by our dear friend, the late and much-lamented Basil Tramplebone—'

'Get a blinking move on, Gristle,' growled a deep, rumbling voice. All eyes turned to the back of the group, where an enormous figure stood. His hulking shadow wavered huge against the rock walls of the cave. His arms hung by his sides and the tips of his black-gloved fingers (fingers as thick as bananas!) reached to a point half a metre below his knees. Everything about him—from his black hobnailed boots, up over his bulky black leather jacket, and on up to the shiny black motorcycle helmet on his bullet head—was oversized. Behind the helmet's visor, his eyes were dark and deep under his heavy brows and his mouth was a wide slit in his flat white face.

'Ah,' said Griswold, with a hint of nervousness in his voice. 'Mr Cudgel—my dear fellow—'

'Don't "dear fellow" me,' growled Cudgel. 'It's cold in here, Gristle. It's cold and damp and dark and I don't care for it. The sssooner I'm out of here, the happier I shall be. Ssso, just get on with it.'

'I sssecond that,' said Mr Flabbit, nodding his head so violently that his long hank of greasy hair came unstuck from his scalp and flapped loose around his coat collar. 'Ssstop patting yourself on the back, Griswold, and tell usss what you have in mind. And do it quickly—our merged rain clouds are sure to be noticed sssooner or later and I don't want the Wizards' Guild knowing where I am, thank you very much.'

Griswold ground his teeth with annoyance. He cleared his throat and started again.

'Fellow wrathmonks, we are gathered here to discuss a plan which will lead to the ultimate dessstruction of the evil Ssstubbs family—'

There was an immediate reaction. The wrathmonks twitched and shook with rage, muttering and snarling like a pack of angry dogs. *'Ssstubbs!—We hate the Ssstubbses!—They got my friend Hogsbottle!—They're Guild's pets!—Think they're better than usss!—Dangerous, that's what they are!—Filthy, horrible beastsss!—We'll get them!'*

'Friends, friends!' shouted Griswold over the noise. 'Lisssten to me! That is why we are *here*! To devise a plot to rid oursssselves of these foul creatures! That is why Judge Cedric and I sssought the *thing*! For, with the *thing* in our possession, we have a powerful tool, which will aid uss in sssubduing the Ssstubbses! Basil himself sssubdued the Ssstubbses for ssseveral years, using thisss very object that I hold in my hands!'

Griswold held out his two pudgy little hands and the wrathmonks shuffled forward to look. A small cloth bag lay on Griswold's sweaty palms.

'What's in there, then?' said a skinny young wrathmonk, with long, wispy yellow hair and a scruffy, straggly, blond beard.

'A great treasure, young Draggle,' said Griswold, proudly. 'It once adorned the head of an actual

Gorgon. It is the mummified head of one of Medusa's sssnakes.'

'Yeah? But… how do we know that's what it is?' said Draggle. 'I mean to sssay—that could be anything in there, couldn't it? Like… like a pebble or something. Let's have a look at it.'

Griswold hissed in disgust. *Really, what a sorry collection these wrathmonks were! They had the brains of a herd of goats!*

'We cannot look at it, dear friends,' he said, with all the patience he could muster. 'If we do, we shall be turned inssstantly to ssstone. That is what the Medusa head does, you sssee. Merely retrieving the thing from the ruins of dear Basil's house brought Cedric and me to the brink of peril. However, if used properly, it is a fearsssome weapon against our enemies. It is the first of many other weapons we shall use against the hateful Ssstubbses.'

'What sssort of other weapons?' asked a hard-faced, skinny woman in a long black dress. Her shiny black hair was scraped back from her long, thin face and tied in a tight little bun at the back of her head. Her nose was long and sharp, except for the tip, which spread out into a sort of blob, making the whole thing look—from the front at least—rather like a soup spoon. Her mouth was caked thickly with scarlet lipstick and she had painted a pair of high, arched, jet-black eyebrows on her white forehead.

'Excellent quessstion, Mrs Zagreb,' said

Griswold, bowing slightly in the woman's direction. 'We shall use the Medusa head, of courssse—and also all our various individual powers, in particular our exhalation enchantments.'

'He means our *breathing* magic, dear,' said a short, dark man, standing by Mrs Zagreb's side. The man had beady black eyes, thick, wavy black hair, and a small, carefully clipped black moustache. His black suit was pressed and shiny and he had several big gold rings on his fingers. He looked like a black beetle.

'I know that, Zag,' said the woman, sharply. 'I know what "exhalation enchantment" means. Do you think I'm a fool?'

'Of courssse I don't, my dear,' said Mr Zagreb, hurriedly. 'On the contrary, you have a brilliant mind.'

'I mossst certainly do,' said Mrs Zagreb, her scarlet lips drawing back from her teeth in a snarl of contempt. 'A lot more brilliant than yours, that'sss for sure!'

Mr Zagreb nodded nervously and decided to change the subject. 'Our exhalation enchantment will come in very ussseful, I predict.' He turned proudly to the other wrathmonks. 'Our breath is highly corrosive. Particularly my lady wife's. It can ssstrip paint from walls. It can remove varnish from furniture. We find it mossst useful when trying to dissslodge those annoying little price ssstickers you find on merchandise these days—one tiny puff from Mrs Zagreb's lovely lipsss, and the thing almossst removes itssself!'

Griswold tried to look impressed. '*Mossst* useful, I'm sure,' he said. 'We shall certainly find a place for sssuch a talent in my plan. For I have a plan, dear friends—and it's a fine plan. A wonderful, *wonderful* plan. My plan is to—'

And that was as far as he got before the other wrathmonks started to interrupt him.

'I think we should get a really big mincing machine and grind them all up into hamburger meat!' shouted Draggle.

'Nonsssense, young Draggle!' yelled Flabbit. 'Far too complicated. I propose we capture the Ssstubbs family, then buy a sssmall ship, sssail far out to sssea and then sssink it with them ssstill on board!'

'Don't be ssstupid, Flabbit!' roared Cudgel. 'We'd all drown too. And, where are we going to get a ship? No—but I sssuggest we drop them from a helicopter ssstraight down into an active volcano—'

'I don't much care for flying!' squeaked Mr Zagreb. 'Nor does my lady wife. Here's an idea: we could get really big feathers and tickle them to death—'

'Don't talk rubbish, Zag!' barked Mrs Zagreb. 'Tickle them indeed! They might like it! No—we should put them in a cardboard box, full of ssscorpions—'

'We could make them eat coathangers!' shrieked Judge Cedric Hardscrabble, who had been desperately trying to think of some horrible calamity for the Stubbses to experience—and when he couldn't think of anything sensible, now said the first thing that came into his head.

Griswold was flapping his hands in frustration. 'Friends, friends—I beg you—please be patient and listen to my plan—my wonderful, wonderful plan—'

BE QUIET.

The babble of the wrathmonks stopped. All their movements stopped as well—their pacing feet, their flailing hands, their shaking heads—as if they had been somehow frozen in their tracks.

It wasn't a voice—or at least, not a voice that any of them heard with their ears. It was a sound *inside their heads*, a sound that had simply arrived in there without going through their ears at all. An icy sound, cold and hard and dark—like frozen blood. They all heard it in their heads at the same moment and all of them felt a sudden, overwhelming impulse to stop their chattering and listen and wait for further instructions.

The further instructions came almost at once.

REMAIN QUIET. REMAIN STILL. I AM COMING.

The wrathmonks stood like stone statues, not moving a muscle.

There was a shimmering in the shadows, a movement of air and light—and then an extraordinary little figure drifted out of the gloom at the back of the cave.

It was a garden gnome. A perfectly ordinary little garden gnome, obviously made of painted concrete, with a tall, painted-on crimson hat and a little painted-on green jacket and a pair of painted-on, shiny black boots with the tops turned over. The gnome's face was painted too, with jolly red cheeks and a jolly red nose and a pair of sly little eyes with wrinkles at the corners. A clay pipe stuck out of the gnome's long white beard which surrounded the little grinning mouth. The gnome floated a few centimetres off the rocky floor of the cave, drifting steadily towards the group of motionless wrathmonks. When it arrived in their midst, it hovered for a moment, turning slowly in the cold, damp air—and then it settled with a small thump onto the rocky floor.

For several moments there was a stunned silence. Then Griswold Gristle found his voice.

'What is thisss? Is thiss sssome sssort of joke?'

NO JOKE.

Griswold's piggy little eyes blinked in astonishment. The gnome's mouth hadn't moved— *Well, how could it? It was made of concrete!*—but Griswold had heard the words quite clearly—or rather, he hadn't heard them at all, they had simply appeared inside his head, clear as anything …

'Who—who are you? *What* are you?'

I AM THAT WHICH YOU SHOULD FEAR THE MOST.

Griswold glared at the gnome. It didn't look particularly dangerous. In fact, it looked rather ridiculous, standing there with its fixed, concrete grin and its silly little clay pipe.

'I think,' said Griswold, slowly, 'that it should be the other way round. I think *you* should fear *usss*.'

There was a murmur of agreement from the other wrathmonks and they edged a little closer to the gnome, staring at it with angry eyes.

'In fact,' continued Griswold, his voice strengthening, 'I think it would be besst if you left immediately. Thisss is a private meeting. The guessst lissst contains the following names.' And here Griswold pulled a folded sheet of paper from the inside pocket of his black jacket, opened it and began to read in a pompous, official sort of voice. 'Mr Frognell Flabbit, Mr Ssscab Draggle, Mr Buford Cudgel, Mr and Mrs Zagreb, myssself as chairman, of courssse, and Judge Cedric Hardssscrabble as vice-chairman. But you—whoever you are—*you* are not here on my lissst. Therefore, whoever or whatever you are, you are not welcome and I sssuggest you leave at once.'

The gnome simply stood there, unmoving and silent.

Griswold began to feel a little foolish—*he was talking to a concrete gnome, of all things!*

'Very well,' said Griswold, 'I have given you fair warning. Gentlemen—lady—kindly deal with thisss intruder.'

It was young Scab Draggle who made the first move. He stepped forward and hissed, *'Zzzssychhherpsy herpsy globbershmuck!'* At the same moment, a pair of purple beams of light flew from his eyes and smacked the gnome clean in the middle of its forehead.

Nothing happened.

Draggle frowned. That was his best spell—his Blow-Up-Like-A-Balloon spell! The gnome's body was supposed to swell up, getting bigger and bigger and rounder and rounder and then—like an overfilled beach ball—burst with an enormous bang! But it hadn't worked! Now he was drained of his mana—at least until this time tomorrow—and all he had left was his exhalation enchantment. He stepped quickly over to the gnome, bent over the short figure, took a deep breath, and began to blow his stinking breath.

It seemed to last forever, this endless breathing out, and the only indication of any effort on Draggle's part was that—after thirty seconds—his eyes began to bulge a little with the exertion. After forty seconds, there was still no change in the gnome's appearance.

'What is Draggle's exhalation enchantment sssupposed to do, actually?' whispered Mr Zagreb into Frognell Flabbit's ear.

'Sssupposed to make all the hair fall out,' muttered Flabbit, smoothing his greasy comb-over into place.

'It doesn't ssseem to be working, does it?' said Mr Zagreb, under his breath.

'Well, it wouldn't,' said Flabbit. 'That's not real hair. Unlike yours and mine, Zag, old man.' He broke off, stepped forward and touched Draggle's arm. 'Here, that's not going to work, young Draggle. Let me have a go. Watch its nose fall off!'

Draggle stepped aside. Flabbit took his place, glared at the gnome and said, *'Haarrrcky schnaarrrcky oichenblast!'*

A sizzling yellow flame splashed across the gnome's face—then blew itself out, leaving the gnome untouched.

'All right,' said Flabbit, sounding a little disappointed. 'That was my nose-falling-off enchantment and it doesn't ssseem to work. But look at *my* exhalation. I've got a good one, I have. In a couple of ssseconds, it's going to have the worssst toothache of its life!'

Flabbit bent over the gnome and began to breathe on its head. After a solid minute of blowing out—without taking in any air at all—Flabbit was completely deflated and the gnome appeared to be perfectly fine, without any trace of a terrible toothache at all.

'Yeah—well,' said Flabbit, breathlessly. 'It probably hasn't got any teeth, either.'

One by one, the wrathmonks tried their major spells and then, with their mana exhausted, they tried their exhalation enchantments. The only one that made any difference at all to the gnome's appearance was when Mr and Mrs Zagreb were breathing together into its face—after half a minute, a few square centimetres of paint on its crimson hat blackened and peeled away—but, other than that (and by the time all the wrathmonks had taken their turns) the gnome appeared quite unchanged. It stood there, grinning its sly little concrete smile, appearing to be rather enjoying the wrathmonks' humiliation.

Then—

THANK YOU. I AM GRATEFUL FOR THE SMALL GIFTS OF YOUR MANA.

'Who—who—who are you?' stammered Griswold.

I? I AM—THE LAST.

'The lassst what?'

THE LAST—OF THE DRAGODONS.

They all heard it in their heads and they all turned and stared at each other, puzzled frowns creasing their foreheads.

'*Dragodon?*' said Draggle. 'Wozza Dragodon when it's at home, eh?'

'*Dragodon?*' said Mr Zagreb. 'Now, where have I heard that word before?'

'Don't be a fool, Zag!' snapped Mrs Zagreb. '*I've* never heard of it, ssso you *certainly* have never heard of it—and don't pretend you have!'

'*Dragodon,*' muttered Flabbit, rolling the word around on his tongue. 'No, doesn't ring a bell.'

'It's a sssort of motor car, isn't it?' said Judge Cedric.

Griswold Gristle shook his head, impatiently.

'Ssso ignorant, all of you,' he sneered. 'The ssstory of the Dragodons is an ancient legend and, if any of you had ever bothered to visit the Library of the Wizards' Guild and read the hissstory of our race, you would mossst certainly be aware of it. In the golden olden days, the Dragodons were the keepers of the dragons. They possessed great powers, which they used to control the monsssters. It was sssaid that they could ssspeak to them, communicating directly with the creatures' primitive brains. The Dragodons were thus sssupremely important and powerful wizards and no kingdom could exist without employing the ssservices of one of them. Then, according to the legend, these Dragodons became arrogant and began to think they should have more power than even the kings they ssserved—ssso they banded together and went to war, riding their dragons against the world of men. There were great battles and much dessstruction and loss of life—but then, ssslowly and with the help of the wizards and the warlocks and even sssome of the wrathmonks, mankind managed to turn the tide of battle against the Dragodons. One by one they were dessstroyed, along with their dragons, until there was not one left alive.'

There was a long silence. Then Cudgel said, 'I don't believe a word of it.'

'Of *coursse* you don't, my dear Cudgel,' said Griswold, smiling kindly at the huge wrathmonk. 'Nor do *any* of usss. It's jussst a ssstory. A legend. No truth to it whatsssoever.'

IT IS THE TRUTH.

They all turned and looked at the garden gnome. Griswold opened his mouth to speak but the gnome got there before him.

LISTEN AND LEARN, LITTLE WRATHMONKS. THE STORY IS NOT A LEGEND—IT IS HISTORY. THERE WAS A GREAT WAR. THERE WERE MANY TERRIBLE BATTLES. AT FIRST, WE AND OUR DRAGONS WERE VICTORIOUS. THEN, LATER—THROUGH THE TREACHERY OF THE WIZARDS, WE BEGAN TO LOSE THE STRUGGLE. ONE BY ONE, WE FELL. OUR DRAGONS, OURSELVES—ONE BY ONE. EVEN MY OWN GREAT ARCTURION WAS FINALLY BROUGHT DOWN TO EARTH. HE FELL—AND I FELL WITH HIM, FOR I WAS ASTRIDE HIS GREAT NECK. TOGETHER, WE PLUNGED TO THE GROUND. THE FALL FROM THE SKY WAS LONG AND THE ROCKS ON THE GROUND WERE HARD.

The words died away in the wrathmonks' heads, leaving behind a slight aching feeling. Then—

BUT I SURVIVED THAT LONG, LONG FALL. I AM THE LAST. THE LAST OF THE DRAGODONS.

'A Dragodon?' sneered Griswold. 'You? I hardly think—'

I KNOW. YOU RARELY DO, GRISWOLD.

'How do you know my name?' gasped Griswold.

I KNOW ALL YOUR NAMES. I KNOW EVERYTHING ABOUT ALL OF YOU. I CAN CRAWL INSIDE YOUR HEADS AND DIG OUT YOUR SECRETS. YOU CAN HIDE NOTHING FROM ME. I AM YOUR MASTER AND YOU WILL OBEY ME.

'We mossst certainly will not!' spluttered Griswold. 'The very idea! Expecting usss to obey sssome minor magical entity in temporary possession of a concrete garden gnome! Ridiculousss! Quite ridiculousss! And as for your claim to be the lassst of the Dragodons—well, I don't believe they ever existed!'

BE CAREFUL, LITTLE WRATHMONK.

Griswold drew himself up to his full height and looked down his nose at the garden gnome. 'Huh!' he snorted. 'If you're the lassst of the Dragodons, why don't you ssstop hiding in a sssilly little garden gnome and show usss what you really look like?'

DEAR LITTLE WRATHMONK. YOU TALK TOO MUCH. I WILL NOT SHOW YOU WHAT I LOOK LIKE— BUT I WILL SHOW YOU WHAT I CAN DO. I WILL SHOW ALL OF YOU WHAT I CAN DO.

A moment of stillness passed— then a tiny spark of green fire flashed from the bowl of the gnome's clay pipe. The spark darted across the cold damp air of the cave and onto one corner of Griswold's thick lips. Then, like the needle of a sewing machine, it zipped rapidly up and down, moving steadily from one corner of Griswold's mouth towards the other corner—and, as it passed across his lips, it left behind blank, white skin. It was as if Griswold's mouth was being rubbed out by the little eraser on the end of a pencil, and replaced by—well, by *nothing*.

Griswold's eyes got very large and very round and he tried to open his mouth to object to what was being done to him—but he no longer had a mouth to open, so he simply sat there, his snub nose twitching, and his eyes blinking, and the two little ridges of bare skin where his eyebrows would have been if he'd had any moving up and down in a mixture of horror and fury and utter bewilderment at what was happening to him.

Then, when the spark was finished, it left Griswold's face and hovered in the still damp air.

A DEFINITE IMPROVEMENT, GRISTLE. AND NOW FOR THE REST OF YOU.

The green spark zipped to the side of Judge Cedric's forehead. Judge Cedric said, 'Ow,' loudly.

HARDSCRABBLE HANDS OUT FOOLISH SENTENCES. HE SHALL HAVE ONE OF HIS OWN.

The spark moved quickly across the skin towards the right side of Judge Cedric's forehead, writing in blue tattoo ink as it went. I AM A VERY STUPID OLD JUDGE, it wrote, and when it was finished the green spark darted across the cave and hung in front of Draggle's frightened eyes.

WHAT CHARMING HAIR YOU HAVE, MASTER DRAGGLE. WE MUST PUT IT TO SOME USE.

The spark leapt forward and wound itself into

Draggle's long blond hair. It buzzed, like an angry bee, among the dirty locks, braiding them faster than the eye could see—plaiting them into a sort of loop over the top of Draggle's head—then, when it was done, the spark attached itself to the top of the plaited loop and lifted Draggle off his feet. Draggle yelped with pain as he rose up towards the roof of the cave. The spark lifted him higher and higher—and then dropped the loop over a small outcrop of rock that stuck out high on the cave wall. The spark hovered briefly in front of Draggle's pain-filled eyes and then darted back to the cave floor. It paused there briefly, as if deciding whom to visit next. Then it zoomed through the damp air and landed an inch from Frognell Flabbit's nose

FLABBIT BY NAME. PERHAPS FLABBY BY NATURE?

The green spark flew and, moments later, every bone in Flabbit's stout body was turned to a soft jelly and he collapsed in a shapeless heap on the cave floor. He looked like a pile of clothes with a head stuck on the top—and the head had a very worried look on its face.

Mr and Mrs Zagreb were next.

AH—THE PROUD ZAGREBS. THEY MUST BE TAUGHT HUMILITY. THEY MUST BOW BEFORE US.

The spark sizzled to the Zagrebs' eyes—there was some yellow smoke—a squeal of pain from both of them—and, when the smoke cleared, everybody saw that Mr and Mrs Zagreb's eyes had been moved from their usual place and put, instead, on the tops of their heads, underneath their hair. This meant that, if they wanted to see what was going on in front of them, they had to angle their heads over and point their now eyeless faces at the ground—and that is what they now did, bending both their bodies into a permanent bow before the little garden gnome.

Buford Cudgel was the last to receive the treatment. The green spark flew towards Cudgel's great body and then paused there, hovering at the level of Cudgel's broad black leather belt.

MR CUDGEL—WITH HIS GREAT BRUTE STRENGTH. PERHAPS, FOR MR CUDGEL—A LITTLE DAINTINESS? A SUGGESTION OF GRACE? A TOUCH OF DELICACY?

The spark flashed and darted down to Cudgel's enormous booted feet. It zigzagged there for a couple of seconds and then began to move up towards Cudgel's helmeted head, moving rapidly from side to side as it went—and, as it did so, it left behind a transformed Mr Cudgel. The huge wrathmonk's black boots morphed into a dainty pair of pink ballet slippers—the black leather trousers became a pair of shiny, pink tights—Cudgel's thick belt turned into a frilly pink ballet tutu, which stuck out from Cudgel's thick waist like a filmy ruff—his leather motorcycle jacket became a pink, lacy top, decorated here and there with pink satin ribbons—and the black helmet disappeared entirely and was replaced by a little coronet of soft, pink, downy feathers, which fluttered prettily every time Cudgel moved his head. Then, when the spark had finished this final transformation, turning the brutish Mr Cudgel into a very pink (but still very brutish-looking) ballerina, it moved up and hovered over his head. It attached itself suddenly to the top of Cudgel's cropped scalp and lifted him up until he was resting on the points of his toes. Mr Cudgel, with sweat pouring down his broad, flat face, could do nothing but hang there, quivering slightly like an enormous pink blancmange.

There was a short, stunned silence from everybody, broken only by a nervous giggle from high up on the cave wall. For all the pain from his pulled blond hair, Scab Draggle still found the spectacle of Buford Cudgel as a pink ballerina just a bit funny.

Then—

A SMALL TASTE OF SOME OF MY LESSER POWERS. I HAVE OTHERS FAR GREATER. AND NOW, PERHAPS, YOU WILL ATTEND TO WHAT I HAVE TO SAY?

There was a murmur of agreement and a lot of nervous nodding of heads—except for Draggle and Flabbit and Cudgel, none of whom could move their heads at all. Instead, these three mumbled that yes, they were absolutely prepared to listen to whatever was said and would, absolutely *certainly*, agree with *all* of it—if only they could, perhaps, be released from their rather painful (and, in Mr Cudgel's case, extremely *humiliating*) conditions?

VERY WELL. NOW—I UNDERSTAND YOU WISH TO DESTROY THE FAMILY OF STUBBS? EXCELLENT. SO DO I. HOWEVER—HAVE ANY OF YOU EVER MET THE STUBBS FAMILY?

There was more nervous shaking of heads.

I HAVE. THEY CAME TO MY HOME. THEY ARE POWERFUL, PARTICULARLY WHEN ACTING TOGETHER. FAR MORE POWERFUL THAN ANY OF YOU. BUT NOT, OF COURSE, AS POWERFUL AS I. NOTHING IS AS POWERFUL AS I. SO, IF YOU WISH TO DESTROY THIS FAMILY OF STUBBS, YOU WILL DO IT WITH MY HELP. ON MY TERRITORY. UNDER MY LEADERSHIP. AND ACCORDING TO THE PLAN THAT I SHALL DEVISE. DO YOU AGREE TO THIS?

The wrathmonks looked nervously at each other. They were thinking that perhaps this thing, this creature—with its amazing resistance to their magic and its enormous abilities with its own—would make a much better leader than Griswold Gristle who, at the moment, didn't even have a mouth with which to tell them what to do. And as for Judge Cedric Hardscrabble leading them, well—Judge Cedric probably couldn't lead an ant to a sugar lump.

They all looked back at the garden gnome and, together, they all signified their agreement.

EXCELLENT. A WISE DECISION.

The green spark detached itself from Mr Cudgel's scalp, dropping the vast, pink ballerina heavily to the floor. Then it zoomed round the cave, touching each wrathmonk as it passed by. Griswold's mouth reformed on his face—the tattoo on Judge Cedric's forehead faded away—Flabbit's bones became hard again and he slowly pulled himself back onto his feet—Mr and Mrs Zagreb's eyes returned to their proper places—Cudgel's pink satin became black leather once again—and there was a sudden scream from high up on the cave wall as Draggle's hair unwound itself from its braid and released him from the rock peg he'd been hanging on. There was a long wailing cry as the young wrathmonk fell and then a loud thump as he hit the rocky floor. For a moment, Draggle lay still—then, grunting with pain, he sat up, rubbing his back.

ARE YOU NOW READY TO OBEY ME?

There was much vigorous nodding of heads. Flabbit's hair flapped wildly and Cudgel's motorcycle helmet almost fell off his bony skull. Even Griswold reluctantly bowed his head in humble submission.

GOOD. MY FIRST COMMAND—I REQUIRE TO BE TAKEN HOME. NOW. THIS INSTANT. CARRY ME CAREFULLY. ONE CHIP AND I SHALL BECOME VERY ANGRY. VERY ANGRY INDEED. CARRY ME HOME, MY LITTLE MENIALS. I SHALL SHOW YOU THE WAY.

Slowly—and very fearfully—the wrathmonks shuffled forward. With trembling hands, they lifted the garden gnome onto their shoulders. Then, slowly—as if they were carrying the coffin of a great, dead king—they moved towards the distant mouth of the cave.

KiDNaPPeD

Ten days later, the wrathmonks struck.

It happened while the Stubbs family were out shopping. The three of them, and Nanny Flannel, had bundled into the Stubbs car and driven to the nearby town. Sam had parked the big green car in the car park of the local supermarket and then Measle, Sam, Lee, and Nanny Flannel had gone inside and done the week's shopping, which meant that Nanny Flannel told everybody what to get and everybody did as they were told. When they were finished, they had two trolleys piled high with groceries. Sam was pushing one and Lee was pushing the other. As they came out through the supermarket's sliding doors, Nanny Flannel suddenly turned to Measle and said, 'Oh, Measle dear—I've forgotten the tomato ketchup. We can't live without tomato ketchup. Well, *you* can't live without tomato ketchup. We'll have to go back for it. Come on, help me find it.'

'OK,' said Measle, cheerfully. He didn't mind going back for tomato ketchup because it was true—he really didn't think he could possibly live without it. Measle had discovered that almost *everything* (except perhaps chocolate cake) tasted better with tomato ketchup on it.

'We'll meet you at the car,' said Sam, beginning to push his shopping trolley towards the car park.

Lee smiled and started to follow him. 'That's right—leave your dad and me to do all the loading,' she called over her shoulder.

Measle and Nanny Flannel went back into the supermarket. It took them a few moments to find the ketchup and then another few moments waiting to pay for it in the fast checkout lane. Just as Nanny Flannel was handing over the money, they heard the sound of muffled shouting coming from the car park. Then there was a crash of glass, some more shouting—and then the roar of a car engine and the squeal of tyres.

'Something funny going on out there,' said the checkout girl, craning her head round and trying to look out through the tall plate glass windows. 'Sounded like somebody was getting mugged or something.'

Measle felt a sudden fear rush through his body

like ice water. His mum and his dad were out there—and they attracted danger like jam attracts wasps! Without thinking, he began to run towards the sliding doors. By the sound of pounding feet close behind him, he guessed that Nanny Flannel had the same idea.

'Here—you've forgotten your ketchup!' shouted the checkout girl—but Measle didn't hear her. He was already through the doors and was racing across the car park towards the spot where they had left the car. Nanny Flannel followed as fast as she could which, for an old lady her size and shape, was surprisingly fast.

When he got to the Stubbs car, Measle skidded to a halt, panting hard. Sam was there, standing next to his shopping trolley. He was standing quite still and his mouth was open and he had an odd, bewildered look on his face. At his feet there were some pieces of broken glass. Near the front of the car, the other shopping trolley—the one that Lee had been pushing—was lying on its side, with the contents scattered on the tarmac.

Measle tugged at his father's sleeve.

'What happened, Dad? Where's Mum?'

Sam looked down. He stared blankly at Measle. 'What are you talking about?' he muttered. Then he frowned. 'Who are you? What do you want?'

For a moment, Measle couldn't reply. He stared horror-struck up at his father's face. There was something strange about Sam's eyes—they were blank and empty, with no trace of friendliness in them. What was worse—there was no sign that Sam even recognized him.

Nanny Flannel came panting up to join them. 'What happened?' she gasped.

'I don't know,' said Measle. 'Dad's gone funny. He doesn't seem to know who I am.' He grabbed Sam's hand and shouted up into his father's face, 'I'm Measle, Dad!'

'That's an odd name,' said Sam. 'And I'm not your dad.'

'Don't you know me?'

Sam shook his head. 'No... no, I don't.'

'But you must know who I am!' shouted Measle. 'You *must*!'

Sam frowned with puzzlement. 'I think I'd remember you if I did,' he said, slowly. 'I mean—no offence—but you do have the weirdest haircut I've ever seen. I think, if I'd seen you before, I'd remember you—and I don't. Sorry.'

'Dad! I'm *Measle*!'

Sam gently removed his hand from Measle's clutches. 'Measle, yes. You told me that. But why do you keep calling me Dad? I'm not your dad.'

Measle stared up at Sam, his mind racing. Something terrible had happened here—and where was Lee? He looked towards the overturned shopping trolley—there, a few metres from it, were a pair of black rubber skid marks on the tarmac—and the ground there was wet, as if a very small shower of rain had fallen only on that particular spot, and nowhere else in the car park.

Measle looked back at Sam. His father was staring off into the distance, a small frown creasing his forehead. Measle grabbed his father's hands and shook them both hard, forcing Sam to look down at him.

'All right,' said Measle. 'All right. If you're not my dad—then *who are you?*'

Sam smiled—the kind of smile adults put on their faces when a kid asks them what they think is a really stupid question—and then the smile faded and a frightened and bewildered look flooded his face.

'Who am I?' muttered Sam. 'Who *am* I? I don't know. Why don't I know? And who are *you*? And *where* am I? And what's going on?'

'I don't *know* what's going on!' yelled Measle. 'I heard some shouting, then a car driving away fast—and now Mum's gone and you don't know who I am!'

Sam pulled one hand free from Measle's grasp and put it to his head. He rubbed his eyes and then blinked several times. Then he said, 'I don't feel so good. I think I'd better sit down.'

Measle opened the car door and he and Nanny Flannel helped Sam into the front passenger seat. Then Measle looked around wildly, searching for somebody who could help him. There was an old man leaning on a walking stick, about ten metres away, who was watching him. Measle ran over to him and said, breathlessly, 'Did you see what happened?'

The old man sniffed. 'Well, yes I did, young fellow. There was this van—all black it was—and these people jumped out—they were all in black, too—funny looking people they were, their faces were so white they looked like corpses—and they threw a bottle at that chap over there and some funny-looking blue gas comes out of it—and then they grabbed this lady and bundled her into the van—and then they scarpered. I saw the whole thing. Making a film, are they? Where's the camera then?'

Wrathmonks! thought Measle. *Wrathmonks have kidnapped my mum!*

Measle wanted to ask the old man more questions but he was already wandering away, in search of a non-existent film crew. Measle ran back to the car. Sam was still sitting there in the passenger seat, with the door open and Nanny Flannel squatting at his feet. Nanny Flannel turned to Measle, a worried look on her face.

'I know what this is, Measle, dear. It's amnesia. Your dad can remember obvious stuff, like how to walk and talk—but he can't remember a thing about his life. It's a complete blank. He doesn't know he's a wizard—and he doesn't remember either of us.'

Measle swallowed hard. 'What are we going to do?'

Nanny pointed at the overturned shopping trolley. 'Where's your mum?'

Quickly, Measle blurted out what the old man had told him and, by the time he'd finished, Nanny Flannel's pink cheeks had turned pale.

'We must get your father home,' she said, her voice shaky. 'That's the first thing we must do.'

'But what about Mum?'

'We don't know where she is, dear. And we can't involve the police—not in wizarding business. That's the rule. No matter how serious, we have to deal with it ourselves. So, come on, never mind the shopping—into the car.'

'But we can't just—'

'Yes, we *can*, Measle dear. We *must*. We don't know where they're taking her, we don't know what they want. What we *do* know is that we must get your dad home as fast as possible—and then we must tell the Wizards' Guild what's happened and *they* will get your mum back, because we certainly can't. All right?'

Measle thought quickly. Nanny Flannel was obviously right—what else could they do? It was just—well—it seemed so cold and unfeeling, just getting back into the car and driving away—

Measle stared hard at the ground, willing himself

not to cry. *This can't be happening,* he thought. *I can't lose my parents again! I've only had them back for a few weeks—and now—no! This can't be happening!*

But it was—it was happening. And there was nothing he could do about it.

He felt Nanny Flannel's hand touching his arm. He took a deep breath and said, 'All right, Nanny. We'll go.'

Measle walked around to the other side of the car. As he was opening the door, his foot kicked against something that was lying on the tarmac. The object skittered away from his foot, making a small metallic sound as it skidded across the ground. Measle looked down. There were the shards of glass from the broken bottle—and there, a couple of metres away, a bottle cap. Without thinking, Measle bent and picked up the bottle cap and slipped it into his pocket. Then he slid into the back seat of the car.

Nanny Flannel had the engine running and, as soon as Measle slammed his door shut, she stamped down on the accelerator pedal and they roared out of the car park.

Three hours later, Measle and Nanny Flannel were sitting on one of the big couches in the living room of Merlin Manor. Tinker, aware that something was wrong, lay on the carpet close to

Measle, his head resting on Measle's feet. Opposite them, on the other big couch, sat two men. One was tall and lean and dark, the other short and fat and fair. Both wore dark suits and plain ties, both had an identical pair of dark glasses perched on their noses and neither of them looked at Measle very much, even when they were talking to him.

The interview was not going well.

'How do you know they were wrathmonks, Measle?' said the tall lean man, sternly. 'Did you see them?'

Measle shook his head. 'No—but there was an old man there and he told me what happened.'

'He told you they were wrathmonks?'

'No—but he told me what they looked like— and I used to know one and, well—it sounded a lot like wrathmonks—and the ground was all wet and so I—'

'And so you jumped to a conclusion?' There was a note of accusation in the lean man's voice.

Nanny Flannel smacked her hand down hard on the arm of the couch. 'He most certainly did *not* jump to a conclusion, Mr Needle,' she said angrily. 'Measle's not a fool—and he lived with a wrathmonk for a very long time. If he thinks they were wrathmonks, then they were wrathmonks. And for what it's worth, I think they were wrathmonks too. Who else but wrathmonks would do such a thing, I ask you?'

The short, fat, fair man grunted and said, 'A professional gang of kidnappers, for one, Miss Flannel. They needn't have been wrathmonks at all. And, if they weren't wrathmonks, then there's nothing the Guild can do about it. Is there, my dear Needle?'

'Nothing at all, my dear Bland,' said Mr Needle.

'Well—but can't you find out where she is?' said Measle. 'Haven't you got something you could look into?'

Mr Bland shot a small smile in Mr Needle's direction. Then he turned back to Measle and said, coldly, 'Something to look into? What sort of something?'

'I don't know—a crystal ball . . . or a . . . or a sort of revealing pool sort of thing, like they have in books and films.'

Mr Bland sighed with impatience. 'The Wizards' Guild possesses neither a crystal ball, nor a . . . a sort of revealing pool thing. I'm afraid there is no magic available to show us the whereabouts of your mother.'

'What about if it's raining—raining in one small place?' said Measle, desperately. 'Like the other day when Dad telephoned you—about the rain on Borgrove Moor? If there was rain like that—well, then we'd know where they were.'

Mr Bland nodded towards the window. Outside it was dark and Measle heard the spattering of rain against the glass.

'Unfortunately,' said Mr Bland, 'it is now raining across much of the country and, according to the weather forecasts, it looks as if it's going to keep raining for some considerable time. Ideal weather for wrathmonks, I need hardly say.'

There was a silence from everybody. Measle slumped dejectedly against the back of the couch and shoved both hands into his pockets. His fingers touched something hard and he pulled out the object and glanced down at it. It was the bottle top he'd picked up in the car park. He turned it over in his fingers. There was writing on the top— Measle brought the thing closer to his eyes and squinted down at the tiny writing—it read *HAPPY DRINKING AT THE ISLE OF SMILES!*

'I think I know where they've taken her,' said Measle, quietly. 'They've gone to the Isle of Smiles. Look—that bottle they threw at Dad—this is the top. I picked it up in the car park.'

He held it out and Mr Needle took it and examined it closely. 'What do you think, Bland?' he said, passing it to his companion.

Mr Bland peered at the bottle top. 'Hardly conclusive, Needle. It could simply have been lying there in the car park, for goodness knows how long—'

'Oh, nonsense,' snapped Nanny Flannel. 'It's from the bottle they threw! Why can't you understand that?'

Mr Bland changed the look on his face—from one with a very small expression of interest in what was going on around him, to one of no expression at all. 'Miss Flannel,' he said, smoothly, 'you must understand that we cannot act unless we have absolute proof that this event happened as young Measle claims it did.'

'And even if we had the proof,' said Mr Needle, 'at the present time, we would be unable to investigate any occurrence that involved the Isle of Smiles. The Isle of Smiles is off-limits for now—and for the foreseeable future. The Guild is most concerned about that report that Mr Stubbs filed, concerning the *alleged* presence of an entity in the area and we have an ongoing investigation into the matter.'

'Ongoing *fiddlesticks*!' shouted Nanny Flannel loudly.

There was a short silence, while the two officials glanced at each other. Each gave the other a tiny, almost imperceptible nod. Then, Mr Bland snapped his briefcase shut and rose to his feet. 'Our business here appears to be concluded, does it not, Needle?'

'Indeed it does, Bland,' said Mr Needle, snapping shut *his* briefcase and then pushing himself out of his chair.

Measle racked his brain, trying desperately to think of something that might convince the two representatives of the Wizards' Guild that he was telling them the truth—but Mr Needle and Mr Bland were already at the door. Both turned and smiled coldly in Measle's direction.

'We are sorry about your loss,' said Mr Needle, not sounding sorry at all.

'Particularly in light of your recent misadventures,' said Mr Bland.

'We trust that your mother will soon be back with you,' said Mr Needle.

'And that your father will make a swift recovery,' said Mr Bland.

Both men bowed slightly at the waist and said, in unison, 'Good day to you.'

The door closed behind them.

'Huh!' Nanny Flannel snorted. 'I might have known it! Wizards' Guild indeed! Fat lot of use *they* are!'

'What do we do now?' said Measle, feeling utterly miserable. He'd been sure that the Wizards' Guild would solve everything in the blink of an eye—and all that had happened was that the Guild had sent along a pair of cold, dry officials who had flatly refused to do anything at all. His mother was gone—and his father was lying asleep in his bed upstairs, heavily sedated with some sort of tranquillizer pills that Mr Needle had produced from his briefcase.

Nanny Flannel patted Measle's hand. 'We wait, dear,' she said, sadly. 'There's nothing else we can do. We wait and see what they want with her.'

The Car

Later that evening, the rain became heavier. It was a cold, windy rain and it drummed down on the old slate roof and spattered against the leaded windows.

The rain went on all through the night and all through the next two days. Measle and Nanny Flannel spent most of those days simply staring out of the window at the steady downpour. Every hour, Nanny Flannel and Measle would go up to Sam's bedroom and peek round the door, to see if Sam was still asleep. He always was.

'That,' said Nanny Flannel, as they returned down the stairs for the umpteenth time, 'was a very strong pill.'

On the morning of the third day, Measle decided that he'd waited long enough.

'I'm going to go and find her,' he said to Nanny Flannel, across the breakfast table in the big kitchen.

Nanny Flannel put down her cup of tea.

'What do you mean, dear?' she said, quietly.

'I'm going to go to the Isle of Smiles and I'm going to find her. I'm going to try and rescue her.'

Nanny Flannel looked at Measle, peering at him over the top of her spectacles, for several seconds. Then she said, 'No, dear, you're not. You can't possibly. Do you have any idea what those creatures could do to you?'

'Yes,' said Measle. 'Yes, I do.'

Nanny Flannel nodded, thoughtfully. 'Yes, I suppose you do, don't you? But Basil Tramplebone was just *one* wrathmonk, Measle—and he very nearly killed you. This time there are *lots* of them. If they caught you—well, I dread to think what they'd do to you! And anyway, how can you be sure that they're on that island at all?'

'I'm not sure at all—but I've got to start somewhere. Besides, I've got a sort of a *feeling* that that's where they are. See, it's closed for the winter, Nanny—and it would be a great place to hide, because of the mana. Dad said there was a mana well there—and they'd like that, don't you see?'

'No, I don't see,' said Nanny Flannel, unhappily. 'And any idea that you might go and rescue her—you're just a boy, Measle! No, no—it's out of the question.'

'But I *must* go, Nanny!'

'But you *can't* go, Measle!'

Measle and Nanny Flannel sat staring steadily at each other for several moments.

Measle was thinking, *How can I get her to see that I have no choice? How can I persuade her to let me go? And, if I can't persuade her, how can I get away?*

Nanny Flannel was thinking, *There's a look in the boy's eyes—I've seen that look before. His father gets it sometimes, when he's determined to do something crazy. His grandfather had it too. It's a look that says—'Don't get in my way, because I shall do what I have to do, and neither you nor anybody else will stop me.'*

Nanny Flannel sighed. She knew it was no use— and therefore she knew what she had to do. She got up from the kitchen table and said, 'Come with me, Measle. There's a little something I think you should learn.'

She led Measle to the dining room and sat him down at the head of the long table. Then she went to the sideboard and opened one of its low doors. She reached deep inside and then brought out a large, heavy glass jar. She carried the jar to Measle and set it down on the table in front of him.

The jar was full of multi-coloured jelly beans.

'Now then,' said Nanny Flannel, planting herself firmly in front of Measle and peering at him fiercely through her little round spectacles.

This is obviously going to be very serious and very important, thought Measle—and I'd better listen very, very carefully—and he put a serious look on his face and sat up a little straighter in the chair.

Nanny Flannel opened her mouth and took a deep breath. Then she said, 'What colour is your least favourite jelly bean?'

'*What?*'

'You heard me, dear—don't pretend you didn't.'

'But—but I thought this was something *serious*! Something about Mum and Dad! What's stupid *jelly beans* got to do with anything?'

Nanny Flannel clapped her hands together twice—*smack, smack!* Then she glared down at Measle, real anger glinting in her eyes.

'Be quiet, Measle, and listen. You only learn things if you listen. If you blabber and jabber all the time, you learn *nothing*—but everybody within earshot learns something. They learn that you're an idiot. Now, I asked you a question and I'd like an answer. *What colour jelly beans do you like least?*'

'Er…I don't know—I like them all…er…the yellow ones, I suppose.'

'Good. Yellow it shall be.' Nanny Flannel held out the glass jar. 'Take out a yellow one,' she said.

Measle did as he was told.

'Good,' said Nanny Flannel. 'Now, I want you to

shut your eyes, stick your tongue out, and put the jelly bean on the end of it.'

Measle opened his mouth and was about to say that he didn't actually feel very much like eating jelly beans at this particular moment in his life— particularly not a yellow one and *particularly* not with his mum held prisoner by wrathmonks on the Isle of Smiles and his dad lying, in a sort of coma, in his bedroom—but then he saw the glint of steely determination in Nanny Flannel's eyes, so he closed his eyes, stuck out his tongue, and put the bean on the end of it.

'Good,' said Nanny Flannel. 'Now, when I say "GO!" I want you to bite into it, chew it up, and swallow it. Are you ready?'

Measle, with his tongue sticking out, could only nod.

'Good,' said Nanny Flannel. 'Right then, Measle— GO!'

Measle retracted his tongue and bit into the jelly bean. The familiar, sugary-lemony taste filled his mouth. Five quick chews and it was gone. Then he heard Nanny Flannel's voice again—

'All done? Good! All right—you can open your eyes now.'

Measle opened his eyes. Nanny Flannel was still standing in front of him—still looking down at him—but now her eyes didn't quite meet his. She seemed to be looking in the general direction of his face, but instead of looking into his eyes, she appeared to be staring at his right ear.

'Lift up your hand,' she said to his right ear, 'and look at it.'

Measle lifted his hand and looked at it—or rather, he looked at where it should have been—

It wasn't there.

Measle moved his hand frantically in front of his face—and he felt the movement of the air as his hand passed through it—but where his hand should have been was—well—there was *nothing*.

'Look at your feet,' said Nanny Flannel.

Measle looked down to where his feet should have been—all he could see was the carpet on the floor.

'What's happened to me?' he gasped.

'You tell me,' said Nanny Flannel, still staring fixedly at Measle's right ear. 'You're not a stupid boy, Measle—you should be able to work it out.'

'I'm ... I'm *invisible*?'

'Ahah—you got it in one!' said Nanny Flannel, proudly. 'Invisible! You—and whatever you're holding on to at that moment. Invisible every time you eat a yellow jelly bean. Well—not *any* yellow jelly· beans, obviously. These are—well—they're rather special. And only to be used in emergencies—they're not for fun, you understand. Besides, the effect doesn't last all that long—you should be coming out of it any minute now.'

Measle stared at where his hand should have been and watched as his fingers slowly reappeared. At first, they seemed to be made out of a thin grey smoke—but as the seconds ticked away, his fingers became more and more solid until, moments later, his hand was back to normal.

'It only lasts about half a minute,' said Nanny Flannel. 'But half a minute of invisibility can come in quite useful at times.'

Measle thought about this for a few moments. Then he said, 'Why did you teach me that, Nanny? I mean—why now?'

Nanny Flannel's face went pinker than its usual pinkness. She took her spectacles off her nose and polished them on her apron. 'Well,' she muttered, avoiding Measle's eyes, 'you never know when it might come in handy.' Then she stopped polishing her glasses. In one swift movement, she perched them back on the end of her nose and then peered over the top of them at Measle. 'Just remember to keep a few of those particular yellow jelly beans in your pocket at all times, Measle,' she said, firmly. '*At all times*, remember. And use them—use them *when necessary.*'

It was several hours before Measle realized what Nanny Flannel had really meant by that remark, and by then it was early in the evening. Outside the windows it was dark. The rain had started again and was pattering against the window panes.

And in Measle's mind a plan was beginning to form.

While Nanny Flannel was busy in the kitchen, Measle went into the dining room. He took the top off the glass jar and began to take out—one by one—as many yellow jelly beans as he could find. He counted them—twelve—and then he stuffed them into his trouser pocket.

Next, he went to his bedroom and took his warmest coat from his clothes cupboard. The coat was a leather jacket, like the sort that fighter pilots in old war films wore. Of all the new clothes Measle had got for his birthmas presents, this jacket was his favourite.

Measle shrugged the jacket on. There was something in one of the pockets. Measle reached in and pulled it out. It was the VoBo. For a moment, he stared at the little brass trumpet, wondering whether or not to take it with him. Then he stuck it back in the pocket. *It's small*, he thought. *It won't get in the way—and, you never know, it might come in handy—*

Measle went out of his bedroom and crept downstairs. He heard the clanking of pots and pans from the kitchen. He moved silently across the dark hall to the front door. He opened it carefully, trying to stop it creaking—and then he slipped out into the wet night.

The garage was off to the side of the big house. Measle hurried through the rain to the great sliding double doors. He pushed them aside and went into the garage. There it was—the huge, gleaming shape of the Stubbs car. Measle went to the driver's side, opened the door, and slipped into the seat. He paused for a moment, feeling the hammering of his heart in his chest. *Was he going to be able to do this?* He took a deep breath, placed the end of his forefinger on the big red button and pressed hard.

The engine rumbled into life.

Measle breathed a sigh of relief. That was the first hurdle—now for the second. He reached for the switch marked A/P and flipped it down.

Yes? What do you want?

The voice came from somewhere behind the polished wooden dashboard. It sounded tinny and very efficient and businesslike—and just a little impatient.

'Well,' said Measle, hesitantly, 'I…um…I want to go to—'

Identify yourself.

'I'm Measle. Measle Stubbs.'

There was a pause, while the autopilot seemed to think this over. Then—

Measle Stubbs—youngest member of the Stubbs family. Identity accepted. Destination?

'Er…'

'Ur'—ancient city of Sumer, located in what is now south-eastern Iraq. Unable to comply with request, for the following reasons. First, there is a small ocean in the way. Second, the city of Ur no longer exists. Please state alternative destination.

'Um…'

'Um'—no such location known. Please state alternative destination.

Wow, thought Measle, *this machine is really picky—*

'The Isle of Smiles.'

'The Isle of Smiles'—destination recognized. Please state magic word.

What? There's a magic word? And the car won't move without it? Oh, great! What on earth could this magic word be?

Measle racked his brains for all the magic words he could think of.

'Abracadabra?'

Unrecognized.

'Shazam?'

Unrecognized.

'Ooglyboogly?'

Now you're just being silly.

Come on—think! The magic word! What's the magic word?—Oh, no! Could it possibly be as easy as that? Well, it's worth a try—

'Please?'

Finally.

And, the next moment, Measle felt the big car begin to move. At the same moment, the headlights came on, shooting twin beams of light out over the drive. The raindrops flashed through the beams and, as the car slid out of the garage, the windscreen wipers came on automatically, flicking rapidly left and right. The huge wooden steering wheel turned slowly and the big car veered away from the house, its tyres crunching softly over the gravel. Slowly, it began to pick up speed as they rolled down the long driveway, the steering wheel twitching this way and that as the autopilot made its small corrections and then, moments later, they were at the big iron gates that led out to the main road, and the car came to a stop. It waited at the junction for several seconds, almost like a pedestrian waits at a crossing—it seemed to be looking left and right, checking if any traffic was coming its way—then it began to move again, turning slowly onto the main road. Once clear of the gates, it began to go faster and Measle relaxed a little, sinking back against the soft leather. He glanced up at the rear view mirror. It was set for his father, who was a lot taller than Measle, so all Measle could see was a reflection of the ceiling of the car. He reached up and adjusted the mirror— and there, in the reflection through the car's rear window, was a distant speck of white in the darkness—a speck of white that seemed to be following them, but the speck was getting smaller and smaller as the car accelerated away from it—

Measle turned round in his seat and stared back through the rear window.

There, far down the road, was Tinker, racing along as fast as his short legs could move, desperately trying to catch up with them.

'Stop!' yelled Measle.

Stop? But we've only just started.

'I don't care! Stop! Please stop!'

I do wish you'd make up your mind.

The big car began to slow down. Seconds later it pulled over to the side of the road and rolled to a halt.

Measle opened the door and a very wet and panting Tinker jumped into his lap.

'What are you doing here, Tink?' said Measle, trying to sound angry—but not quite succeeding, because the truth was that he was very glad to see the little dog.

And Tinker was very glad to see him. It was good to get out of the rain—why, only minutes ago he'd been in the kitchen, sitting close by Nanny Flannel as she clattered about with her pots and pans—and then he'd heard, in the distance, the sound of the car engine rumbling to life and up had gone Tinker's ears—and the old lady had looked down at him and said, 'What did you hear, little dog?'

Tinker had whined softly and had gone to stand by the kitchen door, which led out to the backyard. Nanny Flannel had joined him. She had opened the door a crack and then both she and Tinker could hear the rumbling of the engine in the distant garage.

Nanny Flannel had looked down at Tinker. Her face was pale and her eyes were wide with worry. She said, 'Go on, then, Tinker. Off you go. And, whatever happens, look after him!' Then she'd opened the door a little wider, just enough so that

Tinker could squeeze through the gap—and Tinker had galloped out into the cold, wet night and had raced after the big green car as it crunched down the long drive. He'd almost caught it at the gates, but then the car had turned out into the main road and had picked up speed again and Tinker had strained every sinew in his body, charging after the twin red tail lights, watching them get further and further away—and then the car had suddenly begun to slow down and then stop and the smelly kid (*well, he wasn't quite as smelly as he used to be, but that was all right, nobody's perfect*) had opened the car door and here they were, together again—and perhaps they were off on another adventure, maybe like the one when they were playing with that giant bug on top of the enormous table, which had been great fun and terrifically exciting—and, if that was the sort of adventure they were headed for this time—well then, Tinker was all for it.

'What am I going to do with you?' said Measle, scratching Tinker between his damp ears. 'I can't take you back—I can't risk Nanny catching us. Oh, well—looks like you'll have to come along. Just be a good dog and do as you're told—OK?'

Tinker—being a dog—didn't understand a word of that. But whatever the smelly kid had just said, at least he didn't sound angry, so Tinker barked once, just to show that, whatever was in store for the pair of them, he was game for anything.

Measle pushed Tinker into the passenger seat, turned to face the dashboard again and said, 'The Isle of Smiles, please.'

Are you sure this time?

'Yes! I'm quite sure! The Isle of Smiles—*please*!'

Well—if you're quite sure, said the autopilot, in a slightly huffy voice. Then, a moment later, the car started to move again.

THE GATES

By the time the Stubbs car arrived at the outskirts of the little fishing town, it was past midnight.

The car had behaved perfectly, driving itself at a smooth, sedate pace, obeying every traffic law and never breaking the speed limit. It didn't say anything either and Measle was quite pleased about that—there had been something in the tone of the autopilot's voice that had made Measle feel he was a bit of a nuisance.

For the first half hour of the trip, Measle had sat up very straight in the driver's seat, his hands resting lightly on the steering wheel, trying hard to look as though it was he who was driving the big car. But, what with the darkness and the heavy, pounding rain, there was very little traffic out on the road that night. Measle never once saw a police car—but even if they had met one, the sharpest-eyed constable on the force would still have had a hard time seeing through the dark-tinted windows of the Stubbs car—so Measle began to relax. Tinker had curled up in the passenger seat and, quite soon after joining the expedition, had fallen asleep and, after half an hour of doing nothing but pretending to drive, of watching the windscreen wipers flick steadily back and forth, Measle felt his own eyelids getting heavy—so he let go of the steering wheel, closed his eyes, and lay back against the soft leather of the seat—and quite soon, he too was fast asleep.

Measle woke up when the car stopped at a traffic light. He sat up, peering out through the windscreen. The rain seemed to have stopped and the wipers no longer flicked from side to side. It was dark outside, apart from the traffic lights—which now turned from red, to red and amber—then green—and the big car moved forward smoothly. Measle stared out of the side window at the passing houses. They were all dark, with not a single light showing through their curtained windows. Measle glanced at his watch. Just past midnight. They'd been on the road for over three hours—surely it didn't take that long to get to the Isle of Smiles? But then he remembered the speed his dad usually drove—and it was a lot faster than the gentle pace the car had adopted for the long drive—so perhaps they were only just arriving? A moment later, the car turned a dark corner—and there, in front of them, was the little harbour—and, beyond it, the long causeway stretching out into the bay. Far off, Measle could just make out the dark hump of the island itself.

Hanging over the island was a wide, black cloud—and Measle saw a faint, shifting haze hanging beneath it, which meant only one thing.

Rain.

Wrathmonk rain.

The Stubbs car headed steadily through the small town towards the beginning of the causeway and Measle realized that, unless he did something about it, the car would continue right up to the very gates of the park itself. He remembered that there was a small car park, right down by the sea, near the start of the causeway. It was used when there were too many visitors to the place, when the big car park on the island itself was full up.

Measle leaned towards the dashboard and said, 'The small car park, please.'

The small car park. A wise choice.

Two minutes later, the Stubbs car rolled to a

halt, parking itself neatly in a marked bay right by the car park entrance. The sound of the engine died away.

'Well,' he said to Tinker, who was now awake and sitting up and paying attention. 'Here we are. Now what?'

Tinker wagged his stumpy tail. Measle scratched him behind his fuzzy ears and then peered out through the windscreen.

'It's so dark out there, Tink,' he muttered. 'I can hardly see a thing.'

You might try looking in the glove compartment.

Measle realized that he'd forgotten to switch off the autopilot. And now the machine had made some sort of suggestion—

'What?'

The glove compartment, cloth ears. Honestly. I don't know why I bother.

Measle couldn't help grinning in the darkness. The idea of a rude and impatient car was kind of funny—

He reached over the passenger seat and opened the small door of the glove compartment. His hand fumbled inside—there was something there—

Measle pulled the object out the glove compartment. It was so dark in the car that Measle found it hard to make out what was in his hand. It seemed to be made of soft leather, with two circles of smooth, hard stuff embedded in the material—

It was a pair of goggles. Old-fashioned goggles—

like the kind pilots used to wear when they flew in ancient, open biplanes. Without really thinking about what he was doing, Measle slipped the goggles onto his head—and over his eyes.

Light! He could see! Quite clearly, as if the car was filled with ordinary daylight!

For a moment, Measle actually thought that somehow night-time had been banished and replaced with the day—but then he pulled the goggles up onto his forehead and, instantly, he was back in darkness again. Cautiously, Measle slipped the goggles back over his eyes—and the light returned. He looked about him—everything in the car—and, indeed, everything *outside* the car—seemed to be lit by a soft, filtered daylight.

Measle pulled the goggles off his head and stared at them. Once again, he couldn't make out a thing. Then Measle remembered that there was an overhead light in the Stubbs car. He reached up and switched it on.

The goggles were odd. The leather was soft and brown—but it was the lenses of the goggles that were a little strange. They were dark and shiny and highly reflective, like a pair of small, round mirrors. *Obviously something to do with Dad's magic*, thought Measle. *Maybe he uses these goggles when he wants to be secret—perhaps when he has to drive without using the headlights? And maybe—just maybe—they might be a bit useful to me?*

Measle slipped the goggles over his head and hung them round his neck. Then he opened the car door and he and Tinker stepped out into the night.

The air outside was cold and damp and Measle was glad he was wearing his leather jacket. Tinker's wiry coat seemed to be keeping him quite warm too or, at any rate, the little dog certainly wasn't complaining—but he kept close to Measle's side as they left the car park. They padded together through the darkness, down to the start of the causeway. Ahead of them, the long, straight, multi-lane highway cut across the black waters of the bay.

It took Measle and Tinker fifteen minutes to walk the length of the causeway and, for the last two hundred metres, they both moved very slowly. When they were thirty metres from the gates, Measle slipped the goggles over his eyes and, with them, he could see clearly in the darkness.

That was how he spotted the wrathmonk.

Scab Draggle was cold and tired and very damp. He was also rather irritable, because Frognell Flabbit was late. Flabbit was late for the third time that week and Draggle was fed up with it.

He and Flabbit had been ordered to guard the main gate and that's what they'd been doing for several days, ever since they had captured the Stubbs woman and brought her down here to the island. The trouble was, Flabbit kept over-sleeping—*or pretending to oversssleep*, thought Draggle. Flabbit was almost certainly being late on purpose—probably out of jealousy. Jealousy over the hair, of course. *I've got sssuch lovely long blond hair*, thought Draggle, hunching his thin body against the cold, damp air, *and poor old Flabbit is almost completely bald and he tries to hide it with that ssstupid comb-over! Well, jussst because I look nicer than he does—that's no reason for him to be late all the time!*

Draggle looked miserably round at his surroundings. He was sitting in one of the several ticket booths at the park's entrance. Now that the Isle of Smiles was closed for the winter, most of the power was off, which meant that inside the ticket booth there was no heating to be had at all and no light either—which was why Draggle was cold and damp—and very bored, too. He was tired because he'd been there all night and Flabbit should have taken over from him an hour ago and the fact that he hadn't shown up at all was making Draggle very cross indeed.

He turned to the stone statue that was sitting next to him and said, 'When that ssstupid Flabbit fellow gets here, you just lisssten—I'll be giving him a piece of my mind, sssee if I don't!'

The statue stayed motionless, the blank eyes staring out through the small window of the ticket booth. It was a life-size statue of a woman, dressed in what appeared to be a sort of uniform. She had a badge on her lapel—it read 'SUSAN'. Underneath was written 'TICKET OFFICE—THE ISLE OF SMILES'.

When the statue failed to respond, Draggle kicked it irritably.

'Bet that took you by sssurprise, didn't it?' he sneered. 'Of course, not as big a sssurprise as the one you got when we turned you to ssstone, eh? You and all the others we found here. Dear, oh, dear—you should have ssseen your faces! One by one, you all came running up to sssee what was going on—and one by one, well—thanksss to the Medusa head, you all got *done*, didn't you? And now, there's nobody here but usss!'

Draggle stopped suddenly and looked about him nervously. Apart from himself and the stone statue, there *was* nobody in the little ticket booth—but he knew that didn't mean a thing. The Dragodon could be anywhere—*watching him, listening to him—he'd better be careful what he said and did!*

Ever since they had brought the Dragodon back to the Isle of Smiles, the wrathmonks had grown steadily more and more fearful of the creature—a creature they still hadn't seen. They had carried the little concrete garden gnome to the great red roller coaster and had deposited it—under strict instructions—at the foot of one of the massive, red metal columns that supported the rails. **LEAVE ME NOW**, were the words the Dragodon had sent into their heads and, obediently, the wrathmonks had turned away and left it there, in the shadow of the Juggernaut. Over the next few days, they had received detailed instructions—all of them hearing the words in their skulls at the same moment—and they had obeyed those instructions to the letter, for one very simple reason.

They were terrified of it.

The Dragodon had disappeared—at least, the garden gnome that seemed to house the spirit of the Dragodon had disappeared—but the creature was obviously fully aware of everything that was going on. When Mr and Mrs Zagreb failed to obey its instructions to bring an empty Isle of Smiles cola bottle to the base of the Juggernaut's metal pillar, they suffered the most horrible pain in their stomachs for the rest of that day; and later in the same week, Scab Draggle had failed to steal a particular kind of black van that the Dragodon had ordered—and the young wrathmonk had spent the rest of that day writhing in agony on the floor of the ticket booth. All of them had been tortured like this, some for the most minor mistakes, and now they all trod very carefully indeed, living in constant fear of a creature—a creature they had never actually set eyes on—whose whereabouts they didn't know and whose powers they could only guess at.

When Measle saw the young wrathmonk, all by himself inside the ticket booth, he wondered how on earth he was going to get past him.

That the creature was a wrathmonk, Measle had no doubt whatsoever. The same white, white face as Basil Tramplebone's. The same cold, fishy eyes. The same long, bony fingers, the skin the colour of old candles. The same tight black clothes—no, it was certainly a wrathmonk and, if by some miracle it *wasn't* a wrathmonk, then what was a sinister looking young man doing there, sitting in a cold, dark ticket booth, at the dead of night, staring blankly out into the darkness?

And then there was the rain. Where Measle was now crouching, with Tinker pressed close to his side, the night air was heavy with dampness—but no rain was actually falling on them. But there, thirty metres away, a steady downpour dribbled over the ticket booth and, as far as Measle could see, the rain was falling in an unbroken shower all over the island. And that meant only one thing.

Wrathmonks. Lots of wrathmonks.

Measle shivered—but not from cold. For the first time that night, Measle began to realize the danger he was in. He was sure now that he'd been right and that this was where the wrathmonks had brought his mother—*but now what*?

Tinker, sensing Measle's sudden uncertainty, pressed his cold nose into Measle's hand, as if to say, *It's OK, smelly kid—Tinker's here!*

To one side of the booth there was a set of roofed-over turnstiles and Measle remembered—from his last visit to the Isle of Smiles—the clicking sound they made when he'd passed through them. He carefully scanned the whole area, looking for another way in. But the only entrance to the park was through those clicking turnstiles and Measle knew that, if he and Tinker went in that way, the young wrathmonk in the ticket booth would be sure to hear them—

There was movement to one side of the booth and Measle saw a tubby, balding man, carrying an umbrella, push the booth's door open and enter. Another white face. Another pair of cold, fishy eyes. Next to him, Tinker growled deep in his throat and Measle stroked his head and whispered, 'We've got to be quiet, Tinker. Really, *really* quiet. OK?'

The door of the ticket office burst open and Frognell Flabbit stepped into the tiny room. He was holding a soaking wet umbrella and he shook it violently, spattering Draggle with water.

'Here, do you mind?' whined Draggle, jumping out of his chair and wiping the drops of water off his greasy black coat.

'Whasssamatter?' said Flabbit, his pasty white face shining with moisture. 'Ssscared of a drop of water, are you?'

'Now look here, Flabbit,' muttered Draggle, angrily. 'You're late again—'

'Yesss, well—I couldn't find my umbrella.'

Draggle shook his head. 'I don't care about your ssstupid umbrella, do I? I'm cold, and I'm tired, and I'm bored—'

'All right, all right,' said Flabbit, flopping into Draggle's chair and stretching his short, fat legs out in front of him. 'I'm here now, aren't I? Keep your hair on.'

'Oh, I shall indeed,' said Draggle, making for the door. '*I've* always been able to keep my hair on—which is more than can be sssaid for sssome of usss, eh?'

Flabbit nodded seriously. He had no idea that Draggle might be referring to *him*, since he'd always believed that his hairdo was completely convincing and that whoever looked at it would believe—one hundred per cent—that he, Frognell Flabbit, was blessed with a fine and full head of hair. So he nodded and smiled in a superior sort of way and said, 'Yesss—you mean poor old Grissstle, don't you? Poor old Griswold—why, he's as bald as a billiard ball! But you and me, young Draggle—well, we've been lucky with our hair, haven't we? Oh yesss, very lucky indeed—although I think you might be thinning jussst a little bit up on top—'

There was a faint clicking sound from somewhere outside and both wrathmonks heard it clearly through the drumming of the rain on the roof of the ticket booth.

'Whassat?' said Draggle, nervously. He was close to the door and now he rather wished he hadn't jumped out of his chair so quickly. If he'd stayed where he was, old Flabbit would now be near the door—

'That's the turnssstiles, I think,' said Flabbit. 'Sssomebody's trying to get out—or get in. Why don't you open the door and have a look? Have you got the Medusa head?'

Draggle patted his pocket. 'It's right here.'

'In the bag?' said Flabbit, a little anxiously. The last thing he needed was for young Draggle to pull the thing out of his pocket, unshielded by the little canvas bag in which it was always kept.

'Yesss, Flabbit—*coursse* it's in the bag. Think I'm an idiot, do you?'

That was *exactly* what Flabbit thought—but the look on Draggle's face stopped him short of saying so out loud.

'No, no, young Draggle. An idiot—you? Very far from it, young Draggle. Very far indeed.'

Draggle nodded sourly. The whole business about who should have the Medusa head still irritated him. All the others had been given their turn with the thing, each one getting the chance to petrify a certain number of the park employees before passing it along to the next in line. Even old Judge Cedric Hardscrabble had been given a turn—and he'd been so clumsy with the thing that it had been pure good luck that he hadn't petrified *himself*, let alone the rest of them. By the time the Medusa head had come down to Draggle—the youngest wrathmonk in the group and therefore the last to get it—there hadn't been a single park employee left to petrify. And that, thought Scab Draggle, was totally unfair.

But now there was this clicking sound from outside. Perhaps one of the park personnel had somehow managed to escape them! And now he, Scab Draggle, was going to get his chance to use the Medusa head at last!

Draggle cautiously cracked open the door and peered out into the wet night.

Measle froze.

He was halfway through the turnstile, with Tinker in his arms, when the door of the ticket booth opened and the young wrathmonk's head appeared in the gap. Measle could see him clearly through the curtain of rain that fell between the roofs of the turnstile and the ticket booth. He had hoped that the wrathmonks would be too busy talking to each other to hear the clicking of the turnstile but the metallic sound had been very loud—

Measle stood quite still, wondering how much longer the effects of the yellow jelly bean would last.

He tried to do a sum in his head—he'd popped the jelly bean in his mouth at the very first sound of the clicking turnstile—that was about fifteen seconds ago—and now he'd been standing like an invisible statue for at least another five seconds, an invisible Tinker held tight in his arms, while the young wrathmonk peered this way and that, his cold, fishy eyes sweeping over Measle's and Tinker's invisible bodies at least three times in the process—*how much longer before the effects wore off?*

'Anything there?' called a whiny, scratchy voice from inside the ticket booth.

'Can't sssee nothing, can I?' said the young wrathmonk. 'Mussst have been the wind.'

Draggle paused for another moment, his eyes wandering suspiciously—then, to Measle's relief, he shrugged his narrow shoulders and withdrew back into the ticket booth. The moment the door closed behind the wrathmonk, Measle held his hand up to his face and watched as his fingers slowly reappeared. He looked down and saw Tinker's small black nose materialize out of grey smoke and, a moment later, Tinker's eyes gleamed up at him from the folds of his jacket.

To Tinker, the whole experience had been only mildly interesting. First, the smelly kid had insisted on carrying him past the little hut thing (and that was all right because Tinker quite liked being carried about the place, particularly when the ground was all wet like it was round here) and then the smelly kid had disappeared completely— but of course the smelly kid was still there because Tinker could *smell* that he was still there—and, since he was a dog, smell was the only thing that mattered. The rest was quite unimportant. If the smelly kid wanted to act like a window, that was fine by Tinker—*just as long as he don't smell like a window, because windows don't smell of nothin' much and that's not very interestin', now is it? Still, it's nice that the smelly kid can be seen again, because when he was like a window, you couldn't be sure which bit to lick and which bit to bark at—so now that I can see him—*

Tinker swiped his tongue across Measle's nose and, for good measure, gave one, loud, high-pitched yelp of pleasure.

Frantically, Measle grabbed at Tinker's nose to stop him barking again. He dived his free hand into his trouser pocket, yanked out a yellow jelly bean and stuffed it into his mouth. At the same moment, he heard the sound of loud voices inside the ticket booth and, a second later, the click of the door opening. Without looking back, Measle pushed his way through the last few clicks of the turnstile and hurried forward into the wet darkness.

'Oi!' shouted a voice behind him. Then Measle heard, 'Quick, Flabbit! Look at that! There! Sssee that? Whassat?'

How could it be anything? thought Measle frantically, *I'm invisible, aren't I?* He glanced down at his hand—and saw, to his horror, that there was a kind of ghostly outline to his body—an outline that seemed to slip and slide, almost as if it was made of water—

Of course! It was the rain falling on him! In the turnstile, he'd been sheltered by its roof. But now, out here in the rain, the water drops were hitting his body! The drops were actually stopping dead and then trickling over him—over his head, over his shoulders, over his jacket—and where they flowed, they made a perfect, watery sort of outline of his body, and that was what the young wrathmonk could see—

'Oi! You! Whatever you are! Get back here, or you'll be sssorry! Come on, Flabbit—let's get after it!'

Measle heard the sound of flapping, squelching feet racing after him. He tightened his grip on Tinker, put his head down and ran into the

darkness. The rain spattered against his goggles, smearing the lenses and making it hard to see what was ahead of him—so Measle pulled them off his eyes and slipped them down round his neck.

He ran on, twisting this way and that, past the shadowy shapes of the park's attractions. The rides and the booths looked different in the darkness. The night washed away the bright colours they wore in the daytime, transforming them all into darkish grey lumps—and this, combined with their odd, angular shapes, made them somehow strange and a little threatening. Even so, Measle recognized them as he raced by—there was the Gold Mine ride, there the Spinning Saucepans—and there, at the start of the Dinosaur Diver ride, huge and looming in the darkness, was the threatening shape of the enormous, life-size model of the Tyrannosaurus Rex. For a moment, Measle felt a new and greater fear grow in his chest—in the gloom, the monster seemed to be glaring down at him and even starting to move in his direction —but then he thought, *It's not moving, you idiot! It can't move, it's just made of plaster and plastic and steel, it can't hurt you—*

but there's something behind you that can! So he ran faster, past the Log Flume and the Thunderer and on and on, right under the huge, spider-web tracery of the Ferris wheel, and behind him he could still hear the sound of pounding footsteps—but only one pair now. Measle guessed that the tubby wrathmonk was the one who had dropped behind—which meant there was only the thin, young blond wrathmonk to worry about—

Measle raced round a corner and there, in front of him, was the ghostly shape of the carousel. The contraption was still and silent and dark—and even as Measle tore past it, there was something about those garishly painted horses, with their staring eyes and their wide, flared nostrils that made him shudder with a sudden, added terror. They looked alive somehow—as if, at any moment, they would leap from their painted stations and join in the chase—

'Oi! Cudgel! Zag! Anybody! There's sssomething loose in the park!'

Measle threw a look over his shoulder. There, on the far side of the carousel, was the young wrathmonk. He was standing still, his narrow chest heaving as he gasped for air, his fishy eyes looking frantically left and right, his wet hair hanging in straggly blond clumps over his white, white face. Measle ducked down behind the cover of the carousel and backed slowly away. When he felt he was far enough into the shadows of the nearby buildings, he turned again and slipped round a corner, running on down the street as silently as he could, straining his ears for any sound of pursuit. He ran until his lungs felt as if they were about to burst—and then, gasping for breath, he risked a pause. There was no sound now, apart from the steady drumming of the rain. He glanced down at his hand. He was fully visible again—well, that was to be expected—he'd been running for at least a minute.

Measle looked about him, trying to get his bearings. Ahead of him there was a narrow alley between two tall structures. Measle lifted the goggles back over his eyes and, in the resulting brightness, he saw that the nearest structure was the pay booth for the Giant Splash ride and next to it was the back wall of what Measle guessed had to be part of the Go-Kart track. The alley might be a good place to take a breather—

Measle walked quickly into the narrow space. Through his goggles, he could see that the alley ended about twenty metres away, in a high wire fence. Beyond the fence were the hulking shadows of some sort of electrical equipment—obviously part of the machinery that ran the nearest rides.

On one side of the alley, a small booth projected from the wall. There was a kind of awning there, made of red and white striped canvas. It hung over a glassed-in hatch. There was a picture of a bucket of popcorn painted on the hatch and Measle remembered getting a bag of popcorn and a fizzy drink right here, with Sam and Lee at his side, only a couple of weeks ago. In the shadows, on the back wall of the little booth, there was a shelf. On the shelf, acting as a sort of decoration, sat a familiar-looking pink nylon hippopotamus.

A picture of his mum—a smiling, happy Lee—sitting on a bench and holding her prize pink nylon hippo in her arms, flashed into Measle's mind. He felt a sudden lump in his throat. He bent his head and put his mouth close to one of Tinker's fuzzy ears.

'She's got to be here somewhere, Tink,' he whispered. 'But where?'

Measle hurried under the awning, out of the incessant rain. He pulled Tinker out of the front of his leather jacket and put him on the ground—and Tinker wagged his stumpy tail and then sat down and began to scratch his right ear with his back foot.

Slowly, Measle's breathing returned to normal and he began to take stock of the situation. He counted the number of enemies that he knew of—there was the thin, blond wrathmonk, the tubby one (*Flabbit, that was what the young wrathmonk had called him*), and then a couple of other names that his pursuer had shouted out, ('*Cudgel*', *that was one of them—what was the other?—something like Zig, or Zug—'Zag', that was it!*) so, there were at least four wrathmonks

 and probably several more. Measle felt in his pocket for the jelly beans. How many had he eaten already? Two—that meant he only had ten left! He would have to be careful with them if he wanted them to last.

There was the sound of pounding footsteps and Measle huddled back into the shadows. A moment later, he saw Scab Draggle run past the entrance to the alley, his wet hair streaming behind him. Tinker huddled close to the ground and growled softly and Measle quickly put his hand over the little dog's muzzle to quieten him. The sound of the slapping footsteps faded away and Measle bent his head close to Tinker's and whispered, 'You've got to be quiet, Tink. You can't growl or bark every time you see a wrathmonk. You've got to be quiet all the time—OK?'

Tinker licked Measle's nose. He had no idea what the smelly kid had just said but that was all right, wasn't it? *He could do without all this fallin' water though—and it was nice and dry under this roof thingy—*

Tinker heard the distant voices before Measle did and he growled again, softly—and immediately the smelly kid wrapped his fingers round his nose, stopping any further sound from coming out. *Ah*, thought Tinker, *the smelly kid did this before—it happens when I give the smelly kid the warnin'-growly-business—the smelly kid wraps his paw over the old nose—can't do the warnin'-growly-*

business no more—so, the smelly kid doesn't want the warnin'-growly-business—right then, I'll just keep quiet...

Measle huddled deeper into the shadows under the awning as the voices came nearer and nearer.

Five wrathmonks came into view at the end of the alley. Two of the wrathmonks—one thin and blond, the other short and tubby—Measle recognized. The third wrathmonk was huge. He looked to Measle more like an enormous gorilla than a man—and the gorilla seemed to be wearing some sort of motorcycle outfit, complete with a motorcycle helmet on his square, bullet head. The last two wrathmonks had glossy black hair and

neat black clothes and Measle noticed, with a start of surprise, that one of them was a woman. *Well, why not? Prudence Peyser had told them all, back there on Basil's table top, that women could be wizards and warlocks too—but very few ever became wrathmonks. This must be one of the rare ones—*

The small male wrathmonk with the glossy black hair said, 'You're quite sure it came thisss way, Draggle?'

The young blond wrathmonk nodded impatiently. 'Yeah, *courssse* I'm sure, Zag.'

'But what did it look like?' said the skinny woman.

'I dunno, do I, Mrs Zagreb?' snarled Draggle. 'It was invisible, wasn't it? I only sssaw its outline because of the rain falling all over it.'

'But did it appear to be *human*, Draggle?' said Mr Zagreb. 'That's what we want to know.'

'Yeah,' said Draggle, with growing confidence. 'It was definitely human. It was a bit sssmall, though.'

'The child!' said Mrs Zagreb, excitedly. 'It must have been the Ssstubbs child!'

The wrathmonk that looked like a gorilla grunted and said—in a voice so deep that it sounded to Measle as if it was coming from an underground cave—'We ought to be sure, Mrs Zagreb. It could have been anything. Knowing Draggle, it could jussst have been a big rat or sssomething.'

'It was not a big rat!' shouted Draggle. 'I know

the difference between a big rat and a human being, don't I?'

The huge wrathmonk took a step towards Draggle and put a fist—the size of a soccer ball—under the young wrathmonk's nose. 'Don't you raise your voice at me, young Draggle,' he growled—and Draggle took a nervous step backwards.

'I'm sure he didn't mean it, Mr Cudgel,' said Flabbit, soothingly. 'I sssuggessst we assume it *wasn't* a big rat, though. Jussst for sssafety's sssake, eh? I mean to sssay, if it *is* the Ssstubbs boy—well, that's a bit of all right, isn't it?'

'Indeed it is,' said Mr Zagreb, 'and we've got to find him! That was the whole point, wasn't it? The whole point of Grisssstle's plan!'

Measle felt a sudden chill flutter down his spine. *Gristle! Wasn't that the name of Basil Tramplebone's bank manager? Yes! Griswold Gristle! The one who had turned over all the Stubbs money to his horrible guardian! Was he here too?*

'Right,' growled Cudgel. 'We'd better sssplit up. But I dunno how we're expected to find sssomething that's invisible. And come to that, how did he get to be invisible in the firssst place, that's what I'd like to know?'

'It's a wizard family, Mr Cudgel,' said Flabbit, nodding wisely. 'There's no telling what they can do.'

'Well, they can't do anything very much now,'

sniffed Mrs Zagreb in a scornful voice. 'Not without the woman—and we've got her.'

In the darkness of the alley, Measle's eyes gleamed. *He was right! His mum was here! Now it was just a question of finding her!*

'Mr Grissstle sssaid we could use sssome collective magic on this one,' said Draggle. 'He sssaid the Dragodon won't mind for once. What do you think we should do? Any ideas, Flabbit?'

Mr Flabbit was busy trying to stick his loose hank of greasy hair back on his scalp. He smoothed it down with one pudgy hand. 'I don't know any invisible-to-visible ssspells,' he muttered. 'Does anybody?'

All the wrathmonks shook their heads, gloomily. Then Mrs Zagreb narrowed her small black eyes and smiled with her lipstick-caked mouth and said, 'We could enlissst sssome help. Some *mindless* help.'

'You what?' grunted Cudgel.

'Come, I'll show you,' said Mrs Zagreb, moving away and out of Measle's line of sight. He watched as the rest of the wrathmonks followed her and he listened as their footsteps faded into the distance. Only when he could hear nothing but the steady dripping of the rain did Measle dare to relax a little. He took his hand off Tinker's muzzle and whispered, 'Good boy,' into one of Tinker's ears— and Tinker wagged his stubby tail and managed a quick lick of the smelly kid's nose before Measle pulled his face away.

THE HUNT

There was a sudden flash of light in the sky, quickly followed by a low, rumbling sound. At first, Measle thought it must be thunder—but the flash had been quite close and somehow lower in the sky than where lightning usually occurs—and the rumble wasn't quite the same as the rumble of thunder.

'I think they're doing magic, Tink,' whispered Measle into Tinker's ear. 'Big magic too, by the sound of it.'

Measle waited a few more moments but there was no further sound, apart from the drumming of the rain. He looked around at the dark alley. The tarmac shone with wetness. There were scattered piles of used paper cups and paper plates and sodden paper napkins and there, down at the far end of the alley, the tall wire fence. The alley was a dead end. It was, Measle decided, a bad place to be holed up in—but, at the same time, he was reluctant to leave it. At that moment, the alley seemed to Measle to be the only relatively safe place in the whole park.

Measle was wrong.

Sitting in the shelter of the awning, on the cold, damp ground, with his knees drawn up to his chin and his back resting against the wall of the booth, Measle was quite unaware that there was something moving above and behind him. The something was pink and fuzzy and cuddly—*very* cuddly, until you looked a little closer and saw the nasty glitter in the thing's beady glass eyes.

The thing was inching along the shelf in the shadows at the back of the booth. It moved onto a shelf on the side wall, creeping soundlessly along until it reached the glass window at the front of the booth. It bent its head and peered down at the figures of Measle and Tinker below. Then, quite silently, it began to push at the sheet of glass.

The booth's window was hinged at the top, so that it could be swung up and out when the booth was open for business. Bit by bit, the bottom of the window began to move outwards—pushed there by the steady pressure of the pink and fuzzy thing behind it—

Measle didn't discover the danger he was in until a pink, nylon-furred hippopotamus fell, with a soft thump, onto the top of his head.

Instinctively, Measle raised his arms and brushed frantically at the thing that was now clinging to his hair. His hands met softness—a furry, fuzzy softness—and he shoved hard at the thing and felt it lose what little grip it had. He pushed again, harder this time—and the thing flew off his head and landed several metres away, splashing into a puddle on the wet tarmac.

Measle stared at the extraordinary object, his whole body frozen with shock. *How could a pink nylon hippo—exactly the same pink, nylon hippo as the one his mum had won the other day—suddenly come to life?*

Tinker wasn't frozen at all. Tinker was on his feet, the hair on the back of his neck stiff and straight, his lips curled back from his teeth in a snarl. Whatever this thing was—*a squishy-lookin' cushion on four legs!*—Tinker didn't like the look of it at all. He'd seen it before—*it was the same nasty, squishy cushion thingy that the Nice Lady had brought home the other day—and he hadn't liked it then! And now here it was again—and now he liked it even less! At least the one the Nice Lady had brought home didn't move—but this one did! This one was stompin' along on its fat little legs, lurchin' steadily towards him—*

Tinker let out a succession of short, sharp little barks and this brought Measle sharply out of his shocked paralysis. He lurched forward and grabbed Tinker's nose and whispered frantically into Tinker's ear.

'Shhh, Tink! Not a sound!'

Measle pushed Tinker behind him and stood up, facing the oncoming creature. It didn't look very dangerous. Other than the disturbing fact that a pink, nylon-furred hippopotamus had somehow come to life, it was still just a soft, cheap, cuddly toy and, as such, could hardly do either him or Tinker any harm—

Measle took a step forward and reached down to pick the thing up.

And then the pink hippo's mouth split open.

A moment before, the mouth had looked like a simple line of black thread, embroidered into the nylon fur, to give the suggestion of lips—

but now the threads parted and the mouth gaped

open and, in the fraction of a second before the hippo lunged at his hand, Measle saw—lining the front of the open jaws—half a dozen gleaming steel needles. They looked like the sort of needles that a sewing machine uses—

The hippo's head darted forward—and the needles sank deep into Measle's outstretched hand.

The pain was bad. It was like being stung by six large and ferocious bees. Measle gave a sharp cry and yanked his hand away—and, at the same instant, the hippo released Measle's hand, opening its mouth to take another bite—

Measle kicked out at the horrible thing and the toecap of his shoe connected with the snout of the creature, hurling it backwards into the shadows.

Measle hissed with pain and stared down at his throbbing hand. There were three little pinpricks on the back of his hand, and three more on the other side, on his palm—and from each tiny puncture wound oozed a small drop of blood. The stinging feeling was bad—but just about bearable if he didn't think about it too much. *That thing might* look *cute and cuddly*, thought Measle, *but it's really* dangerous—

And here it came again, waddling out of the darkness towards them, its mouth gaping wide, its little glass eyes glittering—

I've got to get rid of it! thought Measle. *I've got to stop it coming after us!*

The creature's pace was slow. Its legs were only five centimetres long and it lurched clumsily from side to side as it advanced. Measle walked quickly to one side and then watched as the hippo turned slowly to face his new position. The hippo's turn was a sluggish business and Measle realized that he could, if he moved reasonably quickly, get behind the hippo before the thing would be able to move to face him again.

'Stay, Tink!' he hissed. 'Sit!' And Tinker, growling very quietly at the back of his throat, obediently sat down. Measle moved quickly round the hippo, out of its line of sight. Then, firmly pushing his fear aside, he darted forward and grabbed the creature by the scruff of its neck and lifted it off the ground.

It was heavy and damp from the rain. The fur felt slimy. The hippo wriggled weakly in Measle's hand, its head twisting from side to side, its mouth opening and closing, the tiny needle teeth gleaming faintly in the darkness—but, try as it might, it couldn't reach his hand—or any other part of him, either.

Holding the writhing hippo at arm's length, Measle ran to the end of the alley. The high wire fence loomed over him. It was high—but not too high. Measle swung his arm back, then forward, releasing his grip on the pink hippo when his hand was at the highest point of the arc—and the hippo sailed through the darkness, turning end over end as it cleared the top of the wire fence.

Then it fell in amongst the electrical machinery with a faint and distant thump.

Measle pulled his rain-smeared goggles down from his eyes and ran back to where Tinker was still sitting.

'Come on, Tink,' he whispered, his voice unsteady with pain. 'We'd better get out of here. I don't know if that thing can climb fences—I hope it can't—but I don't want to wait to find out!'

Measle and Tinker ran quietly towards the entrance of the alley. When they got there, Measle carefully put his head out. To the left was the Go-Kart track, the street beside it empty and stretching away into the darkness. To the right—empty darkness.

No, not empty.

Something was moving.

In the distance, something was moving in his direction. Some sort of mass of crawling things, slow and low to the ground—and there, behind this mass, other similar shapes—it looked as if the ground was swarming with movement—

Measle pushed his goggles over his eyes and rubbed both lenses with the woollen cuffs of his leather jacket, clearing as many of the raindrops as he could from their mirrored surfaces. Then, in the soft light that the goggles revealed, he saw them.

Pink, squashy, nylon-furred hippopotamuses. At least fifty pink, squashy, nylon-furred hippopotamuses were waddling slowly towards him!

And behind the pink hippos came a whole zoo of nylon-furred, multi-coloured, cuddly toys—lime-green teddy bears, lemon-yellow camels, crimson monkeys, blue dinosaurs—all advancing steadily towards him in the darkness, with what little light there was glinting menacingly in their glass eyes—

It wasn't just the one pink hippo that had been brought to horrible life, thought Measle, *it was every cuddly toy prize in the theme park! And, while he might be able to cope with one or two of the creatures, here was a whole regiment of the poisonous things! And if he got surrounded by the things—a few more of those sharp,*

stinging bites and he'd be done for! As he watched in horror, Measle saw four of the creatures break away from the main group and waddle off down a side street—then another four turned off and stomped in another direction.

Mrs Zagreb had said something about getting 'mindless help'.

These things didn't seem to be mindless at all.

They were searching the place.

Searching for *him*.

Panic suddenly seized Measle and, with his brain frozen and incapable of sensible thought, he grabbed Tinker and ran back down the alley and

huddled under the awning once again. By the time he realized that this was a bad idea, it was too late. The front line of the army was passing by the alley entrance. Measle watched them as they went by—they marched in step with each other, a steady, pounding rhythm that Measle could hear through the drumming of the rain. *Thump, thump, thump.*

Then, to Measle's horror, two lemon-yellow camels, a green teddy bear, and a small blue dinosaur broke off from the main body and waddled into the alley.

Tinker growled softly. Measle fumbled in his trouser pocket for a jelly bean and, as he did so, he lost hold of Tinker. The little dog wriggled free, jumped out of his arms, and ran towards the advancing creatures, the hair on his back standing up straight and stiff. Measle, his fingers still searching frantically in his pocket, froze. But it was too late. The leading camel's head turned and its tiny, black glass eyes stared fixedly at Tinker, who was now advancing slowly on the small group, a low, rumbling growl sounding deep in his throat.

'Tinker!' whispered Measle hoarsely. 'Come back!'

Tinker took no notice. *This was too important—what were these thingies? They didn't smell like animals—they smelt more like cushions—wet cushions—but, wet or dry, cushions didn't walk and cushions didn't look at you all funny, not like these cushions, which were lookin' at him very funny indeed—and if there was one thing Tinker didn't care for, that was being looked at all funny—*

The two yellow camels and the green teddy bear came steadily closer. The little blue dinosaur paused for a moment and then turned away and began to stomp back towards the alley entrance— back to where the tail end of the army of soft toys was just then passing by.

It's going to report on what it's seen! thought Measle. *It's going to report that it's found us! I've got to stop it!*

Measle got up from his crouched position and ran towards the end of the alley. He passed Tinker, who was holding his ground—and he skirted by the three advancing creatures. They paused and turned their heads slowly, watching him run by— then they turned back and plodded steadily on towards Tinker.

Measle caught up with the slow-moving dinosaur just as it reached the alley entrance. He bent down and grabbed it by the long blue nylon fur at the back of its neck and lifted it clean off the ground. It was surprisingly heavy and felt horribly cold and slimy—and Measle realized that the steady rain had soaked right through the fur and into the stuffing of the toy, so that it was saturated with water.

Holding the horrible thing at arm's length, Measle ran back down the alley—

And then Tinker attacked his foes.

The little dog decided that walking cushions—soaking wet, walking cushions—were objects that he simply couldn't allow. So he leaped forward, buried his teeth in the nose of the leading camel and began to shake the thing wildly from side to side.

The squashy wet dinosaur in Measle's hand was wriggling, its stumpy legs jerking backwards and forwards. Its mouth gaped open, its head twisting from side to side as it tried to find something to sink its needle teeth into.

Measle ran past Tinker and on down to the end of the alley. There was the high wire fence and, beyond it, the dark humps of the electrical machinery—

Measle swung his arm and hurled the blue dinosaur clean over the top of the fence. It landed with a squishy thump somewhere in the darkness. Other than the sound of its fall, it made no noise. Measle didn't wait to see if the thing was going to come back—he turned to see how Tinker was getting on.

Tinker was in trouble. He'd been so busy trying to shake the leading camel into small pieces that he hadn't noticed the other two creatures beginning to crowd round him and, by the time he felt the pressure of their heavy, wet, soft bodies against him, it was too late. The lime-green teddy bear lunged forward and snapped its steel teeth into Tinker's stumpy tail.

Tinker yelped, high and loud. The stinging in his tail was very painful—but it wasn't enough to make him lose his grip on the camel's nose. He held firm to the camel's snout and went on shaking the creature from side to side with all the strength of his powerful neck muscles—and, at the same time, he began to circle faster and faster, trying to keep his rear end as far as possible from the snapping jaws of the other two creatures.

All the attentions of Tinker's attackers were on the little dog, so neither of them saw Measle approaching from behind them and the first thing they knew about it was when they felt Measle's hands grab the scruffs of their necks. A moment later, they were dangling in mid-air. Tinker, free now to concentrate on the one enemy over which he had complete control, gave one more furious shaking to the camel in his mouth and, in a great shower of wet, fuzzy, nylon stuffing, the head ripped clean off the camel's body. The lemon-yellow torso flew several metres across the alley and landed, on its back, in a pile of discarded food wrappers. Its legs waved feebly in the air. Tinker gave one more furious shake to the head and then let it go—and the head slithered away into the darkness.

Measle ran, with a squirming yellow camel in one hand and a lime-green teddy bear in the other, down to the end of the alley. He hurled the camel over the fence—there was a SQUISH! as it landed somewhere in the darkness—then he pulled his arm back and hurled the teddy bear, listening for the sound of its fall—

The teddy bear flew through the falling rain. Measle had let go of it a fraction early, so the thing went higher over the fence than the other two. It soared over the electrical machinery and then began to fall—and, as it did so, it hit a high power cable that stretched between the tall buildings on either side. There was a sudden, blinding flash of blue-white light, a crackling bang, a great shower of sparks—and an explosion of white kapok stuffing, that fell out of the night sky like oversized snowflakes.

'They are doing too much magic!' screamed Griswold Gristle, peering out into the darkness through the office windows of the park's administration block. 'I sssaid they could do *one* major collective spell—but they've jussst done a *second* one!'

'How do you know that, Griswold?' said Judge Cedric Hardscrabble. The judge was sitting bolt upright in a swivel chair behind a big steel desk and he was pretending that he was in his courtroom, presiding over a very interesting case. 'Where is your evidence, Griswold?' he said, in his best judge's voice. 'Where is your evidence that they are disssobeying you?'

Griswold turned away from the window. 'There was another flash of light in the dissstance, Cedric,' he said, angrily. 'A flash of light and a loud crash. Is that sssufficient evidence for you?'

'A flash of light and a loud crash?' murmured Judge Cedric, narrowing his eyes, in the hope that he would look intelligent and thoughtful. *He looks like a short-sighted old tortoise*, thought Griswold. Judge Cedric opened his mouth again.

'Well, I mussst grant you—it is certainly a *possibility* that they have cast a further ssspell, Griswold.'

'A possibility?' yelped Griswold. 'A *possibility*?'

'It is certainly a *possibility*,' repeated the judge, in his most pompous voice. 'However, there is another explanation, Griswold. Have you consssidered that what you sssaw could well have been caused by... the sssetting off... of a small *nuclear device*?'

Griswold gritted his teeth. Of all the wrathmonks he'd ever known, Judge Cedric Hardscrabble was certainly the stupidest.

'It was *not* a nuclear device, Cedric, small or otherwise,' said Griswold, in as patient a voice as he could manage. 'It was magic! A fairly powerful ssspell, too—and very sssoon after the first one. Where they obtained the additional mana is anybody's guess—I presume they mussst have been very near the sssource to recharge ssso quickly. And that could ssso easily upset his lordship the Dragodon! We cannot afford to disssplease his lordship the Dragodon in thisss manner!'

'Well—what do you want me to do about it?' said Judge Cedric, sulkily.

'We mussst go out there and take charge,' said Griswold, seizing his umbrella and making for the door.

Judge Cedric didn't move. Instead, he settled himself more comfortably in the swivel chair, leaned back, and clasped his hands behind his head. He had no intention of going anywhere. Not now, at least. It was dark out there and cold and, of course, very wet. But here, inside the administration offices, it was nice and warm and dry. The only inconveniences were the twenty or thirty stone statues that littered the offices and the corridors and just got in everybody's way. The statues were all that remained of the administration staff and the security personnel, who had been left behind to look after the Isle of Smiles while it was closed for the winter. Of course, the Medusa head had made short work of them! It had really proved its worth—it had been such fun watching them all, one by one, petrify—

'Well, come *along*, Cedric!' snapped Griswold, now standing in the open doorway.

'I thought I might ssstay here, Griswold,' said

Judge Cedric, in a dreamy voice. The chair was so comfy—

Griswold plastered a sickly smile on his little mouth and put on his most persuasive voice. 'When we capture him, Cedric,' he said, 'perhaps you would be ssso kind as to use your exhalation enchantment on him—before we kill him, that is. I would ssso love to sssee all those horrid boils popping out all over his body and his face! Would you do that for usss, Cedric?'

Judge Cedric was proud of his exhalation enchantment and the thought of using it on a helpless captive was very appealing. He jumped to his feet. Then he took his old bowler hat and his umbrella from the coat stand in the corner of the room and joined Griswold in the doorway.

'Come then, Griswold,' he hissed. 'What are we waiting for? Let usss make haste!'

Half a mile from the administration block, the other wrathmonks were also on the move. They too had seen the flash of blue-white light and had heard the sizzling crackle as the wet teddy bear had exploded in a shower of stuffing but, unlike Griswold Gristle, they had been close enough to realize that this was not magic. This was some kind of electrical short-circuit—and it almost certainly had something to do with whatever it was that they were seeking.

They began to hurry back towards the alley.

GHOULISH GRANGE

Measle stood frozen to the spot as the kapok
stuffing fluttered down around him. Then, a
moment later, the stinging pain in his hand
brought him back to his senses. He ran back down
the alley towards Tinker, who was running in little
circles, trying to catch up with his hurting tail—if
only to give it a good licking. Measle scooped up
the little dog in one smooth movement. Then he
ran with Tinker in his arms down to the alley
entrance. He peeked out—looking left and right: to
the left, he could just make out the tail end of the
soft toy army marching away into the darkness.

To the right was the empty street—but that was the way that the wrathmonks had gone and Measle was sure that the flash and the crackle would bring them back to the alley in a hurry—so, he would run in the opposite direction.

Measle, with Tinker in his arms, slipped out of the alley. Silently, he trotted through the darkness, keeping a good distance between himself and the last line of the marching toys. Quite soon he came across a side street and he ducked into it. It was dark here, like the alley. But this was a proper street, with no high wire fence across it, which meant that Measle and Tinker couldn't be trapped here. They had a clear escape route, just so long as they kept going.

Measle tried to remember where this particular road led to. On his right there was a miniature roundabout with brightly coloured little cars and buses and lorries mounted on it—and there, further up the street, was a small railway track that went in a simple oval. Standing silently in the miniature station was a little bright red locomotive. It had a happy, smiling face painted on the front of its boiler, just above the cow-catcher—and Measle realized where he was. This was the area of the Isle of Smiles where the rides were reserved for the littlest children. Somewhere close by, Measle remembered, was one of those blow-up castles. On the day he and his parents had come to the park, it had been full of squealing, laughing, bouncing toddlers—yes!—there it was, just round a bend in the road. It was still and silent now and a lot of the air had leaked out, so that the castle drooped and sagged, almost as if it was made from melting ice cream—

There was a distant, clattering sound, coming from somewhere behind them.

Measle turned slowly and Tinker poked his snout out from the folds of Measle's jacket and sniffed the air suspiciously. The clattering sound was getting steadily closer. It was a very odd noise—as if a hundred wooden hammers were tapping away against the hard ground. The hammers tapped with no apparent rhythm—just a steady, irregular *tap-tap-tap, clatter-clatter-clatter—*

Tinker growled, his nose twitching furiously. The stinging in his tail was forgotten. There was a slight breeze that was blowing in their direction and Tinker caught a sharp smell on the damp air.

Wood.

Lots and lots of wood.

And paint. Shiny sort of paint. Now, where have I smelt that smell before? Not long ago, neither! Just a short while—when the smelly kid was carryin' me—it was when we was runnin' around that big round thingy—with all them horsey-looking thingies on it!

Measle couldn't smell anything other than the cold, wet air—but he could see clearly through the darkness to the spot where the street joined the road they had just vacated. And there, just coming into view, trotted a brightly-painted, wooden carousel horse.

It paused for a moment and, as it did so, it was joined by another horse—then another, and another—until a small crowd of the creatures jostled for space at the junction of the two roads.

Measle watched in horror as the leading carousel horse flared its nostrils wide. Slowly, the yellow head turned this way and that. The mouth was open and gaping and Measle could see the bright red, lolling tongue of the thing. Its eyes were wide and staring and unblinking and it moved its head with a certain stiffness—as if movement of any sort was strange to it. The pole that had attached it to the platform of the carousel was still upright in its body, sticking up from the middle of its back and down through its belly, the end just clearing the ground beneath.

Measle shuddered. The pink hippos—and the lime-green bears and the lemon-yellow camels— they were bad enough. But these things were a lot worse. The hippos and the bears and the camels could bite and they could sting, but they were soft and light and (one by one, at least) fairly easy to throw over a nearby fence. But these horses were made of wood and wood was heavy and hard! And then there was the size of the creatures—they were taller than Measle by a good margin and dwarfed little Tinker completely! And last—but far from least—was their speed. *They may be made of wood,* thought Measle with growing despair, *but these are horses and horses can run really fast!*

All the carousel horses were now turning their heads this way and that, their staring eyes peering through the rain and the darkness, their nostrils flared wide to catch any scent on the damp air. It was lucky for Measle and Tinker that it was a dark night and that the breeze was, at the moment, blowing in their direction, otherwise the horses would have been certain to see them and smell them. As it was, the horses went on milling around at the junction of the two streets, as if unsure which way to go next.

Very carefully—using as little movement as possible—Measle reached into his trouser pocket and took out a yellow jelly bean. Slowly, he raised his hand to his mouth and popped the jelly bean onto his tongue. A quick chew—and it was down his throat. Then Measle turned and began to run, as silently as he could, his invisible feet skimming over the wet road like a ghost.

He passed the drooping castle and headed fast towards a big dark building that loomed large at the far end of the street. It was a spooky looking place—with tall chimneys and a steeply sloping roof. Beneath the roof, the eaves were ornately carved and the windows looked like the sort you see in old churches. The whole thing reminded Measle a little of the horrible house where he'd spent so many miserable years with Basil Tramplebone. There was a short path that led to the tall front door—and at the start of this path was a sign that read

For a moment, Measle wondered if perhaps it was here that the wrathmonks were holding his mother prisoner? Unlike the rest of the rides, here was an actual house—and it was weird enough and grim enough and generally nasty enough to suit the wrathmonks' purposes—whatever they might be—

Measle's thoughts were interrupted by the sound of wooden hooves on the roadway—a sound that was getting rapidly louder and louder. Measle risked a quick glance over his shoulder—and there, not a hundred metres behind him, came the carousel horses at full gallop, heading straight for him! How they knew he was there, Measle couldn't imagine—perhaps the wind had changed, perhaps they had seen his ghostly outline—but there was no time for thinking, there was no time for anything, except to run—run as fast as he could towards the only place that might offer him even the smallest degree of safety—

Ghoulish Grange.

By the time he reached the sign and the start of the short path that led to the front door, Measle felt that his lungs were about to burst. The added weight of Tinker, still stuffed down the front of his leather jacket, increased his exhaustion. Panting heavily, Measle passed under the sign and staggered up the path. The sound of the wooden hooves was almost deafening—the carousel horses could only be a few metres behind him now! He reached the heavy door and slammed his shoulder against its wooden panels—

It didn't move. Measle rammed his shoulder against it again—nothing. *But—how had it opened before? When he and Sam and Lee had been here—only a few days ago?—it had just swung open as they approached, with a lot of amplified creaking and groaning from its rusting iron hinges, and a ghostly voice had* boomed out, 'Welcome to Ghoulish Grange, my hideous house of horrors! Abandon hope, all ye who enter here!' Obviously, the whole thing worked on some sort of sensor beam that detected the approach of visitors—and now, with the power off all over the park, the beam wasn't working—

The clattering of the hooves was right behind him and Measle turned, his back to the door. There, right in front of him, was the leading horse.

Its wide, unblinking eyes bored into his and Measle realized, with a start of horror, that the effects of the jelly bean had worn off and he was no longer invisible—and, even if he could somehow have reached into his pocket for another jelly bean, it was now too late. The horse was rearing up onto its hind legs, its front hooves pawing at the air. A shrieking, whinnying sound came from its gaping mouth—then, it lunged forward, its front hooves slicing through the air towards Measle's head. Desperately, Measle threw himself sideways, like a goalkeeper leaping for a football—and the wooden hooves whistled past his ear and slammed against the door. There was a groaning, splintering sound—and then the whole door suddenly fell inwards, torn from its locks and its hinges by the sheer weight and power of the carousel horse's attack.

The horse took a step backwards and reared once more—and in the moment before its hooves came smashing down again, Measle—clutching Tinker tight to his chest—scrambled on hands and knees through the opening and into the deep shadows of the building.

With Measle on all fours, Tinker found himself no longer being held tight to the smelly kid's chest—so he wriggled free and slipped out of the front of Measle's leather jacket and onto the concrete floor. He thought for a moment of turning back and confronting these strange, woody-smelling creatures that were attacking him and the smelly kid—*they looked like horsey thingies and they ran like horsey thingies and they even sounded like horsey thingies—but they didn't* smell *like horsey thingies and that was all that mattered! Like, back on the table top, when that giant bug was after them, it had smelt like a giant bug, which was why there'd been no question about going after the nasty great thingy! But these horsey thingies smelt of wood and paint and that wasn't right! That wasn't the way things were supposed to be! And when things weren't the way they were supposed to be then, on the whole, runnin' away was a good idea—a couple of quick barks first though, just to show who's really the big boss round here—*

Tinker yelped twice and then darted off into the shadows and Measle scrambled to his feet and raced after him. There was a moment while the carousel horses seemed to be bewildered by the unexpected turn of events—then the leading horse shouldered its way through the opening, its hooves sounding hollow against the fallen door.

In here it was pitch dark but Measle quickly slipped the goggles over his eyes—and now (helped by the fact that raindrops were no longer distorting his vision) he could see exactly where he was—and where he needed to go. In front of him was the queuing area—five rows of steel bars set in the concrete floor, that channelled the visitors to Ghoulish Grange ride in a zigzag pattern. Measle remembered how it had been on the day they had visited the Isle of Smiles—this whole space full of happy, smiling faces, the sound of laughter everywhere around them—and the slow, shuffling feet of the crowd as the queue inched its way towards the rear of the area, where the passengers got on and off the little trains— little trains that were shaped like *coffins*, Measle remembered. At the time, they had all found that quite funny and Sam had even made a joke about *his* coffin being far too small for him—('Look at this, Measle! Fat lot of good this is! I can't even lie down in it!') but now, it wasn't funny any more. Nothing was funny any more—

A loud clattering of wood on concrete jerked Measle back into action. Ahead, he could see Tinker blundering about under the steel railings. The little dog kept bumping his nose against the metal poles and then shaking his head and trying again—and Measle realized that Tinker, in this total darkness, couldn't see a thing. But Measle could—

The leading carousel horse stumbled into the queuing area, its head jerking to and fro, its painted wooden eyes staring in the blackness. Behind it, the rest of the horses began to push their way forward, crowding the creature in the front, pressing against it—and the leading horse turned and snapped its wooden jaws at the noses of those behind it. When they didn't move away, it bucked and lashed out with its rear hooves and there was a loud crack! of wood on wood.

Measle ran forward, away from the snapping jaws and lashing hooves. He scrambled over the first metal barrier—then the second—then the third—

Behind him, he could hear a commotion of clattering hooves. He glanced back and saw the leading horse settle back on its haunches, the powerful muscles in its hind legs rippling. Then the creature launched itself forward and up—it soared through the pitchy darkness, clearing the first barrier easily—and the second—and now it was dropping down, its hooves thrust forward for the landing and heading straight for where Measle was crouching!

Desperately, Measle threw himself under the fourth barrier—rolling across the narrow space— under the fifth and last barrier—and, behind him, came a great splintering crash! as the carousel horse's body landed across the third line of rails. The creature floundered there, its legs flailing wildly, its head jerking madly back and forth as it tried to pull itself up and away—but Measle, in a quick glance over his shoulder, saw that the wooden body of the creature, draped over the iron railing, had broken almost in half. There were jagged splinters of wood sticking out from around its painted saddle and the vertical steel bar that had connected it to the carousel platform was bent almost double—

In the pitch darkness, the rest of the carousel

horses had no idea of the dangers in front of them. All they could hear was the frantic snorting and whinnying of their leader, somewhere up ahead—so, one by one, they all leaped forward, crashing together in a great jumble of splintered wood. Three survived the collision—and they began slowly to pick their way round the obstacles that lay between them and their prey.

Measle crawled forward as silently as he could. The three remaining carousel horses might not be able to see him but they could certainly hear him—and could perhaps *smell* him, too, so the sooner he put some sort of barrier between the creatures and himself the better. In front of him was the platform and the rails—and a line of little coffins on wheels. The wheels rested on the narrow rail lines that led to a pair of tall, arched doors. The doors were made of iron and were massive—the kind you might find in a medieval castle, designed to keep out a whole army of invaders—*the kind that could certainly stop a few wooden horses from breaking through—so that was where he should head for—but first, where was Tinker?*

Measle looked around frantically—and there was the little dog, sitting right by the leading coffin, pawing at his bruised snout. Measle ran forward and scooped him up—and Tinker gave a small yelp of surprise at being grabbed, without any warning, in this total darkness—and then, realizing who was holding him, he shot out his tongue and flipped it over Measle's nose.

'Shh, Tink,' whispered Measle, holding the little dog tight to his chest. He glanced back and saw three carousel horses slowly blundering their way along the zigzag path between the barriers. Measle realized that, if they didn't take it into their heads to try jumping again, these three remaining horses would be through the barriers in less than a minute.

He pushed his way past the line of coffins and reached the huge doors. He put his hands flat against them—*yes, they were cold, like iron or steel!*—and pressed hard—but it was like pressing against a mountain. Nothing moved beneath his straining hands—and meanwhile, the clattering of the hooves was getting nearer and nearer—

There—on the other side of the rail, on the opposite platform where the passengers disembarked—a sort of hatch in the wall! The hatch door was ajar and, beyond it, a rectangle of darkness—

Measle scrambled over the line of coffins and knelt down by the opening. Holding tight to Tinker, he pulled at the small door with his spare hand and the door swung sideways, revealing a metal tunnel that ran for several metres before curving away into darkness. Measle guessed it was some kind of ventilation shaft, or perhaps an access tunnel of some sort. Without looking back,

Measle crawled into the narrow space and began to inch his way forward. Where this shaft was leading, he had no idea—but it was away from the danger behind him and Measle was pretty sure that horses—wooden or otherwise—couldn't crawl through tunnels as narrow as this one.

The tunnel bent to the left and then carried on a few more metres, before ending in a metal grating. The grating looked pretty flimsy and Measle reckoned he could probably kick it out with his feet—but first, he inched up close and peered through.

The inside of Ghoulish Grange was huge—a great empty space, through which the rail lines of the coffin ride looped to and fro. The lines ran past creepy cemeteries and open graves—the mechanized skeletons and ghosts that popped out of them and gibbered at the passing coffin trains were still and silent now, as were the mummies in their Egyptian tombs and the trolls under their sagging stone bridges. It was strange, thought Measle—when he and Sam and Lee had been on the ride, with the skeletons jumping out at them and the ghosts clanking their chains, the mummies lunging with their bandaged claws and the trolls clutching with their knobbly green hands—it had all been such fun and not scary at all. But now, with everything still and silent like this—it was a very scary place indeed. To Measle, the tunnel seemed a better hiding place, what with its steel walls and narrow confines—a carousel horse could never fit in here although from the crashing and clattering that was coming from the tunnel entrance, the surviving creatures seemed to be trying quite hard—

As a precaution, Measle pushed against the metal grating and he felt it bend beneath his hand. *So, in an emergency, he could probably break through. With any luck, he wouldn't have to—this was as good a hiding place as any and he certainly didn't fancy spending any time in the cemeteries and the tombs of Ghoulish Grange—*

From the folds of his jacket came a soft growl.

'What is it, Tink?' whispered Measle—and Tinker pushed his nose out of the depths of the jacket and sniffed the still air.

Wet cushion! Another stupid wet cushion! More than one, actually! And close by! Too close—

Tinker wriggled free and slipped out onto the metal floor. Measle could see the little dog clearly in the pitch darkness. The hair on his back stood up in a ridge and his ears were flattened on his skull. He was facing away from the grating, staring blindly back up the tunnel. Measle shifted his gaze and peered in the same direction—there was nothing there. But now Tinker was growling again—a low, menacing sound from deep in his throat. The curve in the shaft decreased the distance that Measle could see—only a few metres, in fact—so he leaned sideways, trying to look around the bend—and there, crawling steadily towards him, came three crimson monkeys.

Their nylon fur dripped with rainwater. Their mouths were stretched wide in silly grins, revealing the line of steel needles. Their big round eyes were blind in the darkness—and on they came, slowly feeling their way round the curve in the tunnel, coming steadily nearer and nearer—

Tinker burst out with a flurry of short, sharp barks and the three monkey heads swivelled towards the sound.

Frantically, Measle turned and lashed out at the metal grating with both feet. He kicked again—and again—and the flimsy lock on the edge of the grating gave way and the whole thing swung to one side with a tinny crash.

'Come on, Tink,' hissed Measle, grabbing Tinker's collar and pulling him hard towards the rectangular hole.

Tinker wanted to stay and fight but he couldn't see a thing and his paws couldn't get a grip on the smooth metal floor of the tunnel—and the pull on his collar was powerful—and the smelly kid sounded pretty determined—'Come *on*, Tink!'— so, reluctantly, Tinker turned away from the approaching monkeys and allowed himself to be dragged out of the tunnel. He and Measle landed with a tangled thump on the side of a plaster slope and together they rolled down the little hill until they were brought up with a bump against a weathered, mossy tombstone.

For a moment, Measle lay still. Some of the wind had been knocked out of him by the fall and he was having trouble getting his breath back—but Tinker was nudging at him with his nose and then he heard the soft, wet shuffling sound as the three crimson monkeys slipped out of the tunnel and then slithered down the low wall. Measle turned his head and saw the monkeys rolling—just as he and Tinker had rolled—down the slope towards him. He scrambled to his feet, grabbed Tinker and ran a few metres from the tombstone, until he was brought up short by an open grave in front of him. The grave was about two and a half metres long and one and a half metres wide—and it was deep, at least three metres to the bottom. Measle's goggles showed him what was down there. A plastic skeleton, with red glass eyes, was lying in the bottom of the pit, supported by some sort of lifting equipment. Measle remembered the moment (it seemed so long ago!) when he and his parents had passed this way before—his mother had screamed when, as their little coffin had rattled by this very spot, this same skeleton had suddenly reared up out of its grave, its red eyes flashing and its long, bony arms waving over their heads. Lee had screamed and then she had laughed—and then screamed again when Sam had turned to her in the semi darkness, his face pulled into a monster grimace, his eyes crossed and his tongue sticking out and his teeth glowing white in the darkness—

Behind him came the same slow, wet, slithering sound. Measle whipped round—the crimson monkeys were crawling towards him, carefully feeling their way in the pitch darkness. From the folds of Measle's leather jacket came a soft growl. Tinker could smell these three wet cushions—he could smell that they were coming closer and closer—*but how was he supposed to fight 'em if he couldn't see 'em? And all this being carried about everywhere—it was nice, but enough was enough! Didn't the smelly kid realize he had legs? Perfectly good legs too—and four of 'em, which was a lot better than two, thank you very much! Particularly when there was cushions to fight! So, let's do a bit of the old walky-walkies now, shall we?*

Tinker started to wriggle inside the jacket, trying to get free—but Measle tightened his grip, because Measle had just had one of his ideas, and this particular idea (while not being one of his big ones) still required Tinker to be unmoving and quiet, at least for a moment or two—

Measle glanced quickly at the open grave, measuring the width of the pit with his eyes. He reckoned it was only a couple of metres at most—

not a problem if he took a run at it—

Measle took two steps towards the approaching monkeys and then turned. He tensed the muscles in his legs, pulled Tinker's wriggling body tight to his chest and leaped forward. In three steps he was running—and in four he was in the air, his jump carrying him clean over the deep pit. He landed with a thump safely on the far side, right by the narrow rail tracks. Quickly, he turned and crouched down and watched as the three monkeys crawled nearer and nearer.

Tinker managed to wriggle free from the folds of the leather jacket. He pulled himself out of the zippered front and dropped lightly to the floor. He was as blind as the monkeys—but his keen nose told him which way to face.

Tinker growled again and the growl ended in a little yelp and the three crimson monkeys turned their heads towards the sound and came crawling forward, a little faster now.

The sound of their shuffling bodies, somewhere close by in the darkness, caused Tinker to break out in a series of sharp, furious little barks. *Here they came—nasty, wet crawlin' thingies that didn't smell like anyfink he could remember ever smellin' before—I'll let 'em know who's boss!* And Tinker took another deep breath and let out another flurry of furious barks.

And the crimson monkeys turned their heads towards the sound—and now they had something to aim for! Something to kill! Something ahead of them, somewhere out there in that velvet blackness—

The three monkeys lifted their nylon front paws from the floor and stood up on their hind legs. They bared their steel needle teeth. Then, together, they sprang forward in a shambling, scurrying run.

They didn't see the gaping pit in front of them. The only indication that it was there at all was when they felt the ground disappear beneath their nylon feet—and then it was too late.

One by one they dropped soundlessly into the black hole, landing with squishy plops on the skeleton at the bottom. There was a moment of silence—then Measle heard the soft, wet slithery sound again. He and Tinker cautiously approached the edge of the pit and peered into its depths. There, crawling over the long white bones of the skeleton, were the monkeys. They looked up, smiling their crazy smiles. Then they felt their way to the walls of the pit and reached up for a handhold of some sort, with which to pull themselves out of the grave.

But the walls were smooth. The builders of the ride had known that the insides of the various open graves would be invisible to the passing riders, so they had made the walls out of painted steel—and painted steel was impossible to climb, even for crimson monkeys with nylon paws. The three horrible creatures clawed and scrabbled and made little jumps into the air in order to try to catch hold of the edge of the pit but all their efforts were in vain.

Measle edged away from the grave, so he wouldn't have to look at the slithering, clawing, jumping things. When he and Tinker had backed away about ten metres, they couldn't hear them any more either—and that made Measle feel a bit better.

He turned and looked around at the huge cavernous space. In the soft light of his goggles, Ghoulish Grange didn't look creepy at all. It was just a vast, open space, with a high domed ceiling, filled with obviously artificial corpses and skeletons and zombies and trolls, with crumbling bridges and tottering, ivy-covered walls and ancient graveyards—all made of painted plaster— with a looping pair of railway tracks that wound backwards and forwards and round and about until they disappeared under another pair of tall, steel doors on the far side of the building. It was just a mechanical thing, a place designed to amuse ...

Not even a little bit scary.

Well, perhaps a bit.

It wasn't the plastic and plaster inhabitants of Ghoulish Grange that were making Measle nervous now. It was the steady pounding sound that was coming from the great steel doors nearby—a rhythmic clang-clang-clang of wood on iron. Measle guessed what it was—the three remaining carousel horses had reached the doors and were hammering against them in unison, their wooden hooves crashing against the metal in a steady rhythm—and Measle wondered for a moment if animated creatures like cuddly toys and carousel horses ever got tired? Or could they just keep on going and going until either they—or the thing they were assaulting—finally broke? But one look at the great steel doors—a pair at the entrance and another pair at the exit—reassured him. Nothing was going to get through them, which meant that he and Tinker were reasonably safe for the time being. Of course, with all this noise, it was likely that the wrathmonks would soon be arriving on the scene—

Measle shuddered. He didn't want to think about that. Cuddly toys and carousel horses were bad enough, but he'd evaded them all so far. But wrathmonks were another story. Measle felt a sudden weakness in his knees and he sank down and knelt by the tombstone. Tinker stopped scratching and shaking and plopped down at his side.

Measle felt it several seconds before he heard anything. A slow, thudding vibration on the concrete floor where he was crouching. It was nothing more than a small shaking of the ground— so tiny, in fact, that, had Measle been standing up, he probably wouldn't have felt a thing through the thick rubber soles of his trainers. But, through the thin material of his trousers, Measle felt it plainly.

Something heavy—something very huge and very heavy—was approaching. It was still some way off—Measle had no idea how far but he guessed at maybe a hundred metres—but the faint shuddering of the concrete under his knees was getting stronger and stronger and now even Tinker felt it, because he was tilting his head and staring, with a puzzled look in his eyes, at the ground under his feet.

And then Measle *heard* it too. The sound began to mix in with the steady clanging of the horses' hooves on the metal doors. At first, it was quite faint but it grew quickly louder and louder until it almost obliterated the clanging hooves—Clang! Thump! Clang! Thump! Clang! Thump! Clang! Thump! Clang! Thump! Clang!—Thump!—and then the clanging began to die away, as if the surviving carousel horses had also heard the sound and felt the vibration—and Measle imagined their three wooden heads turning slowly towards the approaching sound, their wooden nostrils flaring, their staring wooden eyes swivelling with fear—

And then all the sounds stopped dead.

There was a deep, dark silence. It was as if the universe was holding its breath—and Measle held his breath, too, his ears straining to hear something—anything!—because this utter silence was more scary than anything he'd experienced before.

But, when the long silence was finally broken, Measle discovered what being *really* scared actually felt like.

The sound began as a kind of low, grumbling, muttering sort of noise—very faint at first so that Measle had to strain to hear it through the walls of Ghoulish Grange—then growing steadily louder and louder, the grumbling and the muttering rapidly becoming an ear-splitting, mind-numbing, blood-freezing roar—and the roar was louder than the loudest roar that the largest and fiercest lion could ever have produced—this roar made Measle's ears ache, it shook the whole huge building that surrounded him, even dislodging dust from high in the domed ceiling—

Measle and Tinker froze at the enormous sound. Tinker's ears were flat to his head and his stumpy little tail was tucked under his rear legs—and *Measle's* legs felt as if they were made of jelly and the blood drained from his face and the spiky hair on his head stood up straight like an all-over Mohawk.

The roar went on and on and on—and then there was a great thumping crash as a huge and heavy *something* apparently hurled itself against the side of the building. More dust began to float down from the high ceiling and a skeleton—posed in the act of crawling out of a nearby coffin— suddenly fell to pieces, its bones clattering on the concrete floor.

Another great, thudding crash and Measle felt the air around him shift as the walls of the building bent inwards under the enormous weight of—well, of whatever it was out there. *Whatever it was, it must be huge!* Measle crouched down and hugged his knees tight to his chest and stared wildly towards the point on the distant wall where he guessed the attack was taking place. Tinker whined softly and huddled closer to Measle—and what was going through his doggy mind was something like—*This was a bit of* not *all right, this was—a bit too noisy and a bit too thumpy and a bit too much of the ground jumpin' about in a nasty way—not that he was scared, of course, perish the thought!—but it was better to be really close to the smelly kid, 'cause the smelly kid might need a bit of support durin' these trying times—*

A third shattering crash—and there, on the far side of the building, a small section of the concrete wall fell inwards and exploded on the floor in a cloud of concrete dust. Another thudding smash—and a larger piece cracked away from the wall and fell—and Measle could see that the entire far wall was now covered in a tracery of cracks—it looked as if a mad spider had woven an irregular web all over the surface—another chunk fell inwards—

And now the darkness inside was no longer the pitch darkness of before, because now a dim light from outside showed through the gaping hole in the wall. Through this jagged opening, Measle could see something huge moving. The thing was so big, it completely filled the hole and all Measle could make out through his goggles was a sort of shifting, rippling surface—there was a suggestion of lumpy skin—brown, lumpy skin—

And then there was a fourth shuddering thud against the distant wall and, this time, a whole section of the building simply caved in with a great dusty crash—and now the hole was no longer a hole—now it was an opening at least fifteen metres high and about six metres across—and Measle could see an enormous pair of back legs, scaly back legs that ended in long, vicious-looking claws—and higher up, at least twelve metres off the ground, was a pair of little arms, completely out of proportion to the rest of the enormous body—and now the whole body of the creature bent slightly and a great rectangular head ducked into sight and it poked its long, teeth-bristling snout inside and sniffed the dusty air.

It was the plastic and plaster and steel Tyrannosaurus Rex from the Dinosaur Diver ride—somehow brought to horrible, mindless life!

The huge head of the thing swung slowly from side to side. Its eyes were glowing a deep red and its jaws were bared, showing the double rows of long yellow teeth. It peered into the darkness and a low grunting noise, like that of a gigantic pig, rumbled deep in its throat.

Measle kept very still. Even in his intense fear he realized that, in this pitchy blackness, it was unlikely that the Rex could see him—*hadn't he read somewhere that scientists believed that Tyrannosaurus Rex had pretty poor eyesight?*—he certainly hoped so, because now the huge creature was pushing its shoulders through the opening in the cracked and broken wall, causing more chunks of concrete to cascade around its scaly feet. It shoved its way through the gap and stood there, its head rearing up towards the ceiling, the claws on its little forearms twitching and clenching, as if the creature was desperate to get its talons on something—anything—just so long as it was alive and juicy, with lots of little bones to crunch—

Tinker (who, like most small dogs, thought of himself as a very large, fierce, and dangerous dog indeed) stood up, his wiry fur bristling on his back. Then, before Measle could stop him, he ran forward and began to bark furiously at the great looming shape in the shadows. As far as Tinker was concerned, this thing had no business invading his space! How dare it! *Great big clumsy thingy, roarin' and bashin' about and makin' a mess all over the place—go on, get out of it! Get out of here, or I'll bite you to death—nasty great thingy with no proper animal scent—horrible, nasty thingy smellin' of plaster and plastic and metal!*

Tinker ran forward a few more metres, still barking furiously. Measle crouched by the tombstone, frozen with terror and quite unable to speak. His teeth were chattering, his tongue felt like a lump of stone, and his eyes were wide and staring. He wanted desperately to call out to Tinker—to make him come back—to make him be quiet—but no part of his body seemed to be working any more—

Tinker was now

standing just a few metres from the tyrannosaurus's massive feet. Tinker's own little feet were planted firmly apart, his stumpy tail erect and bristling, his ears flat to his head. He glared up at the enormous shape in front of him and yowled furiously—and the dinosaur lowered its huge head and glared back, its eyes glowing red in the darkness. Then it opened its mouth and snarled. The snarl sounded like canvas being ripped apart and Tinker stopped barking for a moment, a little taken aback by the strange noise. The tyrannosaurus bent its body, lowering its head even closer to the ground. Then it cocked its head to one side, using one glowing eye to find and identify the little creature below. For a moment, the T. Rex and Tinker stood silently, staring at each other. Both seemed puzzled, apparently uncertain what to do next. Then the tyrannosaurus opened its mouth, revealing the double rows of gleaming teeth. It threw back its head and roared—and the sound crashed and thundered in the enclosed space. The ear-splitting noise broke Measle's paralysis and he instinctively put both his hands over his ears—but even then it was still deafening and Measle could feel the air around him vibrating from the sound waves.

The effect on Tinker of this vibrating thunder was very sudden and very dramatic. He turned, in an instant, from a brave and fearless warrior dog into a quivering, panic-stricken little runaway. It was the sheer volume of the dinosaur's roar that did it. Tinker could cope with pretty much anything—*but not that sort of noise, thank you very much—that sort of noise hurt the old ears and we don't like being hurt—it's quite enough that the old tail is stingin' like billy-o, we don't need sumfink even worse at the other end, thank you very much!—So, where's the exit? Right now, please—where's the rotten exit, 'cause it's time to go, indeedydoody—time to go somewhere else,* anywhere *else, just so long as it is far away from that horrible noise—*

And Tinker forgot all about the smelly kid huddled against the tombstone. All he could think about was his own safety—so, with a sudden yelp of terror, the little dog tucked his stinging tail between his legs and ran blindly in the direction of the dim light that filtered in from outside. Without really being aware of what he was doing or even where he was going, Tinker ran between the huge feet of the dinosaur, ran right beneath the huge stomach of the creature, ran past the long tail that swayed back and forth three metres above his head, ran up and over the great lumps of fallen concrete, ran through the gaping opening in the wall—and out into the cold and the rain and the darkness of the night outside.

For a moment, the Tyrannosaurus Rex stood frozen to the spot, as if it didn't understand what had happened to the little yapping creature at its feet. Then it bent its head and craned its neck round and peered shortsightedly behind itself—*and there, a little flicker of movement, a small shadow racing over the chunks of fallen wall—its prey was escaping!* The huge creature heaved its body round—and one foot crushed a desk-sized piece of concrete to fine powder. Its tail swung in a great arc, smashing to dusty smithereens a long section of brick wall that enclosed a part of the cemetery—and then it was pushing its way back out of the broken building, its massive body dislodging more pieces of the outer wall of Ghoulish Grange. Then, with a grunting sound, the dinosaur was through. Measle saw it swing its head to the left and then to the right—he saw one glowing red eye focus on a distant object—and then, to Measle's relief, he saw the dinosaur lean forward and lurch off in a stumbling, loping run.

The relief Measle was feeling was quickly replaced by a terrible fear for Tinker's safety—but then, a moment later, Measle remembered Tinker's battle with the giant cockroach, back on Basil Tramplebone's table top. Tinker had been so quick and agile and the cockroach had been so slow and clumsy—surely the Tyrannosaurus Rex would be the same? All Tinker had to do was to keep out of the way of those great snapping jaws—out of reach of those ridiculous little arms with their long, grabbing claws—

There was the sound of clattering hooves and Measle looked with alarm back towards the great iron doors. But the sound he heard was no longer the sound of wooden hooves crashing against the iron panels—now it was the sound of wooden hooves running, running *away*—

The remaining carousel horses were giving up! They were leaving!

For a moment, Measle felt a sudden surge of hope. But then the hope faded. The sound of the wooden hooves didn't sound like a retreat. It sounded more like the start of some kind of chase. There was something determined in the distant clattering, something urgent—and that meant it might not be a retreat at all! It was more likely that the carousel horses had been summoned somehow, to join in the hunt for Tinker! And that could mean that all the huge regiment of cuddly toys, with their poisonous steel teeth, were even now turning in the same direction, their wet nylon fur dragging on the soaking ground—a whole army of animated monsters, all with a single idea— to hunt and catch and kill one small, frightened dog.

Measle had always been good at one thing—and that was knowing what to worry about and what *not* to worry about. He knew that the only things you ought to worry about were the things you could change. If you couldn't do anything about the problem, then it was a waste of time worrying about it. And right now, Tinker's running off into the night, with a whole horde of animated fairground creatures trying to hunt him down, was something he could do nothing about. Right now, what Measle needed to do was deal with his own problems.

And that was the problem. What should he do now? *Well—what am I here for? I'm here to find my mum! If she's not here in Ghoulish Grange— and it doesn't look as if she is—then where is she? And, if I've got to search all over for her, how do I get past all those horrible things?*

Measle rubbed at his stinging hand. The pain seemed to be less intense now, which was something, he supposed. All the same, he really didn't want to get bitten again. (*Where's my mum?*) And next time, if there *was* a next time, he might not be so lucky. Next time, he might be surrounded by the horrible things (*Where's my mum?*) and, if he was surrounded, he wouldn't have a chance—

—and, even as these thoughts were racing through Measle's mind, he heard in the distance the sound of voices. The voices were coming nearer and nearer and Measle huddled back in the shadow of the tombstone. It was still very dark inside Ghoulish Grange—but not quite as dark as it had been before the dinosaur had smashed the great hole in the side wall. Now, a faint grey glow filtered in from outside—but surely it wasn't enough light to reveal Measle's hiding place?

The voices were very near now.

Some shapes—human shapes—jostled in the jagged opening in the far wall. Through his goggles, Measle could see them as if it was daylight.

Horrible faces. The same horrible faces he'd seen in the ticket booth and at the end of the alley. There was the thin blond wrathmonk (*Draggle, that was his name!*) and next to him stood the stout one with a long loose hank of hair hanging down his back (*That was Flabbit, wasn't it?*) and crowding in around them was the little black beetle and his skinny wife (*Zagreb—that was their name*) and the huge wrathmonk who was called something like Truncheon—*no, not Truncheon—Cudgel, that was it!* And there, behind this small, jostling crowd, stood two more figures, both peering over the shoulders of the others in an attempt to see into the darkness of Ghoulish Grange. One was small and round, his head a pale blob of white skin, his tiny eyes two little black dots on either side of a short, round, snub nose. The other was tall and thin, with a beaky, jutting nose and a pointed chin. A great mane of white frizzy hair stuck out from under an old black bowler hat.

These were two new wrathmonks. Quickly, Measle counted—seven in all. Were there any more—and if so, how many?

Then Measle heard the voices again.

'Do you think it's ssstill in there?' said Flabbit, his little piggy eyes squinting with the effort of piercing the darkness.

'I dunno, do I?' muttered Draggle, sulkily. 'It's all dark, innit?'

'Your animated hunters have proved to be worthless,' said a voice from the back. It was an oily, greasy, high-pitched, drawly sort of voice—and one that Measle hadn't heard before. It made him shudder and shrink even further into the shadow of the tombstone. It made the rest of the wrathmonks turn towards it and Measle guessed, in that instant, that this wrathmonk was, in some way, a sort of leader. The oily voice started again— 'How foolish of you all—to wassste your mana on such mindless creatures. All of them are now chasing after a harmless little dog—leaving behind the real prey! Which is—I have no doubt—ssstill hiding in there in the darkness! Does anybody have a torch?'

There was a great patting of pockets as the wrathmonks searched for torches—torches they obviously didn't have—and then a general muttering that, no—they didn't have a torch among them.

'Well then,' said the oily, whiny voice, 'you will jussst have to enter and feel your way around— and, if there is anything in there worth catching, then you mussst catch it! Sssimple as that!'

'That's all very well,' rumbled a deep voice (*That's Cudgel,* thought Measle)—'but I don't sssee why it's jussst usss that has to go in there. Why don't you and the judge come in as well?'

A judge? The tall, skinny one with the frizzy hair was a judge?

The oily, whiny voice sounded a little irritated. 'Come now, Mr Cudgel—Judge Cedric and I are in *managerial* positions. Indeed, the word is part of my title—"Bank Manager". That means, Mr Cudgel, that I *manage*. I do not ssscrabble about in the darkness, looking for a sssilly child. Neither does Judge Cedric. We are above sssuch things.'

Measle's thin body tensed. *A bank manager! This must be the wrathmonk Griswold Gristle! And the other one, the judge—his name sounded vaguely familiar. Where had he heard that before? Was it a name his dad had mentioned once? They'd all been having breakfast one morning— yes—that was it! Sam had talked about the wrathmonk judge, the one who had awarded Basil the custody of Measle—he'd called him Cedric Hardscrabble! And here he was! Here they both were—wrathmonk enemies of the Stubbs family! Wrathmonk enemies from way back!*

Mrs Zagreb's voice sounded like nails on a blackboard. 'I have no intention of wandering about in sssuch darkness, Mr Grissstle! Why, I might break one of my beautiful long fingernails! How could you asssk sssuch a thing of a lady!'

And then Measle felt it. A sudden, thudding sensation in his head as each word—unheard by his ears but felt by every fibre in his brain—vibrated in his skull.

HE DID NOT ASK. BUT I DO. AND I DO NOT ASK. I COMMAND.

The unheard sounds died away, leaving behind them a dull ache at the front of Measle's skull. Measle closed his eyes and rubbed his forehead. *What on earth was that?*

Then, the sound of movement from the far wall.

Measle opened his eyes and peered through his goggles—and saw, to his horror, that all seven wrathmonks (without a single one of them voicing any kind of objection) had pushed their way in through the jagged opening and were now beginning to feel their way carefully across the huge space. They spread out in a line, their hands held out in front of them, their feet shuffling slowly forward.

Hurriedly, Measle crawled backwards, putting the tombstone between himself and the slow-moving line of wrathmonks. Each one had a different method of moving in the darkness. The

178

enormous Cudgel stepped slowly, feeling his way with his toes. Mr and Mrs Zagreb linked arms and sniffed the air with twitching noses as they inched along. Flabbit crawled forward on all fours, feeling his way along the ground with his hands. Griswold Gristle and Judge Cedric held back, both making sure that there was somebody in front of them in case of a trap—and young Draggle blundered forward, waving his hands in front of his face, as if he was clearing away cobwebs. He was now well ahead of the others and coming steadily forward—and then suddenly he stepped into nothingness, falling with a squeal of pain down into one of the open graves.

'Ow!' he yelled, his voice echoing in the deep pit.

'What has happened?' demanded Griswold Gristle, stopping where he was. He put his hand out and grabbed Judge Cedric's sleeve. 'One moment, Cedric. There may be danger.'

'I've fallen in a hole,' yelled Draggle. 'I've fallen in a hole and I can't get out! Help me!'

LEAVE HIM. CONTINUE SEARCHING.

Measle pressed his hands to his head. The words had been like hammers, thumping inside his brain and, once again, he wondered where on earth (or out of it!) this unheard voice could be coming from. He peered around the tombstone and saw that the remaining wrathmonks were back on the move again. There was no sound from the fallen Draggle. Cudgel was now the closest to him, with Mr and Mrs Zagreb not far behind. If he didn't do something soon, they would be on top of him!

Measle dived his hand into his pocket and pulled out a jelly bean. Then he carefully and silently shifted his body into a crouch, his leg muscles tensed and ready. He peered round the tombstone and quickly worked out the path he would take: run round that open grave, along the wall, over the troll bridge, jump the far grave, up the hill of rubble—and out through the jagged hole in the far wall—

Cudgel was now only five metres away. Measle could hear his heavy black boots shuffling over the ground—he could hear the sniffing sounds that the Zagrebs were making—

It was now or never.

The Ferris Wheel

Measle pushed the jelly bean into his mouth and bit down on it. In the same instant, he thrust forward with his legs and began to run. There was no point trying to be quiet—speed was what he needed. Speed and the element of surprise—

His route took him near to where Cudgel was creeping blindly forward and, as he got near the wrathmonk, Measle saw just how huge the monster was. Even crouched down as Cudgel was, the wrathmonk towered over Measle as he raced by.

'Sssomething's here!' shouted Cudgel, waving his hands backwards and forwards in the darkness. 'Sssomething jussst ran past me! Ssstop it!'

Measle took no notice. He could hear the pounding of his own feet, could hear the rasping of his own breath and he knew that the wrathmonks would hear it too. But they couldn't *see* him—and that was all that mattered. He raced down the length of the wall, heading fast for the troll bridge—he saw, out of the corner of one eye, Flabbit—still on all fours—slowly changing direction towards him—then he was over the bridge and racing for the grave. Measle realized with a start of sudden fear that the grave was the one that Draggle had fallen into—but it was too late to change his path now, so he ran straight for it and, at the last moment, jumped as high and as long as he could—he caught a glimpse of Draggle's startled face, peering up at the sound of some invisible thing whooshing through the air above him—then Measle landed on the far side of the grave, his legs propelling him forward in a frantic run towards the pile of rubble and the gaping hole in the wall—

'Quickly!' shrieked Griswold's oily voice. 'Quickly back, all of you! It is essscaping!'

Measle risked a quick glance over his shoulder. He saw the wrathmonks turning in his direction, saw them beginning to move towards him—they seemed to be moving more quickly now! There was less fumbling with feet, less groping with hands—now they were stepping forward with more confidence, as if they could suddenly see a little light in the deep darkness—then Measle realized that what they could see was the dim shape of the hole in the wall, which gave them a point to head for—

Measle reckoned he had another five or six seconds of invisibility left before the effects of the jelly bean would wear off. There wasn't a moment to lose! He tore to the foot of the rubble pile and began to scramble up over the loose chunks of concrete. Once or twice he almost lost his footing and, for a couple of those precious seconds, a small section of one trouser leg snagged on a piece of steel reinforcing bar that stuck out sideways from one of the concrete lumps. Measle yanked hard at his trousers and felt the material give way—he was free again!—he scrambled on—the rubble pile hadn't looked this big from the other side of the huge space—nor this steep! Just two more metres to the top! The dim light from outside was very close now! Very close—but not close enough! He wasn't going to make it—

'There! Ssseee? In the hole in the wall!'

'It's that filthy boy!'

'He's getting away!'

'Quickly! After him!'

Measle threw a terrified look over his shoulder. He could see the wrathmonks staring up at him. Griswold Gristle and Judge Cedric each had an arm raised and were pointing at him. Then, together, all six wrathmonks began to stumble towards him. He saw Cudgel pause by the open grave, lean over it and pull Draggle out of the pit by one arm. He saw Mrs Zagreb trip over a tangled tree root and almost fall before Mr Zagreb grabbed her round the waist and held her upright—he saw Mrs Zagreb slap his hand away—he saw Flabbit get to his feet and begin a stumbling run towards him—he saw Draggle fumbling in his pocket—

Measle turned away, forced his tired legs to move again and scrambled to the top of the rubble-heap. Now he was in the gaping hole in the wall—two more steps and he was outside, feeling the cold drops of rain spatter on his head. *Which way to run? The tyrannosaurus had lurched off to the right—*

Measle took off fast down the left-hand street. He ran blindly, with no idea where he was going—just as long as it was as far away as possible from the muffled shouts he could hear behind him. The raindrops spattered against the lenses of his goggles, blurring his vision, until the goggles became more of a hindrance than a help—so Measle pulled them down so that they hung round his neck again. Now the raindrops stung his eyes and his legs felt like a pair of lead weights—but he raced on through the night, turning left, then right, then dodging down an alley and then out again into a broad street—the theme park attractions flew by, their shapes looming in the shadows. His breath was coming in great rasps now and a pain was starting under his ribs. *He had to stop—he had to find somewhere to rest—somewhere safe, somewhere quiet, where he could stop and think—*

Something enormous loomed over him. It was tall and round, with spokes like a bicycle wheel. The spokes were covered with a tracery of metal lattice-work and all round the rim hung swinging wooden seats—it was the Ferris wheel!

Measle slipped on the goggles and stared up. He remembered the ride he and Sam and Lee had taken on it. It was one of the less exciting rides in the park but the view from the top had been spectacular. *You could see all over the island from the top of the Ferris wheel—*

Suddenly, Measle knew what he had to do. But he was going to have to do it quickly, because there, in the distance, were the sounds of urgent shouting—and the sounds were coming nearer with every passing second.

Measle stared up at the huge Ferris wheel. His eyes took in the steel girders that braced the contraption—girders that had convenient-looking holes all the way up their lengths— and these big girders were connected to smaller ones, so that everywhere he looked, there were handholds and footholds, all of them making a climb to the top of the wheel look a very easy business indeed.

Measle ran to the foot of the great wheel and grasped the wet iron of the nearest girder. He pulled himself up to the first hole—a foot in there, a hand reaching for the next one—up a metre, then another and another—hand over hand, foot over foot, up and up—hanging tight to the slippery metal, the rain bouncing on his upturned face—a sudden cold wind gusted by him and threatened to snatch him off this steel cliff—and far below him now, the voices were nearer—*perhaps they were coming out of the alley and starting down the road to the Ferris wheel? Would they see him, a little wet spider a third of the way to the top? Perhaps he should risk one more jelly bean?*

Measle paused in his frantic climb and looked over his shoulder and down towards the ground. It was a long way to the base of the wheel—a very long way—and Measle felt suddenly a little sick and dizzy. His head swam for a moment and his tired fingers began to lose their grip—he swayed, his eyes tight closed—then he shook off the feeling and stared hard down the dark street—*Yes! There in the distance, a group of black-coated figures hurrying through the rain! They would be here in half a minute! He mustn't be seen!*

Measle locked one arm round the girder and pushed his free hand deep into his trouser pocket.

There was nothing there.

Well, there was *something* there.

A hole.

There was a hole in the bottom of his trouser pocket!

Measle could feel the skin of his thigh through the tear. Frantically, he pulled his fingers back into the ruined pocket and felt in all the corners.

Nothing.

The few remaining yellow jelly beans must now be scattered over the wet ground, somewhere between the Ferris wheel and Ghoulish Grange— *somehow, he must have ripped his pocket in the mad scramble up the rubble pile! And now he'd lost his only advantage over the wrathmonks! Without invisibility whenever he needed it, he was almost certainly lost! What to do?* What to do?

The voices were nearer now, almost close enough to make out what was being said. Measle risked another quick glance over his shoulder— the seven wrathmonks were hurrying towards the foot of the great wheel! Measle could see that five of them were trying to shelter under a pair of umbrellas that were held by the remaining two— and that, at this precise moment, the five seemed more interested in getting out of the rain than in searching the dark, wet shadows that surrounded them—

There was still just enough time to do something.

Measle grabbed the girder tight and wriggled his body up and over the edge of it. Now, he was on the *inside* of the girder and it was between him and the approaching wrathmonks.The metal brace didn't fully conceal Measle—it was too full of convenient holes for that—but it did hide a lot of his body from eyes on the ground, while still allowing him to climb the remaining two thirds of the wheel. He was just in time—the wrathmonks arrived at the foot of the Ferris wheel only seconds later and they stopped there, huddled together under the two umbrellas.

Measle kept his eyes firmly on the small group as he slowly inched his way upwards. He could hear them quite clearly, discussing what they should do next—

'I can sssmell the beastly thing,' said Mrs Zagreb,

the end of her nose twitching like a hedgehog's.

'Ssso can I, dearessst,' said Mr Zagreb. 'He is certainly nearby. Perhaps we ought to sssearch the area?'

'Well, of *courssse* that's what we ought to do, Zag!' snapped Mrs Zagreb. 'You always ssstate the obvious, don't you?'

'My dear, I was merely sssuggesssting we—' said Mr Zagreb, but Griswold Gristle interrupted him.

'We should sssspread out,' said Griswold Gristle, clutching tight to his umbrella and wishing the other wrathmonks wouldn't press against him so much, in their eagerness to get out of the rain.

'Sssspread out, yesss,' hissed Judge Cedric. 'Spread out—and ssstick together!'

'How do we do that, then?' sneered Draggle, shaking the water out of his straggly hair. 'How do we sssspread out—*and* ssstick together at the same time?'

'We do it—by *doing* it, young Draggle,' said Judge Cedric, in a superior tone of voice—and Measle thought to himself, *That one isn't very bright, is he?*

'Judge Cedric was using a figure of ssspeech, Draggle,' said Griswold, a note of impatience in his voice.

'It was a figure of *ssstupid*,' muttered Draggle.

Griswold felt his temper rising, so he counted to ten in his head and then said, gently, 'What my learned friend Judge Cedric *meant* was—'

'Never mind what he *meant*, Grissstle,' rumbled Cudgel who, being so big, was quite unable to fit under either of the two umbrellas and was therefore now soaking wet and very irritable— 'Never mind what he *meant*. Let's jussst get on with it!'

'I sssecond that!' said Flabbit, nodding vigorously, so that his hank of wet, greasy hair flapped around his ears.

'Very well,' said Griswold, in a soothing voice. 'Let usss sssearch the immediate area. Mrs Zagreb—how ssstrong is the ssscent? How far should we ssssearch?'

Mrs Zagreb sniffed the air. 'Not more than twenty or thirty metres, Mr Grissstle,' she hissed. 'The beassstly thing is nearby.'

'Thank you, Mrs Zagreb.' Griswold turned to the rest of the wrathmonks. 'Cedric—perhaps you had better ssstay by my ssside. The ressst of you, sssspread out and sssearch. There are many nooks and crannies here, where a sssmall child might hide. And, when you find the horrid creature, sssing out! Sssing out loud! Very well—off we go!'

Measle heard all this as he climbed slowly and silently upwards. By the time the wrathmonks began to move off into the nearby shadows, Measle had reached the very top of the Ferris wheel and was now pulling himself up and into the topmost swing seat. He did this very slowly and very carefully—the seat was wet and slippery and it shifted on its axle every time Measle moved against it—and any movement like that could easily catch the eye of a searching wrathmonk below—but eventually, Measle managed to pull his body up and into the seat. He slipped the goggles off his eyes and lay still for a few moments, working the stiffness out of his aching fingers. The rain drizzled down on him and, for the first time that night, Measle realized he was soaked. Even his leather jacket was sodden with rainwater. His trousers were wet through and he could feel water squelching in his trainers. He was very cold. He was also very tired. His legs trembled from the effort of the long climb and the muscles in his arms were sore and bruised. But at least the stinging pain in his hand had gone away—

Then Measle heard a distant roar. It was an angry, frustrated roar—and, even at this distance, Measle knew that it had come from the throat of the Tyrannosaurus Rex. Cautiously, he raised his head and peeked over the side of the seat, in the direction of the sound. There, in the distance, he could see movement—there, back near the go-kart track!

Measle slipped the goggles back over his eyes and swiped the palm of his hand across the lenses, wiping most of the raindrops away. He saw (still a little blurred, but clear enough) the head, the neck, and the top half of the tyrannosaurus's body looming over the surrounding buildings—and the dinosaur was doing something very strange. It was turning slowly round and round, its ridiculous little arms waving uselessly, its jaws snapping furiously—round and round, in small circles—and then, quite suddenly, the creature reversed its direction and began to turn slowly in the opposite direction—round and round, arms flapping, jaws snapping—another furious roar—

Measle guessed what was going on. Somewhere down there—and hidden from his sight by the surrounding structures—was Tinker. The little dog must be running round and round his huge enemy, probably barking like crazy and nimbly jumping out of range every time the Rex made a lunge for him. Measle remembered back in Basil's train set—how Tinker had distracted the giant cockroach, giving him just enough time to run to the end of the tracks—and now the little dog was doing it again—but this time there were more enemies! There were the three remaining carousel horses, not to mention the whole army of cuddly toys—

The tyrannosaurus suddenly stopped revolving on the spot. It roared again and then lurched off towards the distant loops of the Thunderer roller coaster. Measle guessed what had happened: Tinker must have got bored with running in circles—or else he'd been menaced by some of his other attackers and needed to escape in a hurry—but, whatever the reason, Measle imagined Tinker racing off down the dark wet alleys, with the army of animated monsters in hot pursuit. And, although he hadn't actually *seen* the little dog, the evidence that he was alive and kicking made Measle feel much better. Now, if only he could somehow get rid of his own enemies—the prowling wrath-monks, down there at the foot of the great wheel!

Something was digging into Measle's side—a lumpy object in one of his pockets. Measle carefully rolled his body off the lump, put his hand in his pocket and pulled it out. It was the VoBo.

And then an idea jumped into Measle's brain—and, like all Measle's ideas that came to him in moments of extreme danger, this one too was crammed with risks. The only thing that was different about *this* idea was the number of people he could discuss it with before actually putting his idea into practice.

This time, there was nobody to tell him not to try it.

But, like all Measle's crazy ideas, this one seemed (to Measle, anyway) to be completely brilliant, so he dismissed from his mind any thoughts that it might be a bit dangerous and began to think how he might make it work. *Now, who among the searching wrathmonks far below him should he start with? Nobody seemed to like Draggle much —Cudgel was very grumpy—Mrs Zagreb appeared to be irritable all the time, especially with her husband, whom she didn't seem to care for much—and besides, Mrs Zagreb's twitching nose was the reason they were all prowling about in the shadows down there—so, if he could pull it off, Mrs Zagreb would be the one he'd try it out on—*

Measle peeked over the edge of the swing seat and looked down towards the distant ground. He saw several shadowy figures poking about in the Ferris wheel's machinery—there!—close together, Draggle and Mr Zagreb, on hands and knees, searching the narrow space under the Ferris wheel ticket booth! And ten metres away from them, Mrs Zagreb, standing on her own by an ice cream stall, staring out into the darkness!

Measle lifted the VoBo to his lips, centred the cross-hairs on Scab Draggle and pressed the little button on the brass tube. Then, very quietly, Measle spoke some words into the mouthpiece.

'I sssay, Zag—your wife's nose ain't half big, innit?' said Scab Draggle.

Only—*Scab Draggle hadn't opened his mouth.*

Measle aimed at the distant figure of Mr Zagreb, pressed the button, and whispered a few more words into the mouthpiece.

'You're right there, young Draggle—it *is* big,' said Mr Zagreb's chirpy little voice. 'I've sssseen filing cabinets that are sssmaller. Why, the other day, she tried to give me a kiss and that big old blobby nose of hers went off course and it sssmacked me right in the eye—and I couln't sssee out of it for a week!'

For a moment, there was silence. Then, from the direction of the ice cream booth, a shrill scream of fury! Measle, peering cautiously over the edge of the swing seat, watched as Mrs Zagreb marched furiously towards Draggle and her husband, both of whom were staring at each other with puzzled looks on their wet, white faces.

'How dare you!' shrieked Mrs Zagreb, pointing a shaking finger in their direction. 'How dare you insssult me!'

'But—but—but—' stammered Mr Zagreb, sounding a bit like a motor boat.

'How dare you sssuggest that I have *ever* tried to kiss you!'

Measle swung the VoBo round and the cross-hairs found the huge figure of Buford Cudgel—

'*And* she's ugly,' rumbled Cudgel's voice. 'She's ssso ugly, every time she looks at her watch, it ssstops!'

Another shrill scream of fury from far below. Measle watched as Mrs Zagreb turned on her heel and stomped in Cudgel's direction.

'You brute!' she shouted. 'I shall breathe on you, Buford Cudgel—jussst sssee if I don't! Then you'll be sssorry!'

Griswold Gristle and Judge Cedric Hardscrabble came hurrying out of the darkness.

'What is going on?' bleated Griswold, waving his

little arms about. 'Why all thisss unpleasantness?'

Measle took aim at Griswold and whispered hurried words into the VoBo—

'Why be ssso nasssty to Mrs Zagreb?' This appeared to come from Griswold's mouth—but his lips hadn't moved. Then, with his mouth still closed, Griswold cried, 'Poor lady—she can't help it if she looks like a chewed pencil!'

Another shriek of fury—and now Mrs Zagreb was advancing fast in Griswold Gristle's direction.

'Thisss is intolerable!' she hissed. 'I am not ugly! I am beautiful! I shall breathe on all of you! One by one! I shall burn you all with my breath! You first, Grissstle—you useless little blob! Ssstand ssstill and be breathed on!'

Griswold held up both his pudgy little hands and backed away from the advancing woman.

'My dear lady,' he squeaked, 'I didn't sssay a word! It was sssomebody else!'

Again, Measle took quick aim and then whispered into the mouthpiece.

'No, come on, Griswold,' called the pompous voice of Judge Cedric. 'It *was* you. I heard you clearly—and you're ssspot on! Mrs Zagreb is ugly and ssskinny and ssstupid! In fact, she's even ssstupider than me!'

The cross-hairs centred on Flabbit's stout body—more words were whispered—and Flabbit's smug, scratchy voice came out of the darkness.

'Even ssstupider than Judge Cedric? Wow—

that's really, *really* ssstupid!'

And now it was Mr Zagreb's turn to speak without moving his lips—

'And that's *saying* sssomething!'

Mrs Zagreb stopped suddenly where she was, closed her eyes tight shut and started to scream at the top of her lungs. Mr Zagreb hurried to her side and tried to put his arms around her.

'My dear,' he cried (and this time, his lips moved), 'please try to calm yoursssself! I mussst insissst you *calm* yoursssself!'

Mrs Zagreb shook off his hands and turned on him, her eyes blazing with fury.

'Oh—ssso it's not enough that you inssssult me, Zag!' she hissed, her long fingers clenching and unclenching by her side. 'It's not enough that you allow *others* to insssult me as well! Now you dare to tell me what to do?'

'No, no, my dear,' stammered Mr Zagreb, trying to back away—but Mrs Zagreb had him by his wrist and her long red fingernails were biting into his skin.

'Jussst for that, Zag,' she snarled, 'jussst for that, I shall breathe on *you* first!'

'No, my dear—you mustn't!' shouted Mr Zagreb, trying frantically to free himself from his wife's iron grip. But Mrs Zagreb only held him tighter—and now she was opening her mouth and taking a deep, deep breath—

'If you breathe on me,' screamed Mr Zagreb, 'I

shall be forced to breathe on you *back*, my dear!'

Mrs Zagreb took no notice. She took one more shuddering breath—

—and Mr Zagreb himself took a fast, deep lungful of air—

—and, at precisely the same instant, they both started to blow their stinking breaths towards each other's face.

Measle stared transfixed down at the scene far below. He had no idea what to expect—his only experience of being blown on by a wrathmonk was when Basil had shrunk him down to a couple of centimetres in height and dropped him in the middle of the great train set—and somehow Measle didn't think that was going to happen this time. Hadn't the woman said something about burning them all with her breath? Measle didn't want to see anybody—or anything—being burned but he found himself unable to drag his eyes away from the extraordinary spectacle that was taking place down there on the ground.

Mr and Mrs Zagreb were blowing out their horrible breaths steadily towards each other and, where the breaths met, somewhere in the air at a point equally distant from both of them, the air itself seemed to be turning into something else. At first it was just a thin, swirling mist. Then, rapidly, it became a thick, yellowish-greenish-brownish fog that rolled and twisted into a ball of gas—it seemed to thicken even more and now the colour

was turning to a darker brown and the fog was congealing into some sort of oily liquid that began, slowly at first, to drip down onto the wet ground. Where the thick liquid hit, the ground began to sizzle and bubble and hiss—and a thin plume of smoke began to drift upwards from the spot.

Neither Mr nor Mrs Zagreb noticed this. All they saw was the infuriating fact that neither of their breaths seemed to be having any effect at all, other than making this stupid, rolling, dripping fog that hung in the air between them. So they each began to breathe out harder and their eyes bulged with the effort and the tendons in their necks stood out like ropes and they blew harder and harder—and the only effect this had was to make the hanging ball of fog turn into the brown, oily liquid at a faster and faster pace, so that more and more of the horrible stuff was now dribbling down onto the ground between their feet.

Measle stared down, trying to work out what

was happening. He was glad that neither wrathmonk appeared to be getting burnt but he could see the fog and the oily liquid and he could hear the sizzle as the fluid touched the ground and he could see the little plume of grey smoke rising in the air—but what he couldn't see was what the liquid was doing to the ground, because Mr Zagreb was standing in the way.

What Measle couldn't see was this: the corrosive fluid that was forming from the horrible, stinking breaths of the Zagrebs was actually digging a hole in the ground. Where it fell, the tarmac lifted and bubbled and sizzled and then melted away, leaving a steadily growing pit that had started out the size of an eggcup but was now rapidly approaching the dimensions of a plastic washing-up bowl.

The other wrathmonks were as rooted to the spot as Measle was. This was amazing. None of them had ever witnessed the collision of two exhalation enchantments before, and all of them were fascinated to see what would happen next. Would Mrs Zagreb's slightly more corrosive breath win the day—or would Mr Zagreb overcome her small advantage with his slightly stronger lung power? Either way, it was an extraordinary spectacle—and none of the watching wrathmonks had any intention of moving until it finished, one way or the other—

Mr and Mrs Zagreb went on blowing their horrible breaths at each other and neither noticed the hole that was steadily growing between them. Finally, Mr Zagreb felt the first indication that something odd was happening—a slight movement of the ground under the toes of his right foot. For a moment, Mr Zagreb felt the urge to glance down and see what was going on down there—but he stifled the urge very quickly, because he knew that a moment of lost concentration on his part would mean the end of the battle—and in Mrs Zagreb's favour. So he ignored the odd little crumbling sensation and tried to blow even harder at his wife, who saw the doubling of his efforts and, in return, doubled hers, so that both of them were using all the power in their straining lungs, breathing out and out and out, with never a breath taken in!

And now the hole was almost the size of a toddler's paddling pool and the smoke that was streaming up from inside was obscuring the bottom, so that nobody watching had any idea how deep the thing was—

And then, quite suddenly, the ground crumbled away from under the feet of both Mr and Mrs Zagreb. For a fraction of a moment they both stopped breathing at each other. Their eyes, already popping with the effort, popped even further as they realized that the ground—that had been supporting them—simply wasn't there any more!

And then they fell.

They fell quite silently, because neither of them

had any breath left to scream. They simply dropped down into the dark hole and the thin grey smoke closed over their heads—and they were gone.

There was a long, stunned silence. Then—

'Where did they go?' said Flabbit, leaning forward and peering down into the smoking hole with puzzled, piggy eyes.

'I dunno, do I?' said Draggle. 'Why asssk me?'

'Mr Zagreb?' called Griswold Gristle, taking a cautious step forwards. 'Mrs Zagreb? Are you all right?'

'Oi! Zag!' bellowed Cudgel—and his voice was so loud and deep that the vibrations from it made six centimetres of earth round the edge of the hole shiver and crumble and then fall into the darkness.

'Ssstand back!' shouted Griswold. 'It's not sssafe!'

'But—where does that hole lead to?' said Flabbit, his hank of greasy hair hanging over his face. 'Where's the bottom? How deep is it?'

'How should I know?' whined Draggle. 'All I know is—they jussst disssappeared, didn't they?'

'It ssseems to me,' said Judge Cedric, in his wisest voice, 'it ssseems to me that an *aperture* has appeared in the earth.'

'Yesss, Cedric,' said Griswold, irritably. 'We *know* that. The quessstion is, how deep is it and did Mr and Mrs Zagreb sssurvive the fall?'

There was a long silence as the wrathmonks thought about this.

High on the Ferris wheel, Measle wondered what to do next. His scheme had worked brilliantly and now there were two fewer wrathmonks to worry about. Quite what had happened to the Zagrebs, Measle had no idea—but the fact that they were gone was very encouraging. *Perhaps he could try that trick again?*

And that was where Measle made his big mistake.

He thought for a moment. Then he aimed the cross-hairs straight at Judge Cedric Hardscrabble's long, bony face and whispered into the VoBo's mouthpiece.

'I sssuggessst we all hold hands and jump into the hole together and sssee where they went,' announced Judge Cedric loudly. Unfortunately for Measle, at that precise moment, Griswold Gristle just happened to be looking at Judge Cedric's face and wondering why he had taken him on as his companion—it was occurring to Griswold that the reason he had befriended Judge Cedric was perhaps because every time Judge Cedric opened his mouth, he said something really stupid, which made Griswold look even cleverer than he really was—and here was Judge Cedric saying something that was probably the stupidest thing the old man had ever said—but he had said it *without moving his lips!*

'That's moronic,' sneered Draggle. 'You're a moronic old judge.'

'Yeah,' rumbled Cudgel, clenching both massive fists. 'For once I agree with Draggle. You really are a sssilly old git, aren't you?'

'Positively bonkers,' muttered Flabbit.

'No!' cried Griswold, holding up both pudgy hands. 'No, no, my friends. It wasn't Judge Cedric who sssaid that!'

'Yesss it was,' rumbled Cudgel. 'I heard him with my own ears.'

'But you didn't *see* him sssay it, did you?' cried Griswold.

'How do you *sssee* sssomebody sssay sssomething?' hissed Draggle, all the S's in the question making him sound like an angry cobra. 'You *hear* them, Griswold. Dear, oh, dear—you're getting as ssstupid as the judge, aren't you?'

'On the contrary, young Draggle,' said Griswold, his voice rising with excitement. 'I am cleverer than all of you put together. You sssee, unlike the ressst of you, I was *looking* at Judge Cedric's face when he ssspoke—and he never opened his mouth! Therefore, it couldn't have been him that sssaid that! Don't you sssee? Sssomebody else is ssspeaking—in his voice! In fact, sssomebody else has been doing lots of voices—that was why the Zagrebs quarrelled! All those insssults about Mrs Zagreb—I never uttered any—and I don't believe *any* of usss uttered any! It was sssomebody else!'

'Who?' said Flabbit, looking around uneasily.

'The boy!' hissed Griswold, lowering his voice to

a hoarse whisper. 'It mussst be the boy!'

'Where?' growled Cudgel, peering into the darkness.

'Sssomewhere close!'

'We looked everywhere!' muttered Flabbit, into Griswold's left ear.

'Everywhere,' echoed Draggle into Griswold's right ear. Both he and Flabbit had moved closer to Griswold and they were now squeezed tightly against the fat little wrathmonk, both sheltered by his umbrella and both close enough to whisper so quietly to him that Measle, high above them, could no longer hear what was being said.

Neither could Judge Cedric.

'What are you whissspering about?' he demanded. 'Don't you know it's very rude to whisssper? I once sssentenced a person to *ten years* for whissspering in my court—and he wasn't even the prisoner in the dock!'

'Come here, Cedric!' hissed Griswold. He stuck out a fat little arm and pulled Judge Cedric close to him. 'You too, Mr Cudgel—come closer! We mustn't be overheard!'

The five wrathmonks huddled together under the two umbrellas and all Measle could hear now was their hissing whispers. They sounded like a nest of snakes down there and Measle shifted his position in the swing seat, so that he could angle one ear down in their direction.

But Measle shifted too quickly.

Whether it was because all of Measle's weight was now on one side of the swing seat, or whether it was because there was a sudden fresh gust of wind—whatever the reason, the seat swung suddenly backwards and then forwards—and a loud *squeak* came from its axle.

Measle froze—but it was too late. Both umbrellas rocked to one side and five horrible, wet, white faces stared up in his direction. Measle didn't even have time to pull his head back out of sight before Scab Draggle pointed one bony finger and screamed, 'There! There he is! Up there!'

Measle unfroze and jerked his head back and out of the wrathmonks' line of sight—but then he heard Griswold Gristle's oily voice, calling up to him.

'We sssee you, dear boy! We know you're up there! That was very clever, that little trick you played on usss! You mussst be a very clever boy indeed. We would ssso like to meet you and shake you by the hand—'

'Shake you by the neck!' roared Cudgel's thunderous voice.

'Take no notice of Mr Cudgel, dear boy,' called Griswold. 'He's only joking! Please, come down here, ssso we can all be friends! What do you sssay, dear boy? Won't you come down?'

Measle had no intention of going anywhere. He huddled down in the swing seat. He didn't think any of the wrathmonks were going to climb up to get him—*they didn't look in any sort of shape to do that—so perhaps it would be the safest thing just to lie here and hope they would eventually go away—*

Then Measle felt the swing seat jerk suddenly. It swayed backwards and forwards, squeaking on its axle. Measle peered forward and saw the seat in front of his was swinging too—which meant only one thing: somehow, the wrathmonks had got the Ferris wheel to turn! But it was turning in such an odd way—not smoothly, like Measle remembered from the time he and Sam and Lee had ridden the thing—no, this movement was a series of wrenching lurches, which set all the seats swinging on their axles. Measle could hear the whole massive wheel creaking and groaning under the strain. There was the sound of grinding steel cogs and then a screech of breaking metal, as one section of the central axle was sheared off. The whole wheel lurched a few centimetres to one side. Measle peered over the edge and stared down at the wrathmonks far below.

Not so far below now.

Measle saw that he was moving steadily downwards—and what was moving him? What was moving the whole huge Ferris wheel?

It was Cudgel.

Cudgel's enormous hands, encased in their black leather motorcycle gauntlets, were grasping the steel rim of the Ferris wheel and the giant wrathmonk was heaving the whole contraption round and round in a series of jerks—and each wrenching jerk brought Measle closer and closer to the ground.

What could he do? thought Measle wildly. *Where could he go? Maybe he could get out of the seat—climb back up to the top, find another seat to hide in—but that wouldn't work, because the giant wrathmonk would just keep pulling the wheel round and round—and he couldn't climb that fast anyway—think! Think! If only he had a jelly bean left! If only he hadn't tried that last VoBo trick! If only—if only—*

It was no good. With a great sense of despair washing over him, Measle sat quietly in the bottom of the swing seat and waited for whatever fate had in store for him.

THE
PRISONER

Tinker was beginning to enjoy himself.

At first, sheer terror had made him run from the darkness of Ghoulish Grange and out into the steadily falling rain—and sheer terror had made him run blindly back down the street towards the crossroads, his feet a blur and his stubby tail tucked tight between his short legs.

At the crossroads, his fear slackened enough to bring him to a skidding stop. He turned and stared back up the street—there, in the distance, was the sound of clattering hooves—and there too, the thump, thump, thump of the great monster—and both sounds were coming nearer and nearer—

Tinker had turned and fled, running back the way he and the smelly kid had come. Over the next ten minutes, he ran all over the theme park—and the three carousel horses and the Tyrannosaurus Rex followed wherever he went. Lagging far behind came the army of cuddly toys, moving very slowly now. They were so saturated with rainwater that they could hardly drag themselves across the wet tarmac and several of the horrible creatures were losing their kapok stuffing through gaps in their seams, where the stitching had finally given way.

Tinker's initial terror soon lessened to a point where he could pause and think. He discovered that there was a pattern to the chase and he learned to use it to his advantage. The three carousel horses were the fastest of his pursuers— but they had a hard time running on the wet ground because their wooden hooves made them slip and slide and skid as if they were on an ice rink. Tinker found that, if he let them come fairly close at full gallop, and then if he turned a corner as sharply as he could, the horses—in trying to follow him—would lose all traction and would fall and then slide on their sides across the slippery road until their bodies crashed into whatever obstacle was there at the side of the street. One of them had lost one of its hind legs doing this. The wooden limb had splintered against a low brick wall, breaking off cleanly at the horse's knee and now this lame one staggered along in the rear, trying desperately to keep up with its two fellows.

The Tyrannosaurus Rex was also fast—but it was rather short-sighted and very heavy, so that it blundered about, crashing into things and knocking them over—and when it came to a corner it had to bring its huge body almost to a standstill before it could turn and change direction—so Tinker learned quickly that, as long as he kept moving at a reasonable pace, none of these nasty things were going have much success in catching him. At one point in the chase, at one of the park's larger crossroads, he'd even found enough courage to run in circles, barking his head off, round and round the dinosaur and even under the hooves of the carousel horses—and he'd only given up doing that when he saw, out of the corner of one eye, a slow-moving mob of blue dinosaurs waddling towards him from out of a side street—

Nasty, horrible wet cushions—nasty, horrible horsey thingies—and that nasty, horrible roarin' thingy that obviously couldn't run very well—hardly surprisin', 'cause the horrible roarin' thingy tried to do it on only two legs and every sensible animal knew that it was better on four—right, enough of this roundy-roundy runnin'—quick, off down this road and then zip round this corner—ooh, that was a nice slidin'-crashin'-breakin' noise behind him! And here's the big roarin' thingy again—better get a bit of a

move on—wonder where the smelly kid is?
Funny how you miss him when he isn't
around—hope he's all right—

Oi! Don't think! They're right behind you
again! Run!

'Well, well, well,' said Griswold Gristle, his oily
voice even oilier with pleasure. 'What have we
here?'

Measle stared up at the circle of white, grinning,
horrible faces that were looking down at him. He
still lay flat on the floor of the swing seat—but
now the swing seat was at the lowest point of the
Ferris wheel's arc and the five remaining
wrathmonks, standing on the wet ground, towered
over him.

'Young Massster Ssstubbs, isn't it?' said
Griswold. His lips were stretched in a ghastly smile
and Measle could see the two sets of pointed teeth
on either side of his tiny mouth.

'You—you'd better not come any closer,' said
Measle, in what he hoped was his fiercest voice.
'My dad'll be along in a minute and he'll—he'll—'

'He'll what, dear boy?' said Griswold, raising his
non-existent eyebrows.

'He'll—he'll sort you lot out, that's what he'll
do!'

Griswold thought for a moment and then shook
his head. 'No, I don't think ssso, dear boy. You

sssee, we happen to know that the poor chap has lossst his memory. And how do we know that, dear boy? We know that because of what was in the bottle we threw at him. That bottle contained a concentrated distillation of his lordship the Dragodon's breath, you sssee.'

Dragodon? thought Measle. *What's a Dragodon?*

'And that breath,' continued Griswold, 'like all great wizards' breath, has a unique quality. Basil Tramplebone—who was a very close friend, you know—Basil's exhalation enchantment was able to shrink a thing down to a tiny sssize—but, of coursse, you know that, don't you? His lordship the Dragodon's breath causes sssomething else entirely. His lordship's breath causes complete and utter forgetfulness. Amnesia, in fact. How wonderfully brilliant is that? How marvellously refined! How sssuperbly subtle! Ssso, dear boy, even if your dear father *was* here, without his memory he wouldn't be much use to anybody, would he?'

Draggle sniggered and Flabbit nodded in a satisfied way, his lanky hank of greasy hair flapping round his collar. Measle saw that Judge Cedric Hardscrabble was simply staring at him as if he was a particularly nasty-looking bug and the enormous Cudgel, panting slightly from the effort of dragging the Ferris wheel round, stood as tall as a small mountain, glaring at him from under the visor of his motorcycle helmet.

There was a sudden ominous creaking from the girders and braces of the Ferris wheel.

'Mr Cudgel,' said Griswold, staring up at the Ferris wheel, nervously, 'would you be ssso kind and grasssp young Massster Ssstubbs's collar and lift him out of that ssseat. And then I think we should all move clear of thisss contraption—I fear you have done it sssome ssseriousss damage, Mr Cudgel, and it is no longer sssafe. It could fall at any minute.'

All the wrathmonks—and Measle too—peered up at the Ferris wheel. Its angle was no longer quite perpendicular. It now leaned a little to one side, and every now and then one of its supporting girders let out a small creaking sound.

Cudgel leaned down and took the collar of Measle's leather jacket between one enormous finger and one enormous thumb and, carefully, lifted him out of the seat. Then, he and the rest of the wrathmonks moved away from the Ferris wheel, putting themselves at least fifty metres from the tottering thing.

'Thank you, Mr Cudgel,' said Griswold. 'I think we are out of danger here.' Griswold switched his eyes to Measle's dangling body and smiled. 'Now, dear boy,' he said, obviously enjoying this moment, 'it was *ssso* good of you to come. We all appreciate it ssso much. You have come for your poor dear mother, I sssuppose? You have come to the right place. She is here. But we have been ssso clever,

my fellow wrathmonks and I. You sssee, we
ssseparated your mother and your father because,
together, they represent a ssserious threat to our
little community. *Apart*, however, they are of little
danger to usss. Thusss, the elimination of your dear
father in the car park of the sssupermarket. As to
whom we should kidnap, well, that decision was
made for usss by his lordship, the great Dragodon
himssself.'

'Yeah, well,' said Measle, wondering desperately
what in the world (*or out of it!*) a Dragodon was.
Then he said, defiantly, 'His lordship the … the
Dragodon isn't going to like this, that's for sure.'

'Really?' said Griswold, looking not in the least
bit worried. 'Oh, I don't think he'll mind at all. His
lordship the Dragodon really won't care *what* we
do with you. He has no interest in you—none
whatsssoever! We, on the other hand, have an
enormousss interessst in you. You sssee, it is our
intention to take our revenge for the cruel murder

of poor Basil Tramplebone. And, now I come to think of it, for the murders of poor Mr and Mrs Zagreb as well! All murders that *you* committed, dear boy. His lordship the Dragodon had his own reasons for wanting your poor mother and has, no doubt, dealt with her in a thoroughly sssatisssfactory manner. You, he cares nothing about and, in fact, has allowed usss to do whatever we like with you. And now we have you, dear boy—and, when we've finished with you, your father will be sssimple to deal with. And that, dear boy, will be the end of the sssinissster ssspecies of Ssstubbs!'

Measle had stopped listening to Griswold's oily voice the moment he'd heard the bit about his mother. Griswold had said that she had been dealt with *in a satisfactory manner*—did that mean she was dead?

'What's happened to my mother?' Measle blurted.

'I have no idea,' said Griswold, shaking his head and trying, unsuccessfully, to look sad. Then he turned to the other wrathmonks. 'Do any of you know what might have befallen poor Mrs Ssstubbs?'

'Not a clue,' said Flabbit, cheerfully.

'Couldn't tell you,' rumbled Cudgel—and Measle felt the vibrations of his deep, deep voice through the massive hand that held tight to his collar.

'I dunno, do I?' whined Draggle. 'Why asssk me?'

'*I* know what happened to her,' announced Judge Cedric Hardscrabble, stepping forward. All the other wrathmonks turned towards him with surprised looks on their faces—all except Griswold Gristle, who simply sighed and rolled his eyes towards the sky.

'I know what happened,' repeated Judge Cedric. 'Would you like me to tell you, boy?'

Measle nodded slowly, not sure whether he wanted to hear this.

'Very well—then I shall tell you,' said Judge Cedric, in his most pompous voice. 'Thisss is what happened to your mother. We kidnapped her! There! What do you think of *that*!'

'Yes, we *know* all that, Cedric!' squealed Griswold, flapping his arms irritably. Measle thought he looked like a fat little baby bird, trying unsuccessfully to take off. 'We *know* all that!' he repeated. 'Even the *boy* knows that! But what has happened to her *sssince*, Cedric?'

The judge stared blankly into Measle's eyes. 'Ah,' he said, vaguely. 'As to that, I really couldn't hazard a guess. Perhaps... perhaps she has been ressscued?'

Griswold jumped up and down with irritation. 'She has *not* been ressscued, Cedric!' he screamed. 'She is with the Dragodon! His lordship would never allow her to be ressscued! Why do you never think before you ssspeak?'

Griswold turned back to Measle, his fat, pasty

face twisted with annoyance. 'Anyway,' he hissed, 'I don't really care about what has happened to your mother, dear boy. Jussst as long as—*whatever* it is—it's very nasssty and ends with her death! That's what we want for the Ssstubbs family. A great deal of unpleasantness, leading eventually to death! And now that we have you, dear boy, we can make a ssstart! Ssso, what shall it be, eh? Shall we let young Draggle turn you bald? Shall we have Judge Cedric breathe his horrid red painful boils all over your body? Shall we allow Mr Flabbit to give every tooth in your head the mossst terrible toothache? My own perssssonal exhalation enchantment is enormously effective—rather *too* effective at times! And Mr Cudgel's exhalation enchantment is also very impressive—why don't you tell our young friend all about it, Mr Cudgel?'

Cudgel tightened his grasp on Measle's collar and lifted him higher off the ground, bringing Measle's face close to his motorcycle helmet. Measle could see the giant wrathmonk's hard eyes gleaming at him through the visor. Cudgel turned Measle's head sideways with his other massive hand and whispered, in a voice that seemed to be coming out of the depths of the earth, into Measle's ear. He said, 'If I breathe on you, boy, all the microssscopic germs that live on your body will begin to grow. They'll get bigger and bigger and bigger, until you can actually sssee them. They'll get as big as ssspiders, boy. You'll be completely covered in horrible, wriggling germs the sssize of ssspiders—and those horrible, wriggling germs have to eat something, boy. They have to eat to ssstay alive, boy. Guess what they'll ssstart with?'

'Thank you, Mr Cudgel,' murmured Griswold. 'Mossst amusing. I am sure we should all like to sssee that. Now then, dear boy—which one would you like usss to begin with?'

They all sound horrible, thought Measle. His mind was racing, desperately trying to come up with a way out of this terrible situation—but he couldn't think of anything! There seemed to be no escape!

Then, out of the corner of his eye, he saw Draggle put his hand in his pocket and pull out a small, cloth bag. At the same time, he felt Cudgel lowering him slowly towards the ground, right in the middle of the circle of wrathmonks. When Measle's feet touched the wet tarmac, Cudgel took his hand off his collar and took a ponderous step backwards. Measle could feel the eyes of the wrathmonks staring at him in excited anticipation—all except Draggle, who was fumbling in the cloth bag. Measle saw the outline of Draggle's fingers close around something and his hand began to withdraw from the bag—

'Turn away, everybody!' shouted Draggle loudly and, instinctively, all the other wrathmonks began to turn their backs to him. Halfway into his turn,

Griswold Gristle realized what Draggle was up to and he screamed, 'No! You idiotic youth! Don't use that!'—but he was too late. Draggle's hand emerged from the cloth bag and the young wrathmonk, his eyes now tight shut, held the object out towards Measle.

Measle had no idea what was going on. All he knew was that four of the wrathmonks now had their backs turned to him and the fifth wrathmonk was holding something in his hand—something he apparently wanted Measle to see.

Two voices screamed in Measle's head—and they both belonged to him. The first voice yelled, '*Go on, have a look!*' The second voice shouted, '*No, don't! It could be dangerous!*'

The first voice won. It's very difficult not to look at something that is being held out for your inspection—so Measle leaned forward and peered at the little, grey, wrinkled thing in Draggle's hand. It looked like a snake's head—a little, dry, mummified snake's head.

And then a very strange thing occurred.

Nothing happened.

Griswold, with his back turned and his pudgy hands over his eyes, was shrieking, 'You ssstupid fool, Draggle! A boy made out of ssstone is no use to usss! None of our exhalation enchantments will have any effect! What were you thinking, you cretinous moron!'

And while Griswold was screaming into the

darkness, Draggle was looking very puzzled indeed. A bewildered frown was creasing his forehead. He still had his eyes tight shut—but the fingers that were holding the mummified snake head were now moving all over the object, feeling an entirely new and unexpected texture to the thing. A few seconds ago, it had been rough and dry and a little soft—if you squeezed it, you could feel the bones of the snake's skull bend a little. Now, it had changed. Now it was cold and smooth and hard—like a piece of polished rock. Draggle folded his fingers around the head, hiding it from sight. Then, cautiously, he opened his eyes.

Measle was standing there in front of him—a small, wet boy with sticking-up hair, his eyes obscured by a pair of old flying goggles. *But he ought to be a statue!* thought Draggle, frantically. *A stone statue! But instead, here was a living, breathing, and very obviously alive wet boy, without a trace of statue about him!*

Without thinking, Draggle opened his fingers and looked down at the small object in his hand. Then, realizing what he was doing, he slammed his eyelids shut again. *But wait—he'd looked at it! He'd looked into the tiny dried up eyes of the thing—and nothing had happened to him!* Cautiously, Draggle opened his eyes again and peered down at the snake head again.

It had felt different. Now it certainly *looked* different. Now it had the appearance of a lump of granite, carved into the shape of a serpent's head—

Draggle peered into the cold stone eyes of the thing and then shook it gently, as if it was a watch that had stopped. Then he looked back at Measle— and the small wet boy with the sticking-up hair did something quite unexpected.

Measle grinned at him.

And a hundred and twenty miles away, at the end of a dreary, dingy street, the outer layers of a pair of stone statues (which had been lying like discarded toys on top of a huge pile of black rubble) suddenly cracked and flaked and splintered and then fell away in chunks— revealing, in an instant, two live men in dusty working clothes. Both men blinked and both sat upright, staring down in wonder at their grimy hands and flexing their fingers as if they didn't believe such a thing was possible. Then one turned and looked at the other.

'Is that you, Harry?'

'Yeah. Is that you, Robert?'

'I think so. What happened, Harry?'

'I dunno,' said Harry. 'I just know it's nice to be alive.'

Robert looked around him fearfully and lowered his voice. 'Where are our masters?' he muttered.

'Haven't the foggiest,' said Harry. Then he pointed up to the dark sky—and his voice took on a happier tone. 'But they're not here, that's for sure.'

'How do you know, Harry?'

'How do I know? Because the rain has gone, that's how!'

'So it has,' said Robert, climbing to his feet. 'It looks like we're free, Harry—and the sooner we get out of here, the better I'm going to like it!'

The two men scrambled down the rubble-heap and began to run as fast as they could out and away from the dingy dreary street.

And there were other statues that came to life as well—and these statues weren't a hundred and twenty miles away.

They were much, *much* closer.

'What has happened?' squeaked Griswold, his back still firmly turned away from Draggle and Measle. 'Is it sssafe to turn around?'

'Er…yeah,' muttered Draggle, still staring at Measle with a dazed look on his thin white face.

Griswold and the other wrathmonks slowly turned round. Flabbit was the first to see the little grey object in Draggle's hand and he screamed and covered his eyes. 'Put it away! Put it away!' he shrieked.

Griswold had also begun to cover his eyes—but then he saw Measle, standing there, quite unaffected—and so he slowly lowered his hands and took a step forward.

'What is thisss?' he whispered. 'What has happened here?'

'It didn't work, did it?' said Draggle. 'And now it feels all funny.'

'Give it to me,' said Griswold, holding out one pudgy hand. Draggle handed the snake's head to Griswold and the little bank manager examined it closely.

'It appears to have turned to. ssstone,' said Griswold. Then he looked up at Draggle with fury in his little eyes.

'How did thisss happen, Draggle? What did you do to it?'

'I didn't do nothing, did I?' whined Draggle. 'I jussst pointed it at him, didn't I? Everybody else has had a go with it, haven't they? And now it was my turn, wasn't it? And he should've turned to ssstone, jussst like all the others—but he didn't, did he? I dunno why not, do I?'

Griswold stared at Measle, a little uncertainty replacing the anger.

'What magic did you use, boy? Hmm? Why don't you tell your uncle Griswold, eh?'

Measle knew what had happened—and he also knew that it wasn't magic at all. For several seconds after the event, he had been as puzzled as Draggle had been. It had taken him some moments to work out what exactly the object in Draggle's hand was—but, the minute he'd guessed that it was the Medusa head, he'd known what had happened. The same thing had occurred back in the train set—in the forest—the miniature lake, made of a piece of mirror—he and Basil's other victims had prised up the mirror and he'd slipped under it at the precise moment when Basil Tramplebone had started his cockroach spell—and the spell had reflected off the mirrored surface of the lake and had bounced back into Basil's eyes and Basil himself had been turned into the cockroach—

There was only one difference. That extraordinary incident had been on purpose.

This extraordinary incident was an accident.

It was the goggles, of course. Those brilliant goggles, that let you see in total darkness. And those strange lenses—they were highly-polished mirrored lenses, which reflected anything and everything that fell on their shiny surfaces—including the deadly stare of a dried-up, mummified snake's head from a long-dead Gorgon's skull—

'Ah,' said Griswold, his voice shaking with anger. 'I think I undersssstand.' He pointed with a fat finger at Measle's nose. 'Mosssst effective! I congratulate you, dear boy!' He turned to Cudgel. 'Mr Cudgel—would you be so kind as to retrieve the boy once again? And hold him tight, if you would be so kind.'

Cudgel stepped forward, grabbed the front of Measle's jacket, and lifted him off his feet.

'Thank you, Mr Cudgel,' said Griswold. 'You can always be trusssted to do the right thing. Unlike *sssome*. Unlike *one* in particular.'

Griswold turned on Draggle. 'You moron!' he screamed, advancing towards Draggle and holding the Medusa head in one shaking fist. 'You cretin! You blithering idiot! You've *broken* it! It's *useless*! Thisss preciousss object is now completely *unusable*! Because of your ssstupidity, we have lossst one of the raresssst magical articles in the entire *universe*! You *donkey*! You *dunce*! You drivelling *dunderhead*!'

Griswold had been steadily advancing on Draggle during all this—and Draggle had been steadily retreating from the little wrathmonk's fury. What was making Draggle even more fearful was the fact that the other wrathmonks had stepped in behind Griswold and were also pushing their way towards him—and they all had fury in their eyes.

'L-look here,' stammered Draggle, taking another couple of steps backwards. 'I didn't *mean* to break it, did I? It was an accident, wasn't it? I'm ever ssso sssorry, honest I am—'

'Ho, yesss,' said Flabbit, menacingly. 'I'm sure you're sssorry. But you're going to be even sssorrier in a minute.'

Draggle began to regret being so rude to everybody.

'I don't know how it happened, do I?' he whined. The wrathmonks were getting closer and Draggle took another pace backwards.

'You're going to pay for thisss missstake,' rumbled Cudgel. 'And for laughing at me in the cave on Borgrove Moor.' He was holding Measle as if he was a sort of weapon and he was marching slowly but steadily in Draggle's direction—

Draggle realized—far too late—that laughing at Buford Cudgel was a mistake. He took another step backwards.

'You shall pay indeed,' hissed Judge Cedric, waving a bony finger. 'You are guilty as charged, young Draggle! I sssentence you to a million years in the sssalt mines of Sssiberia!'

Griswold, still advancing steadily, suddenly glanced past Draggle, at something behind the young wrathmonk. Then a gleam came into Griswold's piggy eyes. 'Indeed, yesss, dear Cedric,' he said. 'An excellent punishment! We will sssend him down into the deepest mine in the whole wide world!

Into a great black pit! And we shall do it—*NOW!*'

As Griswold yelled that last word, he made a sudden little jump forward—and Draggle, startled, made a sudden little jump backwards—

—right into the Zagrebs' yawning black hole. Measle caught a glimpse of Draggle's horrified face—then, a second later, the young wrathmonk was gone. But, unlike the Zagrebs, Draggle had plenty of air in his lungs, so they all heard his long, wailing scream as he fell into the darkness. The scream went on for a very long time—and then, when it was very faint and far away, it stopped abruptly.

Griswold turned back from the hole and grinned unpleasantly.

'There,' he whispered, 'a very sssatisssfactory ending, I think. We cannot tolerate incompetence—and besssides, young Draggle was of little use. His exhalation enchantment, for example—making hair drop out! How pointless!'

'Well,' said Flabbit, smoothing down his greasy hank, 'perhapsss pointless for you, Griswold, sssince you don't have any. But for the ressst of usss—' Flabbit left the sentence unfinished. Griswold was staring at him with a very nasty look on his pudgy face, so Flabbit said, hurriedly, 'Of courssse, it was a fitting end for the young fellow. Fancy allowing that to happen!' Flabbit frowned. 'The only thing is, Griswold—how exactly *did* it happen?'

There was a murmur of agreement from Judge Cedric and Cudgel. Griswold didn't answer immediately. Instead, he marched up to Cudgel, who was still holding Measle by the front of his leather jacket, so that Measle's feet dangled several centimetres off the ground.

'Lower the boy, if you would be ssso kind, Mr Cudgel,' said Griswold—and Cudgel dropped his huge hand, bringing Measle back down to the ground and to the same eye level as the little bank manager. Griswold reached forward and snatched the goggles from Measle's head.

'Here,' he said, waving the goggles in the air.'You sssee the lenses? Mirrors! The Medusa head's ssspell was turned back on itssself! A very clever trick—and one that I sssusssspect the boy has used before! How else could he have overpowered our beloved Basil? He has no wizard faculties of his own—'

'What about all the disssappearing business he's been doing?' rumbled Cudgel, staring down at Measle angrily.

'A sssimple bit of Old Magic,' said Griswold.'His father taught it to him, probably. I sssusssspect the boy eats something. Kindly empty his pockets, Mr Cudgel.'

The next thing Measle knew was that he was upside down. His ankles were being held tightly in both of Cudgel's massive hands and he was being shaken up and down until his teeth rattled.

Clink went the little brass VoBo as it fell to the ground beneath him. Measle saw an upside-down Griswold toss his goggles next to the VoBo. Then Measle saw one of Cudgel's huge, booted feet lift up and then stamp down on the goggles, smashing the lenses to tiny pieces. The same thing happened to the VoBo—*stamp, crunch, stamp, crunch*—and then Measle felt himself being turned right side up and felt his feet planted firmly on the ground.

'Thank you ssso much, Mr Cudgel,' said Griswold. There was a touch of sarcasm in his voice. 'I can't help thinking that it might have been a good idea perhapsss to *examine* that sssmall brass object that fell from the boy's pocket *before* dessstroying it. However, the deed is done and I am sure he now poses no further threat to usss. Ssso— now is perhapsss the moment to take our revenge for the death of our beloved Basil Tramplebone.'

Griswold turned to Measle and smiled, revealing his sets of pointed teeth. 'You will be relieved to hear, dear boy,' he hissed, 'that we cannot use any of our primary ssspells on you. Mr Flabbit and Mr Cudgel and the rest of them expended all of their mana when they animated those various creatures—creatures that even now are (sssomewhat uselessly, I feel) chasing after one sssmall dog. Judge Cedric and I must keep our mana in reserve, in case his lordship the Dragodon should require it. Therefore, we can only use our exhalation enchantments on you.'

Griswold brought his fat little face closer to Measle's and, when he spoke again, Measle smelt on the wrathmonk's disgusting breath the faint (but horribly familiar) scent of dead fish, rotten mattresses, and the insides of ancient sneakers.

'However, that won't matter, dear boy. By the time the four of usss have finished with you, there won't be any of you left! We might ssstart with Mr Flabbit, I think. Mr Frognell Flabbit's excellent toothache enchantment is, I believe, wonderfully painful. From there, I think we'll move on to Judge Cedric Hardscrabble's boils. His boils will cover your body and they are very nasssty and hurt dreadfully. Mr Buford Cudgel has already told you all about *his* exhalation enchantment—all those lovely germs the size of ssspiders—and we'll all look forward to seeing that. And then there is mine, dear boy.'

Griswold leaned even closer to Measle and Measle tried to turn his head away.

Griswold whispered, 'Would you like to hear about mine, dear boy?'

Measle was terrified but he was determined not to show it. He shook his head firmly. 'No, I wouldn't,' he muttered, through clenched teeth.

'Oh dear,' hissed Griswold. 'Well, never mind, I shall tell you anyway. I dry you out, dear boy. Everything that is wet inssside you, I dry it out. All your blood, all your tears, all your sssweat—all dried to powder! You become nothing more than a little dried bag of ssskin and bones! Dead, of coursssse. Dead as a doornail—and jussst as dry, too! And, as my exhalation enchantment has this sssomewhat *final* effect, we shall leave it to lassst, I think. And then, when you are no more, we shall drop your poor little dried-up corpse into that very convenient hole over there. Oh, yesss. Ssso, dear Mr Flabbit—you shall be the first. Please, feel free to proceed!'

Flabbit smirked and stepped forward. Carefully, he smoothed back the greasy hank of hair. Then he bent down, his face close to Measle's.

'Sssuch pain,' he whispered in Measle's ear. 'In a moment or two, you will be ssscreaming.'

Measle screwed his eyes tight shut and held his breath. He didn't know if holding his breath would be any use against the spell—but he certainly wanted to put off, for as long as possible, the horrible smell that he knew would be coming his way.

A few seconds ticked by—

Then he heard Flabbit taking in a deep, deep breath.

Here it comes!

STOP.

For the third time that night, Measle felt a word jolting in his head and, had he been doing anything other than waiting with his breath held and his eyes shut, he would have stopped whatever he was doing in an instant—so powerful was the effect of that unheard word. And, in fact, everything seemed to have come to a stop, because nothing seemed to be happening—

Cautiously, Measle opened one eye.

Flabbit was looming over him, his fishy eyes wide and his flabby cheeks bulging. A few beads of greenish-coloured sweat had popped out on his forehead—and Measle realized that Flabbit was having to make a serious effort to keep all that poisonous air inside himself. Flabbit's pasty skin was changing colour too. His face was turning a faint shade of purple and his stout body was beginning to shake slightly, which made the jowls under his double chin wobble.

EXPEL THE POISON, FLABBIT—BUT AWAY FROM THE BOY.

Flabbit turned his head, opened his mouth, and let out a great whoosh of stinking air. Unfortunately for Judge Cedric, Flabbit had turned in his direction and a wispy tendril of this poisonous breath wafted across the judge's beaky nose—

'Ow!' screamed Judge Cedric, clapping his hands over his mouth. 'Ooooh! My teeth! They hurt! Ooh—the pain!' Judge Cedric glared furiously at Flabbit. 'You will pay for thisss, Flabbit!' he muttered through his fingers. Then he took a quick, deep breath and lunged forward, towards Flabbit. When he got to within a few centimetres of where Flabbit was standing, he puffed out his cheeks and then blew out hard, right into Flabbit's horrified face.

This time, it was Flabbit's turn to clap his hands to his face.

'Ow!' he yelped. 'That hurts!' Flabbit took his hands away from his face and Measle saw that horrible red boils were now popping out all over his nose. More followed, appearing on his cheeks and his chin and his forehead, until Flabbit's entire face was covered in a rash of lumpy, red, painful spots.

STOP—THIS—NONSENSE!

Everybody froze instantly. There was silence, apart from a faint moaning from Judge Cedric and a quiet snivelling from Flabbit. Then Griswold said, in a voice that shook with fear, 'Oh, your great lordship—what would you have usss do?'

BRING ME THE BOY.

'The boy? Oh. Y-yesss indeed, your lordship,' stammered Griswold. 'The boy. Immediately, your lordship.' Griswold paused, his eyes swivelling wildly in their sockets. He had no idea what to do next. The Dragodon wanted the boy—but *where* was the Dragodon? There was only one way to find out and that involved some risk—

'We shall bring him at once, your lordship. B-but, O great lordship—wh-where shall we bring him?'

THE JUGGERNAUT RIDE. BRING HIM TO THE JUGGERNAUT RIDE.

'Immediately, your lordship!' cried Griswold. Then he turned to the other wrathmonks. 'Well,

234

you heard his great lordship!' he shouted. 'Cedric, ssstop moaning! Mr Flabbit—don't be sssuch a baby! Mr Cudgel, please be ssso kind and carry the boy—we mussst take him to the Juggernaut ride. Quickly everybody! As quickly as you can!'

Cudgel reached out one massive, gauntleted hand and grabbed Measle by the front of his jacket. Then he swung him under his arm, turned, and began to run. Griswold was already halfway down the street, his short legs pounding the wet tarmac. Judge Cedric, nursing his jaw, was close behind him, his long skinny legs jerking up and down— and Flabbit, tears of pain coursing over his lumpy face, was trotting in the rear.

Measle, tucked under Cudgel's arm, was being jolted up and down and, for the second time that night, he could feel his teeth being rattled in his head. Cudgel had him held round the waist in such a way that Measle's head was facing the ground, so all he could see were Cudgel's enormous, black-booted feet thumping over the wet tarmac as it rushed by.

A few minutes later, Measle felt Cudgel slow down and then stop. Then he felt the iron band that was Cudgel's huge arm lift away, releasing him from its tight grip—and Measle fell to the ground with a thud. He lay there, not daring to move anything but his eyes.

He was inside a small surrounding circle of wrathmonks. All the wrathmonks were staring up at something—so Measle lifted his eyes and stared up too.

Above him, the great looping steel rails of the Juggernaut roller coaster floated in the darkness. In this gloom, the crimson rails had lost all their colour and now looked, to Measle, like the coils of a huge black snake. The coils were supported here and there by gigantic steel pillars, that rose from massive concrete blocks, set deep in the ground.

There was a long moment of silence. Measle peeked at Griswold's face and saw uncertainty there—and a lot of fear, too. The little wrathmonk was peering about in the darkness and Measle realized that he had no idea what to do next.

Griswold took a tentative step forward and whispered, 'O great lordship? Are you there, O great lordship?'

I AM NEAR, LITTLE WRATHMONK. I AM NEAR.

'Wh-what would you have usss do now, your great lordship?'

PLACE THE BOY IN THE LEADING CAR OF THE RIDE, GRISWOLD.

'The leading car? Yesss, indeed, your great lordship! Immediately, your great lordship!'

Griswold waved bossily at the other wrathmonks and Measle felt himself being hoisted once again up and under Cudgel's arm. This time, he managed to raise his head a little and was able to see where they were going. Cudgel was following Flabbit, Judge Cedric, and Griswold and the wrathmonks were threading their way through the steel barriers that led to the ride's twin platforms. Moments later, they were there, gathered in a small group right by the rails. There was a line of the Juggernaut's cars waiting by the platform and, at a nod from Griswold, Cudgel lifted Measle from under his arm and planted him firmly into the seat at the very front of the train. Then Cudgel stepped back to rejoin the other wrathmonks and, together, they all stared down at him with expectant looks on their faces.

Measle wondered what was going to happen next. *The ride won't start up, surely? Not without any power! It can't!*

But it could.

There was a sudden clang! as the tubular steel safety bar, padded with foam rubber, swung up from the floor. It pushed Measle back into the seat, pressing hard—and a little painfully—against his stomach. Measle didn't remember the bar coming back that far—but it was back that far now and it was holding him so firmly that he didn't think he could wriggle free even if he tried.

'Quite comfy?' said Griswold, staring down at him with hungry eyes.

Measle didn't reply. Instead, he looked straight forward and tried to grin, as if he was looking forward to the ride. *I'm not—but I'm going to make them think I am!*

HOLD TIGHT.

The power of the command in his head was so

strong that, instinctively, Measle grabbed the safety bar in front of him. Out of the corner of his eye, he saw all the wrathmonks flex their fingers, as if they too were trying to hold on tight to something—and there was something so ridiculous about this pointless, collective movement that Measle's pretend grin turned into a real one and a little laugh, almost like one of Tinker's barks, jumped out of his throat.

'Ho! Laugh at us, will you?' said Flabbit, furiously. His face was now so red and lumpy that it looked like a big plate of raspberries, with two little swollen eyes gleaming in the middle of it. He stepped forward, his pudgy fist clenched. Cudgel growled and advanced to the edge of the platform and Judge Cedric took one hand from his aching jaws, clenched it into a bony fist and shook it angrily at Measle.

Then there was a sudden jerk that threw Measle's head backwards with a snap. They were off! Measle saw the platform slide past—much faster than he remembered. Certainly much faster than the first time he and Sam had ridden it—and even faster than their second go on it, when Sam had invoked his go-faster spell. The wrathmonks were being left behind—and now the train was moving fast along the short level section—then there was a sudden up-tilting of the leading car and Measle felt himself pressed back into the seat as they began to climb the long, steep ascent to the top. This time though—and apart from this extraordinary rate of speed—there was something different from Measle's previous experiences with the ride. This time, there was no *clank-clatter-clank-clatter* from the chain lifting-mechanism underneath. This time, apart from the thrumming sound of the wheels on the rails, there was an eerie silence—and Measle realized that, whatever was powering the Juggernaut, it certainly wasn't the normal sort of mechanism. This was something different.

He was halfway up the steep hill now and rising fast. Measle threw a quick glance over his shoulder, back down to the group of wrathmonks far below. He could hardly make them out in the gloomy shadows of the Juggernaut's station but he could see that they were still there, their white faces staring up at him. He thought he saw Griswold waving one fat little hand—

Measle turned back and stared at the rapidly approaching crest of the slope. In just a few seconds he would be up there—*and then what?* The ride itself held no terrors for him—not after what Sam had done on their second go on it. But, at the back of his mind, Measle had a nasty suspicion that this ride was going to be a little different. For a start, his car (and, presumably, the rest of the cars behind him) seemed to be *accelerating*—

The air up here was chill and a stiff breeze was

blowing. It threw the rain sideways against Measle's face, stinging his cheek. A slight vibration from the whirling wheels beneath him was making the soles of his feet tingle and his hands, clenched tight to the padded safety bar, began to ache with the cold.

And then, directly in front of his leading car, the rails disappeared from his view—and Measle realized that he was at the top of the long, steep slope.

And now there was nowhere to go but down.

THE DRAGODON

This time, Measle never felt that moment that all riders of ordinary roller coasters feel when they reach the top of the first hill. If you're in the front, there's always an odd sort of pause as the leading car moves over the crest and starts down on the other side. At first, the leading car seems to hang there, going quite slowly because it's being held back by the rest of the cars behind it, which are still being dragged up the final few metres. Then, when the last car crests the summit and starts down the other side, the leading car suddenly picks up speed—and then the ride really begins.

For Measle, the ride had really begun down at the bottom of the first hill, with that initial jerk. There had then been a steady acceleration as he rode towards the top—and no expected pause or slowing down whatsoever as his leading car slid over the summit. Instead, there was one smooth, continuous speeding up, that had started with that first sudden jerk and now continued as he began the long, howling plunge into the darkness below.

The wind blasted against his face and whistled in his ears. It blew his spiky hair straight backwards from his forehead and, without the protection of his goggles, it stung his eyes until Measle felt the tears squeezing out of the corners. *This was fast—faster than ever before! What would happen when they reached the bottom and started up the other side? Would his body be able to take the force?*

The wheels screamed. The cars rocked. Down, down they plunged into the blackness, gathering speed as they fell. Measle, his eyes already half closed against the howling wind, tried to peer into the darkness in front of him—but his goggles were lying in pieces back there and, without them, Measle couldn't see a thing. Somewhere ahead—*and coming up very soon, surely?*—was the bottom of this long, steep drop. Measle tried to remember what happened next—*there was a bit that goes up, then a level bit—then a sudden uptilting as you go into the first loop—*

The screaming of the wheels and the howling of the wind went on.

And on.

And on.

And on.

No! thought Measle. *This is impossible! We must have got to the bottom by now! Nothing takes this long—certainly not the Juggernaut's first drop! No roller coaster in the world has a drop this long! It's impossible! Completely, utterly, totally imposs—*

Measle dragged his eyes away from the pitch blackness in front of him and looked sideways, expecting to see something flashing by—a pylon perhaps, or a section of rail—something, *anything*, that would show him where he was—but the darkness that was in front of him was exactly matched by the darkness that was at his side—

Nothingness rushed past him.

Nothingness lay ahead.

Blackness everywhere. Only the incessant wind blasting into his face and the screaming of the wheels battering against his eardrums told Measle that he was still moving forward at a terrific speed. An idea sprang into his bewildered mind. He twisted his body round as far as the safety bar would allow and stared back towards the way he had come.

Black nothingness there too—but, in the middle of the nothingness, a faint circle of *lighter*

blackness! And this circle was getting smaller and smaller—and then Measle realized what he was looking at.

It was a hole—far, far above him.

Which meant only one thing.

He was underground! And, because the distant hole was getting smaller, that meant he was going deeper and deeper with every passing second!

Measle shuddered with terror and dragged his eyes away from the fast-diminishing circle of faint light. He twisted back in the seat, facing forwards once again. He screwed up his eyes, trying desperately to pierce the velvet blackness in front of him—

There was light ahead.

A pinprick of light, that grew into a tiny circle. The edges of the circle expanded steadily and now Measle could just begin to make out the shapes of the steel rails stretching out in front—

The hole ahead grew bigger and bigger and the light that streamed from it towards Measle took on a quality of its own. It was a strange quality—the light seemed not so much the sort of light you get from a lamp, or even from a sun obscured by clouds—it was more like the kind of light you see coming from the hand of a luminous watch. A soft, greenish glow, rather than a hard, yellow beam—

The circle of light was coming fast towards Measle now and he gripped tight to the safety bar and tensed his body—

—and he was through the hole in a flash—and the greenish glow was all around him, lighting dimly the vast space that now enclosed him.

It was a cave.

An enormous cave, hundreds of metres across—and just as high. Measle looked down over the front of his car and saw the roller coaster rails stretched out in front until—far, far away—they met the floor of this huge space. There were hills and valleys down there, making ripples across the surface of the ground and, far below, beyond the point where the tracks bent to meet the floor, the rails levelled off and ran for several metres across the ground.

And then Measle saw something that made his mind freeze with terror.

The rails stopped.

They simply came to an end, there in the middle of this vast, undulating floor—and Measle knew that, at this headlong speed, his car and all the others behind him would careen off the ends of the rails and run, uncontrolled, across the ground—and they'd hit one of those low hills and would probably shoot into the air—they'd tumble end over end and then crash, in a heap of splintered plastic and steel and wood—and his chances of surviving that devastation were hopeless—

And now the ground was coming up fast. Measle gritted his teeth, closed his eyes, curled both hands tightly round the safety bar and waited for the end.

The wind shrieked. The wheels screamed.

He felt the sudden sensation of his body being pressed down into the seat. Now, he must be racing along the stretch of level rails—the stretch that had looked so very, very short from way up there—

Measle clenched his fingers on the bar and squeezed his eyes as tight as he could get them—

Any minute now—

There was a sudden, smooth, and powerful deceleration. Measle felt his chest being pressed hard against the padded bar and he braced his feet and pushed back with his hands and, as he did so, he felt the wind die down to a whisper. The screaming of the wheels in his ears became a hiss, and then a silence as the Juggernaut train came to a gentle halt. Then there was a clang as the safety bar sprang from his chest and returned to its slot in the floor.

Measle opened his eyes.

There, a few metres in front of his leading car,

the rails stopped. It looked as though whoever had laid them had simply got bored with the process and had gone off to do something else.

GET OUT.

There was no way Measle could disobey those thudding words in his head. He scrambled out of his seat and stepped out onto the softly glowing ground.

STAND ASIDE.

Measle stepped away from the rails. As he did so, he saw the now empty cars begin suddenly to move backwards. He watched in astonishment as they accelerated smoothly away from him, gathering speed as they raced back towards the spot where the rails arced up towards the distant roof of the cave—and there was something very odd about those rails and, for a moment, Measle couldn't work out what it was—then—*of course! There were no supports! No great red steel pillars set in concrete, holding the rails up! Instead, these rails simply hung there in the glowing green air, stretching down in a long, unsupported curve from the tiny black dot in the ceiling of the cave (and, of course, the tiny black dot was the hole from which he'd emerged only half a minute or so ago)—*

The cars had reached the end of the level stretch and had begun to hurtle upwards along those impossibly-unsupported rails towards the far-off roof. Measle watched as they soared upwards, getting smaller and smaller, until they disappeared into the tiny black hole in the cave's ceiling.

And then there was a slithering sound by Measle's feet. He looked down—and saw that the steel rails themselves were now sliding along the ground! The two ends slipped past him, gathering speed as they did so. It was as if somebody was pulling the rails along, hauling them away—Measle watched in bewilderment as they retracted fast—and now they were off the ground and were hanging in the greenish glow, the ends disappearing upwards at a rate even faster than the cars had travelled—and, moments later, the rails were dragged up and through the hole in the ceiling, which then closed with a faint and distant POP!

If Measle had hoped that there was any chance at all that he might escape from the cave by using the Juggernaut again, his hopes now vanished with the sound of that far-off pop. There was no going back now—at least, certainly not via the way he'd come in.

His heart sinking with despair, Measle looked about him. He noted some details that he'd not seen before. The huge cave seemed to generate its own illumination—this strange green glow that shone steadily from the floor and walls—but not from the ceiling, Measle saw. Up there, the surface appeared to be made up of jagged black rock, which was in sharp contrast to the rounded green hills and valleys of the cavern floor. The walls too were made of this luminous material—and they too had rounded shapes and indentations, almost all the way up to the roof. Here and there, on the floor and on the walls, tall outcrops of bare black rock pushed through the pale green covering. There were several of these rock projections scattered across the enormous floor and one large one that stuck out from the wall closest to where Measle was standing. It was about eight metres up the wall—and Measle saw that there was some sort of opening in the wall at the point where this projecting rock met the surface. Even as Measle was staring at this rocky spur, he suddenly noticed movement in the opening—and a moment later, a strange little figure appeared, stepping out of the darkness and onto the rock platform. The figure moved to the very edge and then stared down at Measle.

Whatever it was, it was very old.

Very, *very* old. Measle shuddered. He didn't think he'd ever seen anybody—or any*thing*, come to that—that was as old as the creature that stood, eight metres above him, staring down at him. The creature's face was an ancient face, covered with a mass of wrinkles that criss-crossed the yellow skin in every direction, making the whole thing look like the bottom of a dried-up lake. Even the wrinkles had wrinkles of their own—and they extended all over the creature's scalp, which was mottled here and there with ugly patches of brown skin. Scattered across this crinkled scalp were little clumps of thin white hair, very long, that hung straggling down on either side of the creature's head. Measle saw, with a start of horror, that the thing appeared to have no nose. There were two dark slits where the nose *should* have been—and above them, a pair of blank, black eyes. And what was really horrible about the creature's eyes was the fact that the entire eye was black, with no trace of white anywhere to be seen, so that, unless its head was turned directly towards him, Measle couldn't tell if the creature was looking at him at all. Its ears were nothing more than a couple of little withered scraps of yellow skin and its mouth was a wide, lipless gash that slashed across the lower half of its horrible face like a scar. It had a long, scrawny neck, covered with folds of loose skin—and below the neck, a dusty black robe that hung to the ground and covered the thing's body completely. But the robe didn't conceal the fact that the creature's body was hopelessly out of proportion to its head. Measle saw immediately that, whatever the *shape* of the thing was underneath its robe, its frame was no bigger than his—and quite probably a bit smaller—

'Welcome, Measlestubbs.'

The gash in the lower half of the thing's face had opened like a letter box, letting out the words in a reedy, husky croak. The sound made Measle think that the creature hadn't spoken for a very long time.

And then Measle saw its tongue—and, immediately, he wished he hadn't. The creature's mouth was still open and, quite suddenly and without any warning, two black pointed things, the size of pencils, slithered out of the opening and twitched in the still air. Then they slid from side to side and, a moment later, pushed their way even further out of the creature's mouth—and Measle saw (and this was worse than the thing having no nose) that the two black pencils were joined at the base and so, what he was looking at was, in fact, a tongue that was forked just like a snake's tongue.

The twin black tongues flickered for another moment and then slid back into the mouth and disappeared. Then the creature cleared its throat.

'I hope you won't object if we converse normally?' it said, its thin voice drifting down in the still air. 'I find the projection of my thoughts into the minds of others tiring after a while and, since we are in reasonable proximity to one another, there is no reason why we cannot dispense with telepathic communication and simply hold an ordinary conversation.'

The creature's mouth stretched into an

unpleasant smile. 'Well,' it added, its voice coming more smoothly now, 'as ordinary as is possible, under these *interesting* circumstances.'

'Who—who are you?' stammered Measle, pretty sure that he knew the answer already.

'Who am I?' said the thing, its black eyes boring into Measle's. 'I think you know who I am, Measlestubbs. We have spoken already. I am the Dragodon.'

There was a long pause. It was as if the Dragodon seemed to be expecting some sort of response from Measle and Measle wondered what to say. There was really only one thing on his mind—

'Where's my mother?'

The Dragodon stared down at Measle. For several moments it said nothing. Then the gash in the lower part of its face opened.

'Do you not wish to know what the Dragodon is, Measlestubbs? Or why the Dragodon has brought you here? Or what the Dragodon intends to do with you? Do you have no curiosity about your fate?'

Measle stuck a thoughtful frown on his face and pretended to think about all these questions. Then he shrugged his shoulders and said—with more bravado than he really felt, 'No, sorry—not particularly. But I would like to know where my mum is and if she's all right?'

The Dragodon glared down at Measle, looking

like somebody who has just been on the receiving end of a mild insult. Then—

SIT DOWN.

Measle's legs folded under him and he sat down with a thump.

The Dragodon took a deep, rasping breath.

'I have forgotten how impertinent humans can be,' it said. 'It has been so long—so very long—since I spoke to one. And, when I finally get the opportunity, I find myself conversing with a *child*. And this child expresses no curiosity, other than wanting to know the whereabouts of its *mother*. This lack of curiosity betrays the child's dullness of mind. This child is an ignorant child and must be educated—so sit quietly, Measlestubbs—sit quietly and listen!'

And then, in a quiet and measured voice, the Dragodon told Measle his story. It was the story that Griswold Gristle had told the other wrathmonks in the cave on Borgrove Moor. It was the story written in the first great volume of wizard history, a huge leather-bound book that lay on a forgotten shelf, deep in the library of the Wizards' Guild. It was the story of the rise and the fall of the Dragodons—the great battles and the great defeats—and the story ended with the last of the dragons and the last of the Dragodons—

'We fell, Measlestubbs. My beloved Arcturion and I. We fell from the skies.'

Measle opened his eyes with a start. The images

from that slow, measured voice that had crowded his mind—they'd been so vivid, so real, that Measle had completely forgotten where he was—and what was happening to him...he was vaguely aware that the Dragodon had finished speaking—

'Wha'?' he managed to stammer, staring up at the Dragodon with bleary eyes.

'The last valiant dragon was my beloved Arcturion. His great wing was crippled. It was enough to bring us down. I survived. But it was the end of us all. The Dragodons and their dragons. The kings and their allies—those treacherous wizards—they all decided that, for me—the last of our breed—eternal imprisonment would be the fitting punishment. They found this island, they extended the great cave beneath it and they sealed me inside—and here I have slept for many a thousand years, my only visitors the flocks of seabirds that nest here on the rocky shores. And then, one day, long after we and our deeds were all forgotten, men returned to the island and began to build. And what did they build? A great castle? A palace for an emperor? A fortified city? No! They built a playground for children!'

The Dragodon paused. Measle saw that it was breathing heavily, its narrow chest moving up and down beneath its dusty robe. Its black eyes were narrowed and its slit of a mouth was turned down at the corners. *It's angry!* thought Measle. *Angry with what had become of its island—*

The Dragodon lifted its scabby head and spoke again.

'Whether it was the thunderous sounds of construction, or the foul and filthy insult to my dignity—whatever the reason, I awoke from my endless sleep. The men above were careless. The ground up there is thin in places. They broke through while building one of their ridiculous creations—the thing they called the "Ferris-wheel"—and I found a way out of my prison. Oh, the careless men quickly sealed up the hole they had made but I found another, within one of the great iron pillars of the Juggernaut ride. I began to move freely—but always on the island. I cannot travel far beyond my source of mana. I can contain my thoughts within an object and I can send that object far and wide—but I myself am trapped here.'

The Dragodon paused. Then—

'At least, I was.'

The Dragodon smiled and Measle saw that the thing had no teeth. Its gums were black and its forked tongue flickered between them. *Well, at least it can't bite me to death,* thought Measle. He waited, while the silence between them grew longer and longer—*It's waiting for me to say something!* he thought.

'Well—what's all this got to do with me and my mother?' he said.

'With you, Measlestubbs—very little,' said the

Dragodon. 'I have no great interest in you, other than a passing admiration for your courage and resourcefulness, both of which are remarkable in one so young. I was mildly curious to meet you, which is why I removed you from the clutches of those ridiculous wrathmonks. I have no interest in your father, either. He is a minor wizard and is therefore no threat to me. However, those foolish little wrathmonks were intent on some sort of revenge against your family and I saw a way to use this to my advantage. You see, the only member of your family that has any significance for me is your mother.'

'Why?' said Measle. He pulled himself to his feet. 'And where is she, anyway?'

'She is here, Measlestubbs,' said the Dragodon. 'We *all* are here. All four of us—here in this great cave.'

Measle was about to shout, *Where? Where is she?*—but something the Dragodon had said stopped him short. The Dragodon had said *All four of us*—

'Four of us?' said Measle, looking around.

'Indeed yes,' said the Dragodon—and Measle saw that he was smiling very broadly now, his black gums exposed and his forked tongue flickering between them. 'Indeed yes—you, your mother, myself—and Arcturion, of course. I have not been alone in my prison. Arcturion has been at my side all through the long, dark ages of our sleep.'

'Arc-Arcturion?' stammered Measle. 'You mean—your dragon?'

'Yes, Measlestubbs. My beloved dragon is here with us.'

Measle looked wildly around the great cave, searching for some sign of scales, or teeth, or vast bat wings. There was nothing—only the undulating walls and floor, glowing a luminous pale green. Measle felt a little of his courage returning. If the Dragodon thought that a silly, obvious lie was going to frighten him—

'Where?' said Measle, loudly. 'I can't see any dragon! So where is it?'

'Use your eyes, Measlestubbs.'

Measle stared again, searching the walls and floor and ceiling—*perhaps there's a tunnel somewhere, leading to another cave—no, nothing—*

'I don't see anything!' shouted Measle. 'You're lying—there's no dragon here!'

'But there *is*, Measlestubbs.' *'Where?'*

'Why, Measlestubbs,' said the Dragodon, his reedy voice almost a whisper, 'you're *standing* on him.'

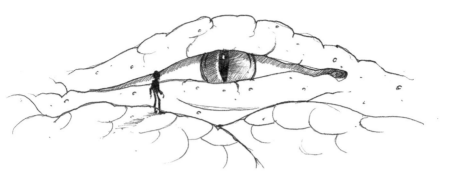

ARCTURION

Griswold, Cudgel, Flabbit, and Judge Cedric were still waiting patiently on the Juggernaut's platform when the command from the Dragodon slammed into their minds.

They had been waiting for something to happen—for some time, they had stood watching the section of rail that entered the platform area from the rear, expecting Measle's train to come hissing back from its journey round the ride. But when a full five minutes had passed, Griswold Gristle had turned to Judge Cedric and said, 'It would appear, Cedric, that the boy is not coming back.'

'Ah,' muttered Judge Cedric, frowning with pain. His hands were still pressed to his aching jaws. 'Then he mussst have essscaped usss, Griswold.'

Griswold sighed. *Really, he must find himself a more worthy companion in the future!* 'No, Cedric,' he said, with as much patience as he could muster, 'no—the car he was travelling in has not returned either, which can only mean one thing.'

'It has exploded?' said Judge Cedric, hopefully.

'No, Cedric. It means that his lordship the Dragodon has him now and will, no doubt, be dealing with him in a mossst sssatisfactory way.'

'His *lordship* has him?'

'Yesss, Cedric.'

'You mean—I won't be able to breathe on him, Griswold?'

'It would appear not, Cedric.'

'But—but my lovely boils!'

There was a snarling sound from Flabbit, whose face was now even redder and lumpier than before.

'They're not *lovely*, you ssstupid old plonker,' he muttered. 'They *hurt*. I jussst hope my toothache hurts you worsssse.'

Judge Cedric sneered at Flabbit and opened his mouth to say something, but Griswold stopped him. He reached up and patted Judge Cedric's bony shoulder. 'Ressst assured, my dear Cedric— his lordship the Dragodon will punish the boy far more effectively than we ever could—'

He broke off—because here, sliding steadily and silently backwards down the first slope of the Juggernaut ride, came the missing line of cars.

They slipped between the two platforms and hissed to a stop. All the wrathmonks stared at the front seat of the leading car.

Measle wasn't in it.

'There, you sssee?' said Griswold. 'The child has been removed—and is, I imagine, caught fassst in the clutches of his great lordship!'

'Ssso it would sssseem, Griswold,' rumbled Cudgel. 'What do we do now?'

The answer came, but not from Griswold.

YOU ARE RELEASED, LITTLE WRATHMONKS. I HAVE THE WOMAN. I HAVE THE BOY. THEY ARE MINE AND WILL BE...EXTINCT...WITHIN MINUTES. I LEAVE THE FATE OF THE STUBBS MALE IN YOUR HANDS. YOU ARE FREE TO GO—SO GO!

That final command was the strongest one they had ever received. Without a word, and with their heads buzzing from the sheer power of the Dragodon's order, the four wrathmonks turned and walked quickly, through the drizzling rain, towards the distant gates.

Measle's legs didn't seem to be working. Sheer terror was paralysing his muscles. He couldn't move his feet—they seemed to be stuck fast to the ground—*but it wasn't the ground at all! It was— it was something else!*

When the Dragodon had said, 'You're standing on him,' Measle had immediately looked down at his feet. Beneath them was the glowing green surface, rolling into the distance like gently billowing waves in mid-ocean—

'Of course, exactly which *part* of Arcturion you are presently standing upon, I couldn't say,' said the Dragodon, coolly. 'Perhaps towards the tail? He has grown considerably over the centuries—increasing his great size by many thousandfolds—and his coils have extended over the floor and walls until even I, his master, can no longer tell the difference between neck or tail, wing or claw. Only when he raises his head will I be able to know for sure which end is which.'

Measle's legs were numb with fear—but his mind and his mouth still worked.

'Wh-wh-why isn't it moving?' he stuttered. 'Is—is it *dead*?' he added, hopefully.

'Not dead. Far from dead. He is asleep, Measlestubbs. He has been asleep ever since we were imprisoned here. His injuries were great and sleep was the only cure. You cannot put a bandage on a Great Worm.'

'G-Great Worm?'

'Another name, Measlestubbs. Occasionally he wakes, if there is food—but he quickly sleeps again.'

'Is—is it g-going to w-wake up soon?'

'Oh yes. He will awake—but only when I tell him to. Not before—so you need have no fear for a few more minutes. You may move freely. Arcturion cannot feel your insignificant weight.'

Measle stared out at the rolling green hills and valleys before him. The strange shape of the landscape now began to make some sort of sense. If you could imagine a faintly luminous, pale green snake, coiled round and over and under itself, it would, perhaps, look a bit like this—but the snake's coils would have to be *huge*, each one at least the width of a soccer pitch—

Measle bent down and put his hand to the glowing surface. It was hard as stone—but it wasn't cold like stone. There was a faint warmth that rose from within, lifting the temperature of the surface just enough to notice—and then Measle thought he felt a faint movement, that tingled against the tips of his fingers—

'Put your ear to his side, Measlestubbs,' said the Dragodon.

Measle bent further and pressed the side of his head against what he still thought of as the ground. Faint, and from far, far away, came an almost inaudible sound. *Thud.* Ten seconds ticked by—and there it was again. *Thud.*

'His heart, Measlestubbs. You are hearing the beating of one of his great hearts. He has four altogether.'

Measle rose slowly, his own heart beating ten times faster. *I've got to play for time!* he thought desperately—

'Where—where's its head?'

'Buried somewhere, deep beneath the coils of his body. When he sleeps, Arcturion prefers the darkness.'

Quick—another question! Keep the Dragodon talking! 'And—and what does it—I mean *he*—what does he eat?'

'Whatever he can get, Measlestubbs. Three foolish little wrathmonks fell through my ceiling a short while ago and I thought Arcturion might enjoy a snack—so I woke him. He snapped them up quickly enough and seemed to find them quite tasty. Then he buried his beautiful head beneath his coils once again and returned to his slumbers. But soon his rest will come to an end. That, Measlestubbs, is where your mother enters the picture.'

'My mother?' said Measle, resisting the urge to stare wildly around in search of her. Instead, he tried to keep his gaze steadily on the Dragodon. 'What's my mother got to do with it?'

'Why, *everything*, Measlestubbs,' said the Dragodon. 'Would you like me to explain?'

Measle nodded. *I've got to keep this going*, he thought, *and for as long as possible—*

The black forked tongue slithered between the black gums.

'Great Worms generate great mana,' said the Dragodon, slowly. 'Their masters, the Dragodons, were able to draw from this mana and use a small part of it for themselves. Thus, our almost limitless powers. But an injured Great Worm is a helpless creature and its ability to generate mana is reduced almost to zero. There is but a small trickle—barely enough to keep the creature alive and, for its master, hardly enough for a dozen spells at a time. The Great Worm must sleep until his injuries are healed and, only then, will his full strength and mana return. I have waited patiently for Arcturion to recover but the process has proved to be a lengthy one. At this rate, it will be another two or three hundred years before his strength and mana fully return. I do not intend to wait that long, Measlestubbs.'

The Dragodon paused, its blank, black eyes sweeping over the hills and valleys of the vast cave. Then it took another breath and said, 'I knew there had to be a solution to my problem. When men came to my island, to build their childish amusements, I was able to move among them. I saw, at once, a means to escape—for both myself and for Arcturion. These foolish men had built a bridge—a path—between this island and the mainland. A path that would allow us to escape our prison. You must know, Measlestubbs, that there was a *reason* the kings and the wizards placed us both on—and within—a piece of land that was surrounded by water. You see, ocean water is death to a Great Worm. It cannot swim across it. Neither can it fly above it. Ocean water is both a barrier—and a weapon—against the Great Worms. And that is why our enemies put us here. But now—now there is a road.'

The Dragodon paused again. Now he was staring down at Measle and the black forks of his tongue were flickering faster.

'I was there that day when you came to my island, Measlestubbs. You and your father and your mother. I sat behind you, I walked behind you, I watched all three of you closely—I brushed against you, I touched your father's shoulder—I learned much—but then, at the end of the day, I managed to make contact with your mother. And, in that instant, I found my answer. Your mother, Measlestubbs—your mother! What power! What great reserves of power! A well of mana—a well that never runs dry!'

The Dragodon was panting now, its narrow chest heaving up and down beneath the dusty robe. *It's very old*, thought Measle. *And very weak—*

'But she's no use!' Measle blurted. 'Not to you!'

The Dragodon turned its head and pointed its blank, black eyes down at Measle.

'Why not, Measlestubbs?'

'Because you've got to be *married* to her! My dad told me that! Otherwise it doesn't work!'

'*Married?*' said the Dragodon, slowly. 'Are you quite sure, Measlestubbs?'

'Of course I'm sure!' yelled Measle—then,

realizing that he ought, perhaps, to deal more cautiously with this creature, he lowered his voice and said, in a small, pleading tone, 'So, if she's no use to you, why don't you just let her go?'

The Dragodon seemed to consider this idea for a moment. Then it shook its wrinkled head.

'No, no,' it said, quietly. 'No—I couldn't do that, Measlestubbs.'

'Why not?'

'Because it is not I who needs her, Measlestubbs. At least, not directly. Your father was perfectly correct—I cannot use her mana. But another can.'

'Who?' said Measle, looking around the great cave.

'Why, you foolish boy—Arcturion, of course,' said the Dragodon, stretching its scar of a mouth into a wide, black-gummed smile.

Measle stared, bewildered, up at the Dragodon.

'What for?' he said. 'What's a dragon need my mother's mana *for*?'

The Dragodon sighed. 'I thought I had explained that, Measlestubbs. If Arcturion can absorb your mother's mana—her endless supply of mana—all his strength and power will return instantly.'

'Yeah—but *how*?' said Measle. 'You can't have a dragon getting married! And, even if you could— well, my mum wouldn't do it! She'd never marry a dragon! And she wouldn't hold hands with one, either!'

The idea was so ridiculous that Measle found

himself right on the very edge of laughing—

'There are other means by which Arcturion can link himself to your mother, Measlestubbs.'

'Yeah? How?'

The forked tongue flickered.

'Why—by *eating* her, of course.'

The four wrathmonks were pushing their way through the clicking turnstiles of the exits when they heard the sounds behind them.

They all turned together—and saw, advancing towards them through the rain, a small crowd of people. Most of the people wore uniforms of some kind and several of them seemed to be holding rough weapons—one man had a broom in his hands, another carried what looked like a garden fork—and the faces of everyone in this small mob looked very angry indeed.

'There they are!' yelled a man, with the words ADMINISTRATION ASSISTANT across the front of his peaked cap. 'That's them! They're the ones who did for us! Let's get 'em!'

The crowd surged forwards. As they came nearer, the wrathmonks were able to read the words on the various badges that adorned their chests and caps—SECURITY, said one—CARETAKING, said another—

Griswold Gristle hissed, 'Of *courssse*! Thisss is that fool Draggle's fault! With the destruction of the Medusa head, the park's personnel have revived! Well, we are released from our duties to his lordship and, therefore, we can use our mana on these interfering fools! Leave thisss to me!'

Griswold took a deep breath and opened his pudgy little mouth.

'*Pedoschkin asphaltiscoop suctobolus!*' he screamed—and instantly a pair of orange beams shot from his tiny eyes. They flashed, sizzling, across the gap between himself and the advancing crowd and then danced around the feet of the mob—and wherever the orange beams touched, the tarmac seemed to soften and then mould itself round the soles of the mob's shoes—and then the thick black tarmac slithered up their legs to just below their knees, so that the advancing crowd was no longer advancing at all—now, all they could do was jerk at their feet, trying to pull them

loose from the sticky, grabbing stuff. But they were held fast now, with nothing left to do but shout angrily at the wrathmonks and brandish their weapons over their heads.

'Hah,' said Griswold, a smirk of satisfaction on his plump lips. 'My Tar Trap spell! They are helpless now!'

'Can I breathe on them, Griswold?' asked Judge Cedric, hopefully. His teeth ached terribly—and the only thing that was going to make him feel better would be to cause a whole lot of pain to a bunch of horrible humans—

'No, Cedric,' said Griswold, firmly. 'There is no time—and besides, we have other fish to fry.'

'Fish?' muttered Judge Cedric. 'Fry? But—do we have a pan?'

'I mean Sssam Ssstubbs, Cedric!' snapped Griswold, pushing his way through the turnstile. 'Sssam Ssstubbs is at our mercy now!'

Cudgel and Flabbit narrowed their eyes and grinned wolfishly. Judge Cedric took his hands from his aching jaws and looked puzzled.

'Sssam Ssstubbs is a fish?' he said, his bushy white eyebrows raised so high that they furrowed his forehead.

Griswold Gristle clucked his tongue impatiently. He reached back through the turnstile and grabbed Judge Cedric by the hand. 'Never *mind*, Cedric! I shall explain on the way! Come—we have no time to lose!'

The other two wrathmonks followed Griswold and Judge Cedric through the turnstiles and then, without a backward glance at the furious shouting from behind them, they began to hurry together across the long causeway.

And the only comfort for the park's personnel—who soon gave up the hopeless struggle against the clinging tarmac—was that the incessant rain stopped falling at last. The heavy black clouds moved off the island and drifted along the causeway, hovering steadily over the heads of the four wrathmonks as they headed towards the distant town.

Tinker was fed up.

Fed up, soaking wet, and very, very tired. He'd been running all over the park for ever, it seemed—and the creatures chasing him showed no signs of giving up. There were only two of the carousel horses now—the lame one had slipped over again and, with only three working legs, hadn't been able to get back up. The Tyrannosaurus Rex was still on his trail though and, once or twice, had almost succeeded in stomping him with its enormous feet. Tinker's own feet were getting sore and his short legs ached with tiredness.

Where's the smelly kid when you need him? he thought, scurrying through the wet darkness. *A dog could do with a bit of a lift—it'd be nice to*

*get off the old tootsies and be carried around for
a bit—not sure how much longer we can keep
this up, the old tootsies and me—*

He caught a faint sniff of a familiar scent.
Somewhere quite close—the smelly kid had
passed this way. There were other, sharper smells
too—odours of dead fish, ancient sneakers, and
rotting mattresses—but it was the scent of the
smelly kid that drew Tinker forward.

*All these problems—like the old tootsies getting
so sore—perhaps the smelly kid could solve 'em?
The smelly kid didn't seem to mind carryin' a
little dog before—perhaps he wouldn't mind
carryin' a little dog again?*

Tinker threw a quick look over his shoulder—
*Oops, here come the two horsy thingies—and
there, close behind, the roarin' monster thingy—
off we go again!*

He pushed his exhausted legs back
into a gallop and headed fast in the
direction of the smells.

'*Eating* her?'

Flicker, flicker went the black forked tongue.

'Arcturion will absorb her well of mana. Her
inexhaustible well of mana—and it will become
his. And *his* mana will become *mine*. Together, we
will be unbeatable.'

Measle's mind was racing. *He had to stop this! Somehow he had to stop it! And, if he couldn't stop this (and there didn't seem to be any way of doing it, other than a miracle) then he had to delay it as long as possible—*

'But—what for? Why do you want to be unbeatable?'

The Dragodon turned its blank eyes down towards Measle.

'Surely *everybody* wants to be unbeatable, Measlestubbs?'

'Yes, all right—but who do you want to beat?'

The Dragodon lifted one corner of its thin mouth in a sneer.

'Why … humanity, Measlestubbs … humanity. Men are fools, Measlestubbs—stupid beyond belief —and they cannot be allowed to control this world any longer.'

'I don't think they're so stupid—'

'Well, of course you don't, Measlestubbs.' Flicker flicker went the tongue. 'You are one of them, after all. One of the cleverer ones, I must admit—which is saying very little. The proof of Man's idiocy lies above us. Who but idiots would spend their time and their riches building a playground for children?'

'It's not just for kids,' muttered Measle under his breath. 'My dad likes it too.'

'You prove my point, Measlestubbs. The mind of Man is a childish mind. That is why I intend to take over. To *run* things again, Measlestubbs, the way we did in the ancient times. That was the Dragodons' destiny—to run things. To rule. To control.'

'To control *what*?'

'*Everything*, of course. As I said, it was the Dragodons' *destiny*. However, their destiny was interrupted for a long, long while—but now it can be ours again.' The Dragodon smiled a small, black smile. 'Well,' it whispered, so quietly that Measle had to strain to hear the words, 'Well, since I am the last of our kind, perhaps I should say—*mine* again.'

Measle thought desperately. 'Well—all right then —but, how are you going to get out? You and your... your Worm? *You* can get out, I suppose— but I don't see any hole big enough to let your dragon out.'

The Dragodon laughed; a dry, dusty chuckle.

'When Arcturion's mana is restored, he will reach his full strength again. Look at him, Measlestubbs! He has been growing steadily during all these endless years! He is vast! He will be the largest creature ever to walk on—and fly above—this earth! Do you really believe that a few metres of rock will be able to hold him?'

'Yeah, well—'(*Think, Measle! THINK!*)'—well, if he does get out—if you both get out—we've got jets—jet fighters—and they've got rockets and machine-guns and everything—'

The Dragodon's dry chuckle became a throaty, rasping laugh.

'I have seen them, Measlestubbs. They pose no threat to either of us. You forget the magic, don't you? I have had a lot of time, Measlestubbs—time to think. Time to develop. Time to practise new skills. I shall not make the mistakes of the past, Measlestubbs. And as for Arcturion—I say again, look at him! Where once his fiery breath consumed an army, now it will incinerate a city! A *city*, Measlestubbs! And you threaten me with puny flying machines?'

The ground (*Not ground! Skin! Muscles! Blood! Bones!*) under Measle's feet shifted almost imperceptibly. It was as if a tiny ripple—no bigger than one caused when you drop a little pebble into the calm waters of a lake—suddenly moved across the surface, passing directly under his feet. Measle's eyes jerked downwards—and then he heard the Dragodon's quiet chuckle.

'He moved, did he? My beloved Arcturion? He must be hungry. Well, perhaps it is time, at long last, to feed him what he needs.'

The Dragodon paused and then raised an arm and pointed to a tall outcrop of black rock that rose from the centre of the cave floor.

'You asked, Measlestubbs, where your mother is. I choose to tell you now. She is there—on the other side of that rock. You may go to her, if you like.'

Measle didn't need any more encouragement than that. Forgetting what he was standing on, he turned and ran towards the distant rock. The ground (*Not ground!*) was smooth but uneven, with short, steep hills and deep, narrow crevasses and Measle had to cross each one in turn, scrambling sometimes on all fours up the slopes and leaping, if they were narrow enough, over some of the dark fissures that lay between them.

At last he neared the rock. It was tall, at least ten metres high, its base the size of a big garden shed. There was no sign of Lee. Measle ran round to the far side of the rock—and there she was—

She was slumped down, sitting listlessly on the ground, her head drooped to one side, her long red hair falling over her face.

'Mum?' whispered Measle. He moved close to her and touched her gently on her cheek. 'Mum?'

Lee raised her head and looked into Measle's eyes. Her face was thin and pale, with streaks of dirt on her forehead. Her own eyes were blank and puzzled and she looked at Measle without a trace of recognition.

'Hello,' she muttered. 'Who are you? Can you help me?'

'*Mum!*' whispered Measle, fiercely. 'It's me—Measle!'

Lee smiled a small smile. 'That's a funny name,' she whispered. 'And I like your hair. But look—I'm in trouble here. Is there any way you think you could get me out? Or are you in the same trouble too?'

'*Mum!*'

SHE HAS RECEIVED A DOSE OF MY BREATH, MEASLESTUBBS. SHE CAN REMEMBER NOTHING—JUST AS YOUR FATHER CAN REMEMBER NOTHING. SHE WILL NOT KNOW YOU.

Measle's head buzzed. For a moment, he wondered why the Dragodon was choosing to communicate like this again—*Of course, it's on the other side of the cave, I couldn't hear it, even if I wanted to*—

Measle looked into his mother's bewildered eyes. He was about to say something—to tell her who he was and who she was and what was happening to them both, when—

AND NOW, MEASLESTUBBS—ALLOW ME TO INTRODUCE YOU AND YOUR MOTHER TO THE MOST WONDROUS CREATURE YOU WILL EVER MEET. HOW SAD THAT YOUR ACQUAINTANCE WILL BE SO SHORT. A PITY—BUT TIME WAITS FOR NOBODY.

There was a moment of silence in Measle's head. Then—

ARCTURION! ACHMAAL! ACHMAAL! MELACHIN! MELOACHIN! ARCTURION! ARCTURION!

The harsh, guttural words were like hammer blows in Measle's head. Lee screwed up her eyes and closed them tight. Then she opened them a crack and peered at Measle. 'That hurts, doesn't it?' she muttered, through clenched teeth. 'What's doing that?'

Measle was about to tell her—but he didn't have time.

There was an upheaval, a massive, rolling, undulating, shifting of the landscape. The entire floor of the vast cave began to move. Slowly, a nearby hill lifted and then shifted to the right. Beyond it, another ridge sank down several metres and then moved steadily to the left. Measle watched, his mouth hanging open, as the floor became a vast plain of moving shapes, valleys sliding past hills, hills sinking and rising like ocean waves—

And then, a hole appeared on the far side of the cave. It was a dark, deep hole, formed by the sudden shifting of a line of mounds, and the sinking and parting of an equal number of ravines—all resolving themselves into a huge circular pit—

—and, slowly, out of this great pit, rose something that Measle, for several moments, was completely unable to identify. It was the size of a house. A big house—Merlin Manor at least—and, as more and more of it appeared from the pit, Measle realized that it might even reach the rough proportions of something as big as Buckingham Palace itself. The top of this enormous object was knobbled and lumpy, a pale, glowing green that matched exactly the colour of the surrounding landscape.

And then there was an eye.

Huge. The size of a double-decker bus. Slanted. Yellow. A narrow, vertical pupil, like a cat's. It was an eye that showed nothing—no fear, no kindness, no interest, no compassion—it was just a cold, expressionless, glowing yellow eye, set in the expanse of wrinkled, lumpy skin that surrounded it—

And then, below the eye, there was a mouth.

Long. Grinning. The tremendous jaws parted a little, showing a line of yellow teeth. Each tooth the length of a tall tree. Behind this forest of fangs, a black, flickering tongue, forked like the Dragodon's—but a hundred, a thousand, a *million* times bigger—

Arcturion raised his great rectangular head from the pit—a pit formed by the endless coils of his body—and slowly turned it from side to side.

Measle shrank back against Lee, feeling the warmth of her body. It was a small comfort—a very small comfort—but without her being there with him, Measle thought he might easily have gone mad at the sight that was filling his eyes.

SAY GOODBYE, MEASLESTUBBS. TO YOUR MOTHER. TO YOUR LIFE.

Measle pressed himself hard against his mother. He heard her whisper against his ear. 'Oh—no—'

ARCTURION! MELACHIN! MELOACHIN!

A long, scaly neck lifted Arcturion's head higher out of the pit and Measle saw that the creature's glaring yellow eyes were now actively searching the ground before it. The immense head glided fifty metres above the floor, twisting slowly this way and that. Any minute now, those eyes would see the rock—and the woman slumped at the base of the rock, and the small boy huddled against the woman, both staring up with eyes wide with terror—

Then the dead yellow eyes of Arcturion saw them.

For a moment, the dragon paused.

But not for long.

More of the neck lifted from the pit and the gigantic block of the dragon's head drifted down towards them. When the front of the jaws reached a point thirty metres from the rock, it stopped. The black tongue flickered out from between the yellow fangs, the twin tips hovering in the air. Slowly, the tongue extended, coming closer and closer. Thirty metres. Twenty-five. Twenty. Ten. Five—

The tips of the forked tongue were shiny with saliva. They quivered in the still air, one now a few centimetres from Measle's face, the other a few centimetres from Lee's. Then, the one closest to Measle darted forward. It almost touched his nose—but not quite. It hung there, trembling slightly, for ten seconds—then it withdrew. Out of the corner of his eye, Measle could see that the

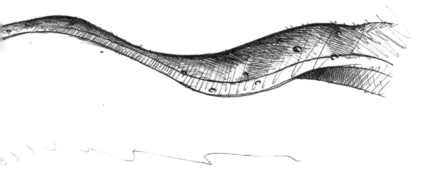

other fork of the great tongue had darted forward in Lee's direction—but this one didn't pull back from her. It moved over her face, still not quite touching her—and Measle realized that (like a snake) it was *tasting* the air that surrounded her. Then, the trembling at the tip of the fork began to move faster and faster. Its vibrations increased until the tip of the fork was moving so fast that it was almost invisible. Then, quite suddenly, it streaked backwards, joining its twin—then the entire length of the great shiny black tongue was drawn away until it disappeared into the forest of fangs in Arcturion's distant jaws.

HE HAS FOUND HER OUT, MEASLESTUBBS. HE KNOWS HER FOR WHAT SHE IS.

SHUT UP! screamed Measle soundlessly, the words staying inside his head. *JUST SHUT UP!*

VERY WELL, MEASLESTUBBS (came the words back into his brain), I SHALL BE SILENT. ARCTURION WILL BE MAKING ENOUGH NOISE FOR ALL OF US.

Measle hadn't taken his eyes off the dragon—and now he saw the creature raise its head towards the roof of the cave—he saw it open its jaws—

A scream—an ear-bending, glass-shattering, ground-trembling scream, like the loudest siren on the biggest ship in the world—came blasting from Arcturion's throat. It made the roar of the Tyrannosaurus Rex sound like the squeak of a sickly mouse. Measle put both hands to his ears to block out the deafening sound. With the sound a little reduced, Measle could make out the actual tone of the scream. It wasn't a scream of pain, or anger, or misery. It was a scream of triumph, like a great war cry—

And then the scream ended and Arcturion lowered his head and began to thrust his jaws forward, across the cave towards them.

Deep in Darkness

Tinker's legs were trembling with tiredness, and his paws were so sore that they were almost bleeding—so, in desperation, he had adopted a new technique with his pursuers and it was working rather well.

He'd found his way to where the scent of the smelly kid was strongest—in a small area round the Ferris wheel. Nearby, in the shadow of the great wheel, was a large, gaping hole in the ground. Tinker had very nearly fallen into it, but he'd seen it just in time and had managed to skid his way round it, his little paws scrabbling against the slick, wet tarmac. Now, on the far side of the hole, Tinker took a breather and watched as the Tyrannosaurus

Rex and the two carousel horses emerged from the corner of a low building and advanced towards him.

The dinosaur—animated plastic and plaster and steel—was incapable of feeling tired; but it could feel *anger*—and the same applied to the carousel horses. They all felt a degree of fury towards the little white creature that was now crouching down, panting, with its tongue lolling from one side of its mouth, on the far side of a black pit that yawned in the ground between them.

The Rex—and the two carousel horses—began to move around the side of the pit. As they did so, Tinker got up and moved too, keeping the same distance between them. The dinosaur changed direction, stumbling against one of the horses and almost pitching it headlong into the hole. Tinker changed direction too and moved back to where he'd been a moment before. Both hunters and prey did this several times and, each time, Tinker simply kept the pit between himself and his pursuers.

The tyrannosaurus's rage increased. No matter what it did, the little white animal stayed out of reach. In a fury, the great dinosaur stamped its massive feet down hard against the ground. Tinker could feel the ground trembling under its enormous weight.

Then Tinker heard a very strange noise. It was a scream—an unearthly, howling screech—and it seemed to be coming from far, far away—

And what was odder still, it seemed to be coming from somewhere deep in the ground *beneath* him. It certainly hadn't been made by the tyrannosaurus, or by either of the carousel horses—

Neither the tyrannosaurus nor the horses took any notice of the sound. Once again, they began to move around the circular pit—and, once again, Tinker simply moved with them. Again, the Rex paused and showed its rage by stamping against the ground—but this time, its great clawed feet stamped very close to the edge of the gaping pit—

And the ground beneath the clawed feet—and the ground beneath the wooden hooves— suddenly gave way. There was a grumbling, rumbling, grinding sound, followed instantly by a sort of whooosh! of rushing air—and that was followed by three high-pitched screams—

A chunk of tarmac, the size of a chest of drawers, hit Arcturion on the head.

For a moment, it seemed that the dragon hadn't noticed the blow. Then, a second—even larger— piece smashed against the end of his long snout—

Arcturion paused in his forward movement and lifted his enormous head.

There, in the distant ceiling of the cave—a hole—and *stuff* was falling down through it— mud, rocks, more lumps of tarmac—and three wriggling creatures too, that screamed as they fell.

And, as they fell down and down and down, dropping closer and closer and closer to Arcturion's great raised head, the dragon instinctively opened his mouth to receive them.

It was this strange, sudden interruption that jerked Measle out of his paralysis. He took in the fact that something was falling towards Arcturion's gaping maw, and that the something (*No—three somethings!*) was distracting Arcturion from his main purpose—and he understood in an instant that this delay, while very welcome, was going to be a short one.

The three distant falling objects disappeared into Arcturion's vast, gaping jaws. Arcturion swallowed. Measle saw the ripple of contracting muscles running down the long throat. Then he saw Arcturion begin to lower his great head towards him—

'Come on, Mum!' he whispered, frantically. 'You've got to get up!'

Obediently, Lee began to struggle to her feet. Measle looked up—and saw that Arcturion was regarding them both, his huge, expressionless eyes boring down on them, as if the great creature was mildly interested to see what these two tiny beings would do next.

Measle's only thought was to put something between Arcturion and themselves—*the rock, obviously—if he could get himself and Lee round to the other side of the rock—*

Lee closed her exhausted eyes and stumbled against him. Thinking that she had tripped, Measle looked down at her feet. There was something there, resting on the ground—small, oval, a purple-ish, blue-ish colour—

It was a jelly bean.

In times of extreme stress, Measle's brain worked very well. It had worked very well back in Basil's train set, and it had worked particularly *quickly* too, mostly in the moments just before Measle's certain death—so quickly, in fact, that Measle had, in the past, managed to *escape* certain death—and his brain worked just as quickly now.

Jelly bean. Blue. Not mine. Must be Mum's. Only one reason for Mum to have a jelly bean—

In one swift movement, Measle bent down, scooped up the jelly bean and pushed it into his mother's mouth.

'Wha'?' mumbled Lee, trying to push the jelly bean out of her mouth with her tongue.

'Eat it, Mum!' hissed Measle. He glanced up. Arcturion's enormous head was on the move again—bearing down on them at the speed of an express train—he could see the jaws beginning to open, he could see the forest of yellow fangs parting, he could see the twin forks of the black tongue flickering deep in the shadows—

'*Eat* it!' screamed Measle—and, at the same moment that Lee bit down on the jelly bean, Measle pushed himself into her arms and wrapped them tight round his body.

And Lee disappeared right before his eyes.

The only way Measle knew that she was still there was the pressure of her slim body against his. He risked a quick glance down at himself and saw—to his great relief—that he too had gone.

Thirty seconds! That's all! So move!

Measle held tight to Lee and together they staggered round the rock, putting its bulk between them and the dragon. Once on the far side, Lee's legs gave way again and she sank to the ground.

Behind them, there was a shattering roar—and this time, there was a very different quality to the sound. This time, instead of a scream of triumph, Arcturion let out (what sounded to Measle's battered ears) a wild shriek of rage.

And it *was* a shriek of rage. The huge creature had been relishing this moment—and then, without warning—

Where was his prey? It had been there, before his very nose, a second ago! And now it was gone! His precious prey! One of the little creatures was small and insignificant and meant no more to him than a grain of rice might mean to an elephant—but the other was rich in mana! Rich beyond measure! Those three tiny morsels that had just fallen out of the sky and into his mouth—and the three soft little wriggling creatures before them—they too had been rich in mana and were giving him a small (and short-lived) degree of his old strength—but this temporary strength was nothing to what the tiny thing by the rock would give him! It had more mana (and more reserves of mana) than anything he had ever experienced! The little thing was so rich in mana, in fact, that he knew instinctively what ingesting that tiny creature would mean to him! Eternal Power! Endless Strength! Infinite Glory!

And now it was gone!

Measle and Lee huddled together in the shelter of the rock as Arcturion let out another, even louder, scream of rage. They felt the ground shudder as the dragon shifted its body—then Arcturion's palace-sized head appeared from round the side of the rock. The great yellow eyes searched the area, the tall, vertical black pupils passing right across Measle and Lee still huddling against the hard stone wall—

Fifteen seconds gone! Do something!

Frantically, Measle freed one of his hands from Lee's encircling arms. He fumbled against her dress, searching for the pocket that he knew was there.

Ah! There it was! Now, please let there be more inside—

Measle's fingers plunged deep into the pocket and touched a small heap of little oval objects. He grabbed a handful and pulled his hand free—then he separated one jelly bean from the little pile in his palm and pushed it between Lee's lips.

'What are you doing?' mumbled Lee, trying to turn her head away. Her eyes were still closed tight. 'I don't like the blue ones—'

'I know you don't, Mum,' whispered Measle, 'but you've got to eat them! Every time I give you one, you've got to eat it! *Don't ask why!*'

There was such a desperate urgency in Measle's voice that Lee felt a strong urge to do as she was told. There was something about this boy, with his funny, sticking-up hair—something vaguely familiar and, at the same time, something very dear and very comforting—

Lee bit down on the second jelly bean—and chose that moment to open her eyes.

She was alone!

No—no she wasn't alone! She could feel *the boy, pressed against her! But she couldn't see him—*

'Where are you?' she hissed.

'Right here, Mum,' came back the answer. She could feel the warm air of his breath against her ear. 'Keep still. Don't move. Don't make any noise. And keep eating the jelly beans.'

Even without her memory, Lee Stubbs was an intelligent woman. She had lost everything—her past, her knowledge, even her identity—and, a moment earlier, she had even been at the point of losing her *life*, it seemed—and then this strange boy had appeared at her side—and, even as the most humongously vast monster Lee had ever imagined was bearing down on her, this boy had somehow managed to drag her out of the path of the great creature—and, not only that, but this extraordinary boy, with the bizarre haircut, had somehow managed to make both himself and her *invisible*—and this succession of fast-moving, impossible events all seemed to be holding out some small hope of survival! So, if this extra-ordinary boy wanted her to eat blue jelly beans, Lee Stubbs was, at the moment, rather inclined to do as she was told—

And now, Arcturion's fury at the loss of his prey was sending the dragon's small brain into a frenzy. His vast head was now darting round the great cave, searching frantically in every nook and cranny, round every projecting rock—and, all the time, the dragon was keeping up a series of piercing screams, each one louder than the last—

The huge coils were shifting fast, rippling across the floor and up the walls. Measle and Lee, huddled in the shelter of their rock, watched as the endless length of the dragon's body slid past. Their invisible hands were pressed hard to their invisible ears. Conversation was impossible. Every thirty seconds, Measle pressed a jelly bean between Lee's lips—

Then, as Arcturion unwound his endless great body, freeing it from where it had lain so still for so many countless years, he suddenly discovered that he was imprisoned. Imprisoned in a space that was too small! Too small to unfurl his great wings! Too small to move properly! Too constricting—the walls and the roof seemed to bear down on him, seemed to close in on him, squeezing him tighter and tighter—

And then Arcturion's fury turned to mindless panic. The volume of his screeching increased, his movements became more and more frantic as he tried to circle the cave—tried to find a way out—tried to stretch his great, black-membraned wings—he managed to free the end of his tail, dragging it up and out from under the heavy coils of his body—and now he began to swing his tail in wide, sweeping arcs. The tail ended in a huge ball of bone, all covered in spikes, which now began to smash against the walls of the cave—SMASH! to one side, then CRASH! to the other—and the walls shuddered and splintered under the blows, big shards of black rock splitting away from the surface and crashing to the floor—and through all this deafening, thunderous, screeching cacophony, Measle and Lee

heard (but only within their heads)—

ARCTURION! ARCTURION! SCHKRAAAST! SCHKRAAAST!

But whatever it was the Dragodon wanted, Arcturion's rage and terror were putting the dragon's brain past commanding. It was unlikely that the great creature even heard the Dragodon's desperate call. If anything, Arcturion doubled his efforts to escape this terrible, confining space, swinging his great tail with ever greater effort, until Measle and Lee could feel the rocky floor shudder and shake beneath them—and all they could do was huddle even closer together, with Measle feeding Lee the jelly beans from a fast-diminishing pile in the palm of his hand—

And then, it happened.

The huge ball of bony spikes at the end of Arcturion's tail swung yet again against the rock wall of the cave—and a massive, rough circle of rock crashed and fell from the surface, leaving a black hole in its place—

A black hole, from which came a sudden trickle of water that dribbled over the edge of the hole—

There was a distant rumble—

The trickle turned to a gush—

Another rumble, closer this time—

The gush turned to a torrent, that spewed from the hole, the water spreading rapidly over the cave floor—

Another rumble, much louder now—

And the torrent turned to a jet—a jet of cold, green water, ten metres across, that leaped from the hole and smashed clear across the great cave. It roared above Measle and Lee, making a sound like a rocket taking off—then it hit the far wall, splashing in a huge circle of white foam.

The water began to spread quickly across the floor.

The first shallow wave reached Measle and Lee, washing over their legs and hands. They both struggled to their feet. Measle lifted his right hand out of the chilly water. He touched the ends of his wet fingers to his tongue—

The water was salty.

'It's the sea, Mum!' he shouted. 'The sea's coming in!' His voice sounded small and faint over the roar of the water and the screams of Arcturion—

And, suddenly, the screams of the Great Worm

sounded different—

Before, there had been the scream of triumph. Then the shriek of fury. Then panic, mixed with rage. Then, just pure panic. To Measle, each ear-splitting howl from the throat of the immense creature had been clear in its meaning. And now—now there was another sound.

This one was a scream of pain.

Measle carefully poked his head out from the shelter of the rock.

It was an extraordinary—and horrible—sight that met his startled eyes. Arcturion had somehow managed to drag the endless coils of his body across the cave, heaping them up against the far wall, piling them higher and higher, his head now brushing the roof—and all in a frantic effort to keep any part of himself from touching the rising waters. But the waters *were* touching him—lapping against the lowest coils that still rested against the cave floor—and there was nothing Arcturion could do about it.

And, where the water flowed against the dragon's skin, the skin turned black. It was as if the water was now acting like fire—or acid, perhaps—burning Arcturion's hide wherever it touched—and, where it touched, the soft, glowing light that shone from the dragon's hide was slowly, but surely, being extinguished. Arcturion's screams of pain were now so high-pitched that they were almost beyond the limits of human hearing—and the only movements from the great creature were his futile struggles to keep his vast body away from the rising waters.

Measle watched as Arcturion managed to free one enormous wing. It was shaped like a bat's wing, with a membrane that was stretched between the long supporting bones—bones that ended in great, curved claws like scythes. Arcturion flapped this freed wing desperately, making a small hurricane of wind that swept over Measle's head with the sound of a train going past. But one wing, in this confined space, was no help to Arcturion. There was no way he could avoid this *wetness*— this terrible wetness that burned wherever it touched and, through his dreadful agony, he began to feel himself gradually weakening. Those parts of his coils which now lay under the water were beginning to dissolve in the corrosive salt water, leaving only the bones behind and, as the sea rose steadily, it engulfed more and more of the great body, blackening the outer skin as it went. And, as it did so, the strange unnatural light from Arcturion's hide (which had, until this moment, lit up the whole cave with its soft green glow) began slowly to dim, plunging the cave into growing darkness.

The huge jet of water—compressed through the narrow hole in the cave wall and then released into the cave, with all the force and pressure of the whole ocean behind it—continued blasting across the cave and smashing in a great fountain against the opposite wall—and now the cold green waters were rising faster and faster—

Already, they were up to Measle's knees. He dragged his eyes away from the horrible spectacle of Arcturion's agonized struggles and looked into Lee's face. She was standing now, her back braced against the rock. She looked at him and smiled.

'We're going to have to swim for it!' she yelled, over the roar of the water. 'Can you swim, kid?'

Measle nodded. *There's only one problem*, he thought. *Where are we going to swim* to? There was only the inside of the cave—

Lee must have seen Measle's eyes as he swept them over the high rocky walls, because she bent her head close to his and shouted, 'There must be a way out!'

Measle didn't look too convinced, so Lee yelled, 'We just let the water take us up! There's that hole in the ceiling—the one all those things fell through!'

Measle nodded. There was only one problem with this idea—what if the water finally reached the same level as the sea that surrounded the island and then rose no further? They could be stuck, floating metres below the hole above them, with no way of reaching it—

There was no more time for thought. The water was up to Measle's neck, so he leaned forward and lifted his feet from the floor. Lee did the same. They clung together, letting the water lift them upwards. The water was very cold and, in a few moments, Measle's teeth were chattering. They were careful to keep the rock between them and the dwindling sounds of distress that still came from the far side of the cave—even half melted away, Arcturion might be still capable of one last effort in their direction—

And now the sea water, rising unbelievably fast, washed over the tip of their rock and Measle and Lee, with their cover submerged, found themselves floating out in the open, in the centre of the cave, with nowhere to hide.

One look told Measle and Lee that the danger from Arcturion was almost past. On the far side of the cave, the dragon was still struggling feebly, but most of his lower coils were gone, dissolved to nothingness in the bitter water and all that was left of the great creature was his long, long neck and his head the size of a palace. The head was drooping, swaying slowly from side to side and the

great yellow eyes were losing their light. In fact, the whole cave was filling with shadows and Measle found he could no longer see the ceiling at all, so dark had it become within the vast space.

MEASLESTUBBS.

Measle felt the word drop into his skull like a small piece of lead. But this time, there was none of the power of command in it. This time, there was a note of pleading—pleading mixed with fear and uncertainty—

WHAT? replied Measle, sending the thought flying across the cave. Was the Dragodon still there, standing on its rock ledge on the far side of the cave?

I AM STILL HERE, MEASLESTUBBS. THE WATER IS RISING. IT IS GETTING DARK. I CANNOT SEE ARCTURION—BUT I FEEL HIS MANA DRAINING AWAY. I AM GROWING WEAKER, MEASLESTUBBS. WHAT HAVE YOU DONE? WHAT HAVE YOU DONE?

Measle paused for a moment, wondering how to respond. Then—

I THINK WE'VE WON, DRAGODON. I THINK MY MUM AND ME HAVE WON!

There was a long pause. Then—

HELP ME, MEASLESTUBBS.

There was no doubt about it. The Dragodon was begging! There was no power in those unspoken words to command any more—just this fearful, defeated begging! And there was something so pathetic in the tone of the request, something so utterly helpless, that Measle, still holding tight to Lee with one hand, began to swim awkwardly towards the distant wall where he remembered the Dragodon's ledge to be.

'What are you doing?' said Lee, finding herself being towed along by this determined boy, whether she wanted to be or not.

Measle didn't reply. He knew what he was doing—he just didn't know *why* he was doing it. He just felt, vaguely, that this was the right thing to do—and that was why he was doing it.

QUICKLY, MEASLESTUBBS. QUICKLY! THE WATERS! THE WATERS ARE COMING! I CANNOT FLOAT, MEASLESTUBBS! I CANNOT FLOAT!

And now there was stark terror in the Dragodon's tone. Measle swam harder, dragging Lee behind him. They swam in silence across the cold, choppy water, the darkness deepening all around them. They could no longer hear any sound from Arcturion and now there was only a faint green glow from the far side of the cave—

MEASLESTUBBS! **MEASLESTUBBS!** MEASLESTUBBS!

The impact of the fear-filled words in Measle's head grew fainter and fainter and fainter—

They swam on. The cave was silent now, apart from the splashing of Measle's arms and legs. The water had long since risen above the hole in the cave wall, risen above the blasting jet, drowning out the deafening roar of its passing—and

Arcturion had fallen silent some time ago. They were surrounded by a darkness that grew thicker with every passing second. Soon, they would be as good as blind—

And then Measle felt Lee's free hand grab his shoulder.

'Measle?' he heard her whisper. 'Measle, my darling—is that you?'

Measle twisted round in the water and stared into his mother's eyes.

They had changed.

Before, they had been the eyes of a friendly stranger. Now—now they were the eyes of his mother, staring back into his with wonder—with relief—with love—with bewilderment—

'Mum? You know who I am?'

'Yes! *Now* I do!'

'And you can remember everything again?'

'Yes! *Everything!* I remember now—I was kidnapped in the car park—the wrathmonks brought me here—the Dragodon—I remember it all!'

'But—but how? *How* do you suddenly remember?'

Lee grabbed both of Measle's shoulders and pulled him close to her in a bone-crushing hug. 'It means that the Dragodon is *dead*, Measle! That's how most spells are lifted! When the caster dies! That means—that means it's dead, Measle!'

'Dead? The Dragodon?'

Lee nodded, her eyes glittering in the darkness. 'There's nothing to go back for, Measle,' she said. 'The Dragodon's gone. We have to save ourselves now. Come on—we've got to try and get out of here. We've got to swim for that hole in the roof.'

Lee took his hand and began to swim back in the direction from which they'd come—and, as Measle felt himself being towed along by his mother's powerful strokes, his whole body suddenly relaxed. A great tide of relief swept over him. He was no longer in charge. He didn't have to do anything—think of anything—come up with any more ideas—or run for his life—not now, now that Lee was back to herself again. She was his Mum again. All he had to do was what she *told* him to do—

The water was very cold. A little wave splashed into his open mouth. It tasted bad—salty, mixed with another strange, metallic flavour. It was like licking an old penny.

And now the darkness was almost complete, surrounding them with velvet blackness—apart from a pale, ragged circle of light high above them. With the wrathmonks gone from the island, the black clouds had gone too and now the moon shone down onto the Isle of Smiles, flooding the whole area with soft, blue light—and some of that light fell down through the hole in the tarmac and cast a circle of blue light onto the water below.

Measle and Lee swam into this circle and stared

upwards. They watched, shivering, as the hole slowly grew bigger and bigger, the sea water lifting them higher and higher towards it.

And then, a few moments later, their hopes died. They saw that the hole wasn't getting any larger. Measle and Lee floated together in the circle of moonlight, staring upwards. The hole was perhaps four metres above their heads—but it might as well have been a hundred miles above them; there was no way that they could reach it.

'I think the water's stopped coming in, Mum,' said Measle, flatly.

'Yes,' said Lee. 'I think it has, too. I'm afraid it doesn't look like we're going to go any higher.'

And now they were getting very tired. They had been swimming, both fully dressed, in this freezing water, for fifteen minutes and now they were treading water, simply trying to stay afloat. Their legs felt heavy and weak and their arms ached with cold and exhaustion and Measle, his mouth dipping for a moment beneath the surface, experienced once again that strange, unpleasant metallic taste on his tongue.

'It tastes funny, this water,' he muttered.

'That's because it's not just water,' said Lee. Her voice was very tired—and there was a trace of uncertainty in it as well. 'It's mixed up with something else, Measle. Try not to swallow any of it.'

'Mixed up with what?'

'Arcturion, love. What's left of him. That's his blood you're tasting. And I have no idea what swimming around in diluted dragon's blood does to you.'

They both heard the rumbling noise at the same instant.

Ever since Cudgel had lifted Measle out of the swing seat, the Ferris wheel had been hanging on by a thread—*literally* by a thread. A thread of steel—the remains of the axle that supported it off the ground. Most of this axle had sheared away under the strain of Cudgel's enormous strength— strength that had overpowered the automatic braking system that had held the wheel immovable ever since the park had closed for the winter. The entire weight of the ride now rested on a thin piece of metal—a narrow strip of steel that had been steadily weakening under the enormous strain of holding the contraption upright.

The scrap of metal had survived the vibrations from the trampling, stamping feet of the Tyrannosaurus Rex. The scrap of metal had survived the shaking and shuddering from the blows of Arcturion's great tail—blows that had caused rippling vibrations which had travelled up in waves from deep below ground, like an earthquake. The scrap of metal had survived (but only just) the last, massive shake from underground when the powerful jet of water had smashed against the opposite wall of the cave. It had survived all these shocks—but each one had weakened it more and more, and now it was at the point of breaking.

And then, simply, it snapped in two.

And it was Tinker who—quite accidentally—caused it to snap.

Tinker had been squatting in the shadows of a nearby refreshment booth wondering, in the vague sort of way that dogs do, where everybody had got to. He felt a sudden itch behind his right ear—so, up came his back leg and *scritch-scritch-scritch* went his claws on the tickling spot. It was a very persistent itch, so Tinker bent his head sideways and scratched even harder and now, at the end of each stroke, his furiously working back leg began to thump on the ground. *Scritch-thump-scritch-thump-scritch-thump!*

With each thump of his leg on the ground, tiny, almost immeasurable vibrations began to run through the ground, spreading, like ripples in a pond, in ever-widening circles. By the time these vibrations reached the splinter of steel—the splinter that was all that held the Ferris wheel in position—they were so weak that even the most sensitive of instruments would have had difficulty picking them up.

But, weak as they were, they were enough.

There's a phrase, '*The straw that broke the camel's back*'. Well, the effect—on the Ferris wheel—of the vibrations from Tinker's back leg thumping on the nearby ground fitted that phrase perfectly. The metal splinter was, by now, so fragile that these minuscule pulsations that travelled through the ground and then up the metal frame were just enough to cause the over-stressed atoms of steel to fall apart.

There was a faint *twang!* from somewhere near the axle of the wheel. Then the whole Ferris wheel made a small lurch downwards. Tinker watched, puzzled, as the great contraption swayed from side to side. Then, gravity took over. With a groaning, creaking sound, the huge disc slid forward, off the supporting pillars—and the rim of the enormous hoop touched down on the ground. Then slowly, majestically, like a gigantic bicycle wheel, the thing began to roll forward.

It rolled, ponderously, to the edge of the gaping hole.

Then, slowly, it toppled in.

With a grinding, crunching sound, it sank down into the pit. It looked, to Tinker's astonished eyes, as if it was going to continue sliding down into the hole until it disappeared altogether. But then, with a third of itself inside the deep depression, the edge of its leading rim grated against the far side of the hole. Several pieces of tarmac broke away from under the rim and the wheel sank another metre. Then, it stopped. Its steel latticework groaned under the strain. It settled another couple of centimetres and then stuck fast.

When Measle and Lee heard the rumbling sound, they both instinctively began to paddle backwards as fast as they could, out of the circle of moonlight and into the relative safety of the deep shadows beyond. They watched as the hole above them suddenly filled with darkness—then they saw the great mass of steel sinking fast down towards the surface of the water. Chunks of roadway fell around them, sending up fountains of water into the air, and it was only by the greatest good luck that neither Measle nor Lee was hit by any of the falling debris.

Then, just as the bottom of the great mass of steel touched the surface of the water, there was a grinding, crunching, creaking sound—and the wreckage of twisted metal came to a halt.

'What *is* that thing?' whispered Lee.

'It's the Ferris wheel, Mum!' yelled Measle, his voice echoing round the cave. 'I climbed it! All the way up! *So can we!* It's easy! Come on!'

Lee didn't need any more encouragement than

that. Ignoring the aches in their arms and legs, they swam quickly to the shattered wheel. They dragged themselves up and out of the icy water and began to climb. Within a few seconds, the hole was just a couple of metres above their heads.

And that was when they saw the small white head, with a pair of fuzzy ears and a shiny black nose—and an alert and curious pair of eyes—staring down at them from the edge of the hole.

'Oh—h-hello, T-t-tink,' said Measle, his teeth chattering together from the cold. 'I b-b-bet you've been having f-f-fun, haven't you?'

THE WRATHMONKS' REVENGE

A very large and very powerful motorcycle, with a battered old sidecar attached to one side of it, turned off the main road and passed between the open gates of Merlin Manor.

The motorbike was painted a dull black. Under the massive petrol tank was a huge black engine, which made a steady *thrump, thrump, thrump* noise through the rusty twin exhaust pipes that stuck out at the back.

Low in the sky—and directly over the motorbike—hung a circular black cloud. A gentle drizzle fell steadily onto the machine and its occupants.

For all its power, the motorbike was going very slowly indeed. Cudgel was the driver. Behind him, on the pillion seat, sat Frognell Flabbit. Flabbit's face was still just as red and lumpy as before and it looked even more like a plate of raspberries than ever. Flabbit was holding tight to Cudgel's waist. Flabbit couldn't get his arms all the way around the enormous wrathmonk, so he was forced to cling onto the bottom edges of Cudgel's leather motorcycle jacket.

Griswold Gristle and Judge Cedric Hardscrabble sat, squashed together, in the sidecar. Judge Cedric held the remains of an umbrella, but it had long since blown inside out and was now no use to anybody at all. All four wrathmonks were very wet.

Since there was only the single seat in the sidecar, Griswold was perched on Judge Cedric's bony knees—and he was very uncomfortable indeed. He'd been very uncomfortable ever since they had set off. This was partly because he was soaking wet, partly because Judge Cedric's knees were rather sharp—but it was mostly because something very strange seemed to have happened to the sidecar's single wheel. Instead of being round, like a normal wheel, the sidecar's wheel was square. The rim was square and the tyre that surrounded the rim was square as well. This meant that, instead of running smoothly along the road, the sidecar bounced up and down with every quarter turn of the misshapen wheel.

Thumpsqueak—thumpsqueak—thumpsqueak it went, jolting Griswold and Judge Cedric up and down so hard that Judge Cedric had to hold tight to his bowler hat to stop it falling off. The juddering, up-down movement of the sidecar was also transmitted to the motorbike itself, so Cudgel and Flabbit were nearly as uncomfortable as the pair in the sidecar. Flabbit's comb-over had long since unstuck itself from his scalp and was hanging long and loose and dripping by the side of his head.

The square wheel meant that Cudgel had to drive very slowly. He'd been driving very slowly for a very long way.

'Thisss is all your fault, Flabbit!' he snarled over his shoulder, as they crept jerkily up the long gravel drive towards Merlin Manor.

'How's it *my* fault, Mr Cudgel?' said Flabbit, plaintively.

'You let the van run out of petrol, didn't you?' rumbled Cudgel. 'There we were, driving along, you lot in front in the van, me following on my bike—then, all of a sssudden—right in the middle of nowhere, sssputter, sssputter, sssputter—and your tank's empty!'

'I ssstill don't sssee why that's my fault,' said Flabbit.

Griswold opened his mouth. Being jolted up and down like this made it hard to say anything, but he was determined to join in this discussion. 'You—

were—s-s-ssupposed—to—be—in—charge—of—
the—van,' he managed to stutter. 'That—includes—
the—p-petrol—tank—Mr—Flabbit.'

Flabbit began to look a little angry.

'Now look here,' he said, 'what about what the
judge did, then—eh? Nobody is sssaying anything
about that, are they? All right—I grant you, the van
running out of petrol might have been a *bit* my
fault—'

'*A—b-bit?*' stuttered Griswold.

Flabbit ignored him. 'But thisss ssstupid square
wheel was nothing to do with me! Ho, no—thisss
ssstupid sssquare wheel was caused by a certain
judge, wasn't it? Why is nobody sssaying anything
about that, eh?'

'Cedric—has—apologized—for—that.'

'Not good enough!' snapped Flabbit. 'I mean to
sssay—ssso, we run out of petrol and—well—
thank goodness for Mr Cudgel and his motorbike,
that's all I can sssay, because our journey is hardly
interrupted at all. We all pile on—a bit of a
sssquash, but never mind—then a few miles
further on, and through no fault of myssself, nor of
Mr Cudgel, his sssidecar wheel gets a puncture.
And Mr Cudgel is jussst getting ready to mend it,
when a certain judge decides to try a bit of his
magic on it!'

'Well—he sssaid—he wanted—to change—the
wheel,' muttered Judge Cedric, sulkily and under
his breath, so that only Griswold heard him. 'He

sssaid—he wanted—to *change* it—ssso I—changed it—for him!'

'Yes, well—never—mind—all—that,' stuttered Griswold. 'We—are—here—now. Perhaps—Mr—C-Cudgel—we—might—ssstop—here—and—w-walk—the—ressst—of—the—w-way?'

Cudgel brought the lurching motorbike to a halt and switched off the engine. All four wrathmonks breathed a collective sigh of relief. Flabbit slid off the back of the pillion, Cudgel swung one enormous leg over his saddle, Griswold pulled himself shakily off Judge Cedric's knees and then helped the judge out of the sidecar. Then, their legs wobbling slightly, the four wrathmonks trudged up the drive to the front door of the big red-brick house.

Griswold Gristle took a deep breath. He looked at his fellow wrathmonks and said, 'Are we all ready?'

The other three wrathmonks nodded.

'Very well,' said Griswold. 'Let us proceed with our final mission.' He raised his hand and pressed his stubby forefinger against the doorbell button. There was a distant ringing sound.

Several seconds passed. Then they all heard the sounds of slow, shuffling footsteps and, a moment later, the heavy door creaked open.

Sam Stubbs stood in the doorway. He was in pyjamas and a dressing gown and his feet were bare. His hair was tousled, he had several days' growth of stubble on his face, and his eyes looked sleepy and bewildered.

'Yes?' he said, in a weak voice. 'What can I do for you?'

Griswold Gristle stepped forward, rubbing his fat little hands together. He had a beaming smile on his round face and his tiny, piggy eyes were gleaming.

'Hah, Sssam Ssstubbs!' he cried. 'It is not what you can do for usss! It is what we can do for *you*! In fact—that is precisely what we are going to do —we are going to *do* for you! What do you think of that, eh?'

'Er… I'm not sure I understand,' said Sam, mildly. He rubbed a hand across his eyes. 'Who are you, anyway?'

'Allow me to introduce myself,' squeaked Griswold. 'I am Griswold Grissstle. These are my colleagues—Mr Buford Cudgel, Mr Frognell Flabbit, and my learned friend, Judge Cedric Hardsssscrabble!'

'Nice to meet you,' said Sam. 'Now, if you don't mind—I think I'd better go back to bed. I'm not very well, you see.' He began to close the door, but Cudgel stuck out one huge, booted foot and jammed it in the doorway.

'Not ssso fassst, Ssstubbs,' he rumbled. 'We've got business with you.'

'Indeed we have,' said Griswold. He peered up at Sam, his head cocked to one side. Then he said, in a slightly sorrowful voice, 'It's sssuch a pity that you have no memory, Sssam Ssstubbs. If you only knew who and what we are! The fact that you don't makes our revenge a little less sssweet, I'm afraid.'

'Then—why don't we tell him, Griswold?' said Judge Cedric.

Griswold stared at Judge Cedric in wonder. It was the first sensible thing his friend had said in months.

'Excellent idea, Cedric!' he said. Then he turned back to Sam. 'Ssso, Sssam Ssstubbs—my friends and I are wrathmonks. Vasstly sssuperior beings to mere wizards, of which order you happen to be a very *minor* member. We are your enemies, Sssam Ssstubbs—and we are here to dessstroy you!'

'Oh dear,' said Sam. 'Must you?'

'Yesss! We mussst! We would have done it sssooner—but for various mishaps on our way here! Not that those mishaps have delayed usss at all, sssince it was necessary, anyway, for usss to wait a day and a night in order to recharge our powers. We *disss*charged our powers on various pressing matters, Sssam Ssstubbs—*sssome* of usss dissscharging them rather more effectively than *others*, it mussst be sssaid.' (And here Judge Cedric turned his frizzy head aside and stared innocently out into the distance.)

Griswold took another breath and went on, 'And now, after a sssomewhat uncomfortable night sssleeping together on the floor of the van—we are fully recharged! Fully recharged—except for *one* of usss, who unfortunately wasted all his precious mana on deforming an innocent *wheel*. However, that is of no consssequence, sssince there are three of usss absssolutely *brimming* with mana! And … we are here, to take our revenge!'

'Oh,' said Sam, nodding thoughtfully. He glanced down at Cudgel's boot, which was still stuck in the narrow gap between the edge of the door and the door frame. 'Wow,' he said. 'What big feet you've got.'

Griswold turned to the other wrathmonks.

'Sssee how ssstrong his lordship the Dragodon's exhalation enchantment is!' he whispered. 'This absssurd wizard doesn't even undersssstand what is about to happen to him!'

'Yeah—well, let's get on with it, Grissstle,' grumbled Cudgel.

'Very well,' said Griswold. He took a step backwards—and the other three wrathmonks all took a step backwards as well. Then Griswold raised his hand and pointed a fat finger at Sam.

'Sssam Ssstubbs!' he cried, 'you are sssentenced to death—'

Judge Cedric tapped him on the shoulder. 'That'sss what *I* sssay, Griswold.'

'Be quiet, Cedric!' snapped Griswold. 'You have no mana left and are therefore not part of thisss moment!' He glared at his friend and then turned back to Sam. 'As I was sssaying—you are sssentenced to death, Sssam Ssstubbs, by order of the Great Order Of Wrathmonks! Prepare to meet your doom!'

'What—now?' said Sam, smiling a small smile.

'Yes—now!' shrieked Griswold. Then he narrowed his little eyes and yelled, *'Dwaaargen Skaaargen Onglepoise!'*—and, immediately, twin beams of electric blue light sprang from his eyes and flashed towards Sam—

And Sam brought his left hand out from behind the door frame and held it up, the palm of his hand facing the wrathmonks—

And the twin blue beams smashed against Sam's outstretched palm, and then splashed, like a fountain, against his skin, the beams breaking into little glowing blue streams, that slid and dripped from his hand and then disintegrated into nothingness.

Griswold stepped back another pace, his round, white face creased with confusion.

'Ah,' he said, uncertainly. 'Well—it would ssseem that, while you may have lossst your memories, you have not lossst your abilities, Sssam Ssstubbs. That, I asssume, was an inssstinctive reaction?'

Sam smiled gently and said nothing.

Griswold shook his head. 'Well, what a pity,' he said, sadly. 'That was my famous Turn-Inssside-Out Incantation. I should ssso like to have watched you turn inssside out—a sssplendidly disssgusssting ssspectacle! However, your low quality defensssive magic has sssomehow managed to block it. But your magic won't help you—not any more! You sssee—you have used up your mana, Sssam Ssstubbs! As have I! Neither of usss has a drop of mana left! Of coursssse, I could always resort to my exhalation enchantment—but I really feel you deserve more than that. Ssso—with both of usss drained, that would mean a ssstalemate, Sssam Ssstubbs. That is, if it was jussst you and I facing one another! But, it is not jussst you and I, is it? No—there are three more of usss!'

Griswold paused and glanced, with a look of irritation, in Judge Cedric's direction. 'Well—*two* of usss, at any rate. However, my colleagues, Mr Buford Cudgel and Mr Frognell Flabbit, have, between them, more than enough mana to dessstroy you, Sssam Ssstubbs! Ssso—I leave you to them! Gentlemen?'

Griswold gave Cudgel and Flabbit a small bow and stepped to one side. Then, Cudgel and Flabbit both stared grimly at Sam.

'My Brain-To-Porridge Incantation, I think,' said Flabbit.

'My Lightning-Ssstrike-To-The-Head Incantation, I think,' rumbled Cudgel.

'Together, my dear Cudgel?' said Flabbit.

'Together?' growled Cudgel. 'Yesss—why not!'

Both wrathmonks opened their mouths and spat out their spells in unison.

'*Groinduckle Groanduckle Spinglebunce!*' screamed Flabbit.

'*Bellicoop Zimbaldrum Armitramp!*' roared Cudgel.

A pair of pink beams shot from Flabbit's eyes and sped towards Sam.

A pair of yellow beams shot from Cudgel's eyes and sped towards Sam.

Sam Stubbs raised a finger and tapped it against the outer panel of the front door. Then, in one fluid movement, he simply swung the door shut in the wrathmonks' faces.

The four beams—two pink, two yellow—smashed against the heavy door, splashed outwards across its surface and then dripped and drizzled harmlessly down towards the ground, fizzling away into little tendrils of coloured smoke that floated away in the still air.

There was a long silence as the four wrathmonks stared in bewilderment at the closed door. Then Griswold recovered himself.

'Mr Cudgel!' he shrieked. 'It would ssseem that our foe has sssome unsssusssspected reserves! Our only recoursssse now is to use our exhalation enchantments on him! Kindly use your great ssstrength and sssmash that door to pieces!'

Cudgel took a step forward—but, as he did so, the front door swung open again.

'Now, I'd really rather you didn't do that,' said Sam, smiling apologetically. 'I'm sorry—but it's a nice door and I would prefer to keep it in one piece, if you don't mind.'

'Breathe on him!' screamed Griswold, dancing furiously from foot to foot. 'We mussst all breathe on him together!'

The four wrathmonks each took a step closer and all of them opened their mouths and prepared to fill their lungs with air—

And then Sam swung the front door wide open—as wide as it would go, revealing everything that was in the great hall of Merlin Manor.

And the wrathmonks gaped in horror.

Sam Stubbs wasn't alone.

Lee Stubbs was standing by Sam's side. Sam's right hand (hidden behind the door until this moment) was held tightly in her left. Her free right hand rested on Measle's shoulder. Nanny Flannel hovered in the shadows behind the three of them, with Tinker at her feet. Tinker had a large beef bone in his mouth and he was trying to growl at the intruders and chew the bone at the same time.

At last, Griswold Gristle found his voice.

'But—but—but—' he stammered. Then he raised a trembling finger and pointed it at Lee and Measle. 'But—you're dead!'

'Apparently not,' said Lee. 'You must be thinking of somebody else.'

'The Dragodon, probably,' said Measle. *'It's* dead, I know. Dead as a doornail.'

Sam stepped forward, out of the doorway. Lee

stepped with him, still holding tight to her husband's hand. They both stared severely at the frozen wrathmonks.

'You've all been very naughty little wrathmonks,' said Sam, quietly. 'You've been making dreadful nuisances of yourselves. You've been bothering my wife and my son, you've turned a whole bunch of innocent people into stone statues—they're all right now, no thanks to you—you've smashed a perfectly splendid Ferris wheel—and now you turn up at my house on a horrible, smelly, broken down old motorbike and start chucking dangerous spells about. Well, we can't have that sort of behaviour, you know. We just can't. Sorry—but there it is.'

Sam raised both his arms and made a few complicated hand movements in the air. Then he said, '*Circumretio Infragilistum Bolenda!*'

There was a shimmering in the air over the wrathmonks' heads. Startled, all four of them looked up—and saw a shining, silvery net materialize out of nothing. It hovered there for a moment—and then, quite soundlessly, it dropped down onto the wrathmonks. The edges of the net fell to the ground and then slid under the wrathmonks' feet, gathering itself together like the strings of a shopping bag.

'Oi!' yelled Cudgel, punching his great fists at the net. 'Lemme out!'

The net drew tighter and now the wrathmonks were beginning to feel the squeeze.

'G r i s w o l d — k i n d l y remove your foot from my face,' said Flabbit, struggling to pull himself free.

'I do believe that thisss is sssome sssort of *net*!' shouted Judge Cedric. His bowler hat was being shoved down hard on his head and was beginning to squash his pointed ears. 'Are we going fishing?'

'Mr Cudgel!' squeaked Griswold. 'Kindly ssstop waving your great fisssts about! That was my *eye*!'

The net tightened and tightened around them, until it was difficult to work out which of those wriggling hands inside it belonged to which of those wriggling arms—or if that shiny bit over there was one of Cudgel's boots or a section of his motorcycle helmet.

Then, with the four wrathmonks wrapped tightly together in a neat ball of tangled arms and legs and bodies and heads (they were encased so tightly, in fact, that they could hardly breathe and certainly couldn't say anything), Sam made another small gesture with one forefinger and the whole silvery mass slowly rose a couple of metres into the air and then hovered there, bobbing gently up and down.

Sam turned his head and called back into the hallway of the house.

'Mr Needle! Mr Bland! Ready when you are!'

Mr Needle and Mr Bland appeared out of the shadows and walked quickly out into the daylight. Mr Needle spoke briefly into what looked a little like a walkie-talkie and, a moment later, a large white truck crunched round from behind the house and drew up by the front door.

Measle noted, with interest, that the truck had no driver.

Mr Needle put on a pair of thick leather gloves. Mr Bland opened the rear doors of the truck and Mr Needle carefully pushed the hovering, netted ball of wrathmonks into the cargo space. Then he and Mr Bland swung the doors shut with a clang.

Mr Needle and Mr Bland turned and looked at the Stubbs family.

'Excellent work, Mr Stubbs,' said Mr Needle, coldly.

'Most efficient,' said Mr Bland, in the tone of somebody who thinks he could have managed the whole affair a lot better.

'We'll take it from here,' said Mr Needle, pulling the leather gloves off his hands. Then he walked to the driver's side of the truck and climbed in.

Mr Bland smiled a wintry smile.

'We shall be making a complete report to the Guild,' he said, 'and I have no doubt that they will be in touch. I imagine that, in addition to the regular fees, there will be a generous bonus. Allow me to congratulate you all. Good day.'

Mr Bland raised his hat, made a shallow bow and then joined Mr Needle in the front seat. A moment later, the truck moved off, crunching its way over the gravel, and gathering speed as it headed down the long drive to the distant gates.

There was a long silence as the Stubbs family watched it go. Then, when the truck turned out of the gates and was at last lost to view, Measle tapped his father's arm.

'Yes, son?' said Sam, smiling down at him.

'I was just wondering, Dad—'

'What were you wondering, son?'

Measle grinned up at his father.

'Well,' he said, slowly, 'what I was wondering was this: they've left their motorbike behind, haven't they?'

'So they have,' said Sam, shading his eyes and peering down the driveway, where the big black motorbike was parked. 'Horrible thing. Well, it's no use to them now. We'll just have to get rid of it.'

'Mm. I was wondering,' murmured Measle, slowly, 'whether we could...er...whether we could keep it?'

'No, Measle,' said Sam, shaking his head. 'No—I don't like motorbikes.'

'Don't you, Sam?' said Nanny Flannel, in a surprised voice. 'Oh, I do. In fact, I used to have one when I was a young girl. I used to go all over the place on it. It was lovely.'

'That's beside the point, Nanny—'

'Justin Bucket used to take me on the back of his motorbike,' said Lee, dreamily. 'It was such fun. We'd go really *fast*.'

'Yes—well, that's why I don't like 'em,' said Sam.

'Why?' said Lee, grinning wickedly. 'Because they go fast? I thought you like going fast?'

'I do.'

'Why don't you like them, then?'

'Well, if you *must* know,' said Sam, in a dignified voice, 'I don't like 'em because Justin Bucket took you for rides on his, that's why.' Sam turned away, trying to hide the fact that his face was going a little red. He pointed to the distant machine. 'Besides, look at that sidecar wheel—it's useless.'

'I expect we could mend the wheel,' said Measle.

'No, we couldn't,' said Sam. 'Besides, the whole thing is *filthy*.'

'We could polish it up—get it all nice and clean,' said Nanny Flannel.

'I daresay we could,' said Sam. 'But we won't.'

'We could buzz around the estate on it,' said Lee. 'It'd be fun.'

'I daresay we could,' said Sam. 'But we won't.'

'But, Dad—' said Measle.

Sam held up his hand. 'No, no, *no*,' he said, firmly. 'No motorbikes at Merlin Manor. Never! The whole thing is absolutely, completely, utterly—and finally

—out of the question.'

Well—there was only one thing left to do, thought Measle. *Use the WORD. The extraordinary WORD. The amazing, effective, and magical WORD, that sometimes works miracles! The WORD that can change History! The WORD that can move mountains! The WORD that can—*

'Please?' said Measle.

There was a very long silence. Even the birds in the trees fell quiet. The seconds ticked by. Everybody held their breath.

Then—

'Oh, all right then,' said Sam.

Ian Ogilvy is best known as an actor—in particular for his takeover of the role of The Saint from Roger Moore. He has appeared in countless television productions, both here and in the United States, has made a number of films, and starred often on the West End stage. His first children's book was *Measle and the Wrathmonk*—and he has written a couple of novels for grown-ups too: *Loose Chippings* and *The Polkerton Giant*, both published by Headline. His play, *A Slight Hangover*, is published by Samuel French. He lives in Southern California with his wife Kitty and two stepsons.

Measle Stubbs is best known as a bit of a hero—in particular for his triumphant role as the charge of evil wrathmonk, Basil Tramplebone. Measle's latest appearance has been his nail-biting encounter with the evil Dragodon. Having rescued his mum from the Dragodon's clutches, Measle is now relaxing at home (well, for a while at least).

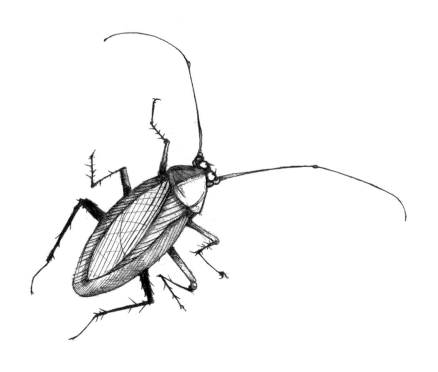

FROM:
MEASLE
AND THE
WRATHMONK

iSBN 0 19271952 1

Measle Stubbs was ten and a half years old. He was small, thin, and bony. Most of the time, he was as hungry as a very hungry horse. He had a short snub nose, high cheekbones, a pair of eyes coloured a deep, emerald green, and (when he felt like it) a wide and friendly smile. His hair was brown and stood up all over his head in spiky tufts. It was the oddest haircut—long where it should have been short, short where it should have been long—and the reason it was like this was because Measle cut his hair himself, using a blunt and rusty kitchen knife, with which he sawed and hacked at his hair whenever it got so long that it fell in his eyes. Apart from being the most uneven haircut imaginable, it also hadn't been washed in a very long time. Neither had his clothes and sometimes he smelt pretty bad, particularly when the weather was warm. It wasn't warm very often where Measle Stubbs lived. Measle Stubbs lived in a cold and horrible house. It was not Measle's choice to live there; it was *circumstances.*

The horrible house was at the far end of a dreary, dirty street full of dirty, dreary houses—but three things set this house apart from all the others. The first was the way it looked—all black, with a tall, pointed roof, tall dark narrow windows like blind eyes, and tall, soot-caked chimneys that looked like dirty fingers pointing at the sky. The other houses in the street just looked dingy and dreary but Measle's house looked as if something bad had happened in it—and, quite possibly, something bad could happen there again tomorrow.

The second fact that made it different from the other houses in the street was that it was the only one that was occupied. All the other houses had been deserted by their owners a long time ago and their doors and windows boarded over. If you stood at the far end of the street and looked down its length, you'd have thought that every house there was abandoned and derelict. But if you looked a little harder, you might have seen—down at the far end of the street—a faint glimmer of light from an attic window, which was the only indication that there was anybody living in the street at all.

The third fact that made the house different from all the others was also the strangest: all day and all night, winter, summer, autumn, and spring, there was a small, black cloud that hung, never moving, over the dismal roof, dribbling a steady, constant stream of rain that fell only on the house where Measle Stubbs lived and not at all on any of the others in the street.

The house belonged to Basil Tramplebone and Basil Tramplebone was Measle Stubbs's Legal Guardian. Measle lived in the house with just his Legal Guardian for company—and his Legal Guardian wasn't good company at all; in fact, his Legal Guardian hardly spoke because he hated everybody—but that was all right because everybody who had ever met him hated Basil Tramplebone. He was very tall and thin and he always wore black clothes. A black coat and a black shirt and a black tie; black trousers and black socks and black shoes. His greasy hair was black and he parted it in the middle and plastered it down on his head with black shoe polish. The only things that weren't black about him were his face and his hands: Basil's face was very white, as though all the blood had been drained out and replaced with milk. His eyes were like fish eyes—staring and blank and very, very cold. His long, bony hands were the colour of candles and the skin was so dry that it rustled when he rubbed his palms together, which he did when he was pleased. Basil Tramplebone wasn't pleased very often, so the rustling noise didn't happen very often.

If the outside of Basil Tramplebone's house was grim and gloomy and depressingly ugly, the inside was even worse. It was so ghastly that Measle only dared go into three rooms—the kitchen, the bathroom, and the attic. All the rooms in the house smelt bad—each one in a different way—but at least being in the kitchen and the bathroom and the attic didn't frighten him half to death. He certainly didn't dare go into the room that was supposed to be his bedroom. There was a huge black oak wardrobe in there, full of clothes that weren't his. They felt damp and smelt of mildew. Once, Measle had got up enough courage to sort through the clothes. He stopped doing that when he found the jacket. It was made of some sort of rough material and it had *three* sleeves—two in the usual places and a third that stuck out at the back. When he finally got up the courage to ask Basil about it, Basil told him to mind his own business—but if he *must* know, then all the clothes in the wardrobe had been left there, over the years, by visiting friends of his, some of whom were, perhaps, a little *different*.

The wardrobe was in one dark corner of the room and a great, black bed that looked like a coffin was in the other. There were black velvet curtains over the windows and the glass in the windows was painted black, so you couldn't see out at all and, what with the black painted walls and ceiling and floorboards, it was one of the gloomiest rooms you can imagine and one that would certainly give you nightmares if you tried to sleep in it—so Measle didn't try at all. Instead, he slept on a pile of old rags in the kitchen, right up by the ancient iron stove, which was the only place in that dreadful house that was warm.

Measle hated Basil Tramplebone and, of course, Basil Tramplebone hated Measle, because Basil Tramplebone hated everybody. He only looked after Measle because Measle's mother and father had been killed by an encounter with a deadly snake when Measle was four years old, leaving poor little Measle an orphan.

The story about the deadly snake had come from Basil who, in Measle's experience, always told the truth. But in this case, Measle wasn't so sure—perhaps because he badly wanted his parents to be alive. So, deep in his heart, Measle was certain that his mother and father were still around somewhere and that, one day, they would come back to him. Meanwhile, his parents had left a lot of money in the bank and now it was all Measle's—but a judge had said that Measle was too young to have control of all that money and too young to live by himself and had appointed Basil—who said he was Measle Stubbs's fourth cousin twelve times removed and, therefore, Measle's closest living relative—to look after him and his money. The odd thing was, (although Measle had been too young to remember this now) the judge had looked a little like Basil. The same black clothes, the same cold, fishy eyes, the same white, white face. He'd even talked a bit like Basil too—and, every time he'd looked at Basil, he'd smiled like a crocodile—as if he was approving of everything that Basil said.

Of the three rooms that Measle could bear to be in, the attic was his favourite. The bathroom smelt bad and the water that came out of the taps was brown, with green, floating bits in it, so Measle didn't bath very often. At least there was a window in the bathroom and, sometimes, Measle would stand on the cracked lavatory seat and look out of the window at the dismal railway yards that were behind the house and dream of living somewhere else.

The kitchen was warm and dry but it smelt of rotten cabbages and was infested with enormous cockroaches. Some of them were so big that, when Measle stepped on them, they didn't go *crunch* under his foot like the smaller ones did—they simply wriggled about in a disgusting way until Measle took his foot off them and then they scuttled away under the stove, quite unharmed.

As far as the attic was concerned, Measle had only recently discovered it, because Basil had never allowed him to go up there before. *Something* interesting had certainly been going on up that narrow flight of stairs, because Basil spent many hours in the attic and for a long time Measle used to stand at the bottom of the stairs and listen—and, occasionally, he'd heard sounds that he couldn't explain to himself. And then, one day, about six months earlier, Basil had said, 'Come with me, Measle,' and then he'd led the way up the cramped, steep staircase and into the extraordinary attic room—and Measle's jaw had dropped in amazement at what he saw.

It was the biggest—and probably the best— miniature railway set in the world.

From that moment, the attic became the one room in the house that Measle actually didn't mind spending time in. It was still a scary room—there was something in there that lived up in the rafters. Measle had seen movement up there among the dark beams of wood and, once, a pair of red, glowing eyes. What the something was, Measle didn't really want to know—just so long as the something stayed up there out of sight and never put in an appearance. At least there were no cockroaches in the attic—in fact, there were no insects of any kind up there, which was odd because the rest of the house was crawling with them.

Measle was fascinated by the train set. Somehow, Basil Tramplebone had managed to build a miniature version of the dismal railway yards on a huge table, right in the middle of the attic. The table was so big that there was only a narrow gap all the way round between the edge of the table and the attic walls and it was a good thing that both Measle and Basil were so thin, otherwise they could never have fitted in the narrow space. Everything on the enormous table was accurate, down to the smallest detail—the coal yard had a mound of tiny chips of real coal, the street lights shone with a sickly yellow light, and there was a constant, tiny stream of dirty water flowing in the miniature gutters—but further out, away from the town, Basil had changed the look. Instead of rows and rows of cheap, sooty houses (which Measle could see beyond the railway lines if he looked out of the bathroom window) Basil had created a forest of tall pines, with the trees set so close together it was hard to see between them. It was very dark and gloomy, with strange little houses here and there in clearings in the woods. The houses were quite different from the grimy houses round the railway yards. They were made of little logs, with stone chimneys and porches on the front and Measle decided that, if he was an inhabitant of the place, he'd much rather live in one of them than in the depressing town.

When Basil played with his train set—and if he was in a good mood—he would let Measle come up to the attic to watch. From the very start of being allowed to watch Basil play with his trains, it was obvious to Measle that Basil didn't care for anything modern. There were no electric commuter trains, no long-distance diesel trains. Everything about the set was old-fashioned and all the locomotives were steam engines from an age gone past. There were two sorts of trains—passenger trains and freight trains—and each one was detailed to the smallest degree. When Measle sat on a chair and watched, he would stay very quiet and still (because Basil Tramplebone hated noise and fidgeting), and he would look down at the layout and, every time he did so, he saw something new in the scenery and that's what he liked best about coming up to the attic and watching Basil play with his trains.

One day, he saw that Basil had made a little plume of smoke to come from the chimney of one of the cabins in the woods; another time, Basil had built a water tower by the side of the tracks and, when one of the freight trains stopped underneath it, the tower let out a tiny trickle of water that filled the boiler of the engine. Once, Measle noticed that Basil had added a lake in the middle of the forest—not with real water this time, which was a disappointment, but with a mirror embedded in the surface, surrounded by the little pine trees. It looked realistic enough, and the way the mirror reflected the dark pine trees and the rocks of the shoreline was probably more effective than if the lake had been made with real water. Measle had to admit that Basil was good with his hands. It seemed as though Basil could make just about anything, so long as the thing was very small. Sometimes Measle was amazed at the details of all the scaled-down objects—every window in the houses looked like real glass, every leaf on the trees looked as if it would certainly drop off when autumn came round and every worn paving stone on the dirty pavements looked as if it had been trodden on by countless shuffling feet.

There were quite a few people in the model too. The painted plastic figures were positioned about the train set, doing all the things that people usually do—shopping, gossiping on street corners, standing

on station platforms waiting for trains. There were a few animals as well—a little black and white dog sniffing round a lamp-post, a cat lounging on a windowsill and, deep in the forest, a family of three black bears walking in a line near the lake.

When Basil Tramplebone played with his trains, he always ate a whole box of glazed doughnuts and drank a gallon of pink lemonade out of a plastic jug—and some of the crumbs and some of the sugar and an occasional drop of lemonade would fall onto the table top. He kept the box and the jug close by his side. Measle never got a doughnut or a glass of lemonade because Basil never offered him any and Measle didn't dare ask. Measle would stare at the crumbs, hoping that Basil would perhaps want to go to the lavatory and then, while he was gone, Measle

could sneak over and lick his finger and dab up the crumbs and the sugar and eat them—but Basil never seemed to go to the lavatory at all, even after eating a whole box of glazed doughnuts and drinking a gallon of pink lemonade, so Measle never got the chance.

Measle Stubbs missed his mother and father badly. He couldn't remember what they looked like, because their unfortunate encounter with the snake had happened when he was very young but, all the same, he wished it was them who were looking after him and not Basil Tramplebone. Basil Tramplebone didn't like looking after anything or anybody—apart from himself and his train set, of course. He looked after himself and his train set very well indeed. He fed himself the best steaks and gave Measle the fat from round the edges. He always made chips for himself but plain boiled potatoes for Measle—and sometimes they weren't cooked all the way through and were hard in the middle. Basil Tramplebone's black socks were made of silk and so were his black boxer shorts; Measle didn't have any socks and only two pairs of underpants and the elastic had stopped working in both of them. But it was the train set that Basil cared for the most and he spent hours and hours and hours working on it and tons and tons and tons of Measle's money on the most expensive equipment he could buy.

Measle didn't mind so much about the money spent on the train set because the train set was probably the best in the world and he liked looking at it. On the other hand, he didn't like Basil spending all that money on silk socks and silk boxer shorts, when all he had were two pairs of underpants with broken elastic—and he *certainly* didn't like Basil buying the best steaks and chips with Stubbs money and then not letting him have any. Measle thought that was totally unfair.

One night, while he lay curled tight up against the stove, an idea came to him. He hadn't been able to get to sleep because the cockroaches were having a party—or what sounded like a party if cockroaches had them—under the stove. There was a lot of clicking and rustling and tap-tap-tapping of cockroach feet and he couldn't sleep with all that noise going on, so he decided to think instead. That was when the idea came to him. It was a brilliant idea. It was, he admitted to himself, also a dangerous idea but the best ideas often are and Measle was prepared to take the risk.

The next day, at lunch (Basil was having fried sausages and bacon and chips and ketchup and Measle was having a piece of stale bread and a paper cup of water) Measle said, 'Oh, Mr Tramplebone, sir, the bank called this morning. They want to see you.'

'The bank?' said Basil. He stared at Measle with his fish eyes. 'When?'

'While you were still asleep, sir,' said Measle, who was good at lying. 'Something about some extra money.'

'Money?'

'Yes. To us, of course. They want to see you about it. The man said something about investing it.'

'Invesssting?' Basil always hissed like a rattlesnake whenever he said the letter S.

'Yes, Mr Tramplebone. He said it was too much just to leave in an ordinary bank account.'

'Too much?'

'Yes.'

'I shall telephone them.'

'Yes, sir—but the trouble is, the telephone doesn't seem to be working any more, sir.'

'Not working?'

'No, sir.'

The reason the telephone wasn't working any more was because Measle had taken the plug out of the socket. He watched nervously as Basil tried the phone. Basil listened to the earpiece for a moment and then hissed like a snake.

'What a nuisssance.' He put the receiver down. Then, he put on his long black coat and picked up his long black umbrella, which looked like a sleeping vampire bat.

'I'm going out, Measle,' he hissed. 'To the bank. Behave yoursssself. Do nothing. Nothing at all.'

Basil hardly ever went out. He had all their food delivered from the local supermarket and bought all his clothes and stuff for the train set from catalogues, so he never needed to leave the house at all. In fact, when the door closed behind him, Measle realized that this was the first time he could remember ever being alone in the house and, for a moment, he felt scared. Then he said to himself, 'What can a house do to you? It's not like it's a burglar or a murderer or a mugger or anything, so what can it possibly do to you?' That made him feel a little better, but not a lot.

He looked through a crack in the front door and watched Basil stride down the path to the street. A small piece of the black cloud that hung over the house detached itself and began to follow Basil. It dribbled a little shower of rain on Basil's open umbrella. At the end of the path, Basil turned right, which was the way to the better part of town, where the bank was. Basil was going to have to walk the whole way, because they didn't have a car and there were no buses that came out to this side of the railway yards. The bank was about a mile and a half away, which meant that Basil was going to have to walk three miles and, even with his long, spider legs, that was going to take some time.

It was enough time, thought Measle. More than enough time.